D1759738

I See You

TATJANA GENYS

BALBOA.PRESS

A DIVISION OF HAY HOUSE

Copyright © 2024 Tatjana Genys.

All rights reserved. No part of this book may be used or reproduced by any means, graphic, electronic, or mechanical, including photocopying, recording, taping or by any information storage retrieval system without the written permission of the author except in the case of brief quotations embodied in critical articles and reviews.

Balboa Press books may be ordered through booksellers or by contacting:

Balboa Press
A Division of Hay House
1663 Liberty Drive
Bloomington, IN 47403
www.balboapress.com.au
AU TFN: 1 800 844 925 (Toll Free inside Australia)
AU Local: (02) 8310 7086 (+61 2 8310 7086 from outside Australia)

Because of the dynamic nature of the Internet, any web addresses or links contained in this book may have changed since publication and may no longer be valid. The views expressed in this work are solely those of the author and do not necessarily reflect the views of the publisher, and the publisher hereby disclaims any responsibility for them.

The author of this book does not dispense medical advice or prescribe the use of any technique as a form of treatment for physical, emotional, or medical problems without the advice of a physician, either directly or indirectly. The intent of the author is only to offer information of a general nature to help you in your quest for emotional and spiritual well-being. In the event you use any of the information in this book for yourself, which is your constitutional right, the author and the publisher assume no responsibility for your actions.

Print information available on the last page.

ISBN: 978-1-9822-9903-3 (sc)
ISBN: 978-1-9822-9902-6 (e)

Library of Congress Control Number: 2024902795

Balboa Press rev. date: 02/08/2024

Finally!! What took you so long??
Days I have been lying here, or could have been years...
I must have lost count.
Dusting away on this godforsaken shelf waiting for
the right time to come...

CHAPTER 1

Nate 2 years ago - how it all began

"Finally!! What took you so long??" I am taken aback by the words staring at me. "Days I have been lying here, or could have been years… I must have lost count"

"Waiting for what?" I ask, turning the book upside down to monitor it more closely. No title, no name, no description. Weird… If I didn't know any better, I'd say someone lost their journal. But no one writes their journals like this, do they?

"Dusting away on this godforsaken shelf waiting for the right time to come," continues at me through the pages. I rub my eyes. I should really get more sleep.

"Tap tap tap…" Another paragraph emerges. "Raindrop after raindrop gliding down the glass panel, before disappearing from my view. Calming somehow… as if I could be *calm* right now. "Enough!" I want to scream.

It sounds agitated… "Enough of what?" I ask more to myself than anyone else. I know only too well what it means to feel uneasy, but why would whoever wrote this, not be calm? "Pitter-patter, pitter-patter, click clack, click clack, click clack" it continues, ignoring my inner dialogue. "Footsteps approaching, hundreds maybe even thousands, always in a rush, not seeing anything or anyone. "STOP!" I want to shout.

I can't decide if it's sad or angry. But at who? And why? It feels so strange, I must read on.

"Stop doing the same thing over and over, without real purpose or impact. Stop wishing you would have done more, seen more, visited more, laughed more, slept more… or actually been happy. When was the last time you were happy?"

I turn the page but there is nothing else. A blank page stares back at me, ending as abruptly as it began. I scratch my head. Pretty sure the book was written front to back when I opened it.

I look around, but there's no one there, I am the only person standing in the little bookstore off Stanton Avenue. God knows what brought me here today or why I set foot here in the first place. I was on my way home from work when something caught my eye in the window, but now that I look back at it, there's nothing there. Maybe I'm losing my mind…

"Don't worry about it," comes back at me through the pages, "I'm getting ahead of myself. You don't have to answer it yet."

I think back to the question. When *was* the last time I was happy? I scramble my brain for a date. Few years ago? Distant memories wash off in front of my eyes. When my son was born… couldn't believe my luck back then. I push that thought aside quickly.

When I open the book again, I find a new paragraph inside.

"It can't just be anyone you know? It's not as simple as that."

I follow the spaces between the lines as the shapes form slowly and find a pair of eyes looking back at me. "You look surprised," comes back observing, followed by a giggle. A giggle? I must be going mad.

"But of course! We haven't been formally introduced yet. Where are my manners…"

"We?" I ask.

"Yes, you and me." Her reply is matter-of-factly. "Who else would I be talking to…?"

She rolls her eyes.

"We?" I repeat.

"Didn't we just cover that?" she almost sounds annoyed. "You will need to do better than that my friend, we don't have all day. Soon you will understand that nothing is a coincidence."

I hesitate and look around, in search of a hidden camera. I've heard they do all sorts of tricks these days. "You got me!" I exclaim, lifting my arms waiting for someone to jump out from behind the grey curtain. Nothing changes. Seriously, does anyone even work here??

"You found the key?" Her voice continues reluctantly. I look down at my left hand holding a small golden key and nod.

"Unlocked the lock?"

I nod again, feeling its weight resting heavily inside my right pocket.

"Didn't you read the small print at the back?"

I freeze and turn the book upside down quickly, scanning it for a clue, and am met with a frustrated exhale.

"No use doing it now... Seriously, why are people so illogical? Always do things first and think later... Well, it is what it is. Guess I have to fill you in instead. Sometimes the best journeys are the ones you never see coming anyway." She pauses for a moment.

"Congratulations, you are 'it'! You look different than I imagined... Not that I knew what to expect of course, but different somehow." A big smile appears on the page. The irony of a book telling me that doesn't escape me.

"But you will do just fine. Optics are an illusion, beauty fades and I am more interested in your soul anyway."

I tilt my head as she continues, a question mark playing on my forehead.

"I want to see the real you, the true you. The only one who really matters. You ready?" Before I get a chance to respond, she continues. "Good. Now let's get started."

"Get started with what?" I finally ask.

"Haven't you figured it out yet my friend? You and I will change the world together."

I flip the page.

"You're here!" She sounds relieved. "Now that you decided to stay, I can fully fill you in. But I must stress: Staying alone is not enough. You will need to make a choice. Decide to come along with me and there is no turning back. No looking away when it gets hard. And *it will* get hard. There will come a time, every part of your body will want to get away. Unsee what it's just seen. *That* is the commitment you give, breaking your word will have fatal consequences." A sharp inhale breaks the silence between us. "Good. Now that that's covered, let's get right to it, no time to waste. We have already wasted too much. Choose fast my friend and wisely I urge you, I will never give you this option again."

Panic rises in my throat. "What exactly am I deciding on?"

"No time for questions," she simply replies. "Use the pen inside the key and sign down below. Or close the book, bury the key, forget it ever existed and never return. You have ten seconds to decide."

My hands bring the key closer mechanically, spotting the sharp edge of one of their teeth as my eyes scan the paper in front of me.

Contract for Nathaniel Bennet:

I double blink. Nathaniel Bennet. That's me. Or my birth name rather, named after my great grandfather. No one calls me that of course, I have been Nate for as long as I can remember.

How does she know my name?

> *I hereby consent to fully immerse myself in this experience. To push myself beyond imagination and challenge everything I believe in. To enter with an open heart, and mind, and commit to bravery, especially when faced with my biggest demons.*

Big bold underlined letters have **N A M E** written beneath it, leaving space for me to sign. My throat goes dry. I know a thing or two about fears... I close my eyes and take a few deep breaths. *This is madness*, crosses my mind. *Am I seriously considering this?*

"Five seconds," she warns me.

I mean, nothing about this seems right. Or even legit, to start with...

"Two seconds," more forceful this time.

But it has my name written on it. My palms start sweating as I grip the pen hard. One eye closed, peeking through the other, I scribble my name on the piece of paper at the last second. Just in time to see my signature burn onto the page and the last part written in tiny letters underneath it

P.S: No guarantee this won't impact your sanity or that you will make it out alive. All activities are taken at your own risk and all responsibility will be held against no other but yourself.

~

Annabelle

"You did it!! Congratulations, you passed the first test." She claps her hands in excitement.

"That's it?" I ask, standing exactly where I was. "It was just a test??" I half expected to land in a different galaxy, fight off sea monsters or at least get to slay a dragon. *Unlikely*, I know… but nothing about this seems very likely. Was this a joke??

A tiny foot steps slowly out of the book, followed by another, forming the shape of a little girl. Big brown eyes stare innocently back at me, a combination of joy and relief playing on her face.

"Looks like you *are* the chosen one after all," she exclaims, ignoring my rant. "Now let me introduce myself. My name is Annabelle, and I am 2190 days old." She pauses for a moment giving me time to collect my thoughts. "I only have a few talents, but they are my very precious ones. I can see the soul of people."

"You can do what?" I ask, only half listening.

"You heard me," she simply remarks "and you will soon see for yourself. But for now, I need you to pay attention." She snaps her fingers at me. "Watch closely, wherever we go." She opens the backdoor and gestures to follow her. "Do you tend to see people or are they just bodies moving past you? Ever stop to watch the person next to you or start a conversation with someone you don't know?"

I think about it for a brief moment, my brain still trying to rationalise what it just saw. I used to. Before… I swallow hard. It's not that I don't care anymore… but keeping it together takes most of my energy these days. I look back at Annabelle, remembering everything I should be doing right now.

"People never cease to surprise me, you know?" she continues, oblivious to my thoughts. "They do the funniest things, the loveliest things and then the ugliest things… all within the blink of an eye. But you are different my friend, I have a good feeling about you." She gives me a long look as we step on the pavement and shakes her head softly, as if to shake off a thought.

I look around. A riverbank stretches out in front of us, surrounded by luscious green grass and big leafy trees. The bustling noise of the city faintly audible and buildings cramped one next to the other disappearing in the far distance.

"Where are we?" I ask.

"I really don't know," she replies honestly, holding onto the seam of her white dress. "I never know where it takes us… and it doesn't tend to matter very much. What tends to be more important is who we meet along the way and how we respond when we do." She looks at me eagerly. "Now let's get to work! What do you see?" The excitement in her voice is contagious.

"I see a riverbank," I state matter-of-factly.

"Aaand?" she continues enthusiastically.

"Trees… ducks… clouds?" I continue, noticing her surprised expression.

"Oh dear… this will be harder than I thought," she adds quietly. "Shall we call this a warm-up?" She looks at me hopeful. "Why don't you try again, look closer this time. Pay attention to the smallest of details. Feeeeel into it."

I close my eyes and take a deep breath.

"Calm your mind," she whispers in my ear. "You will need to see beyond the obvious."

When I open my eyes again, colours, graphs, and shapes playfully emerge in front of them. I notice people walking their dogs, kids laughing chasing after a ball, a couple sharing a kiss on the park bench. It feels… *happy.* Annabelle smiles at me broadly.

"There. That's better," she adds softly. "Did you also see the fishermen down by the riverbed?" I nod. "He looks very content, doesn't he? You know what they say: Want happiness for a day, go fishing. Want happiness for life, help someone else. Which brings me to my next point." She straightens her shoulders.

"Did you also see the man on the other side?"

I follow her gaze. "The one in the ruffled clothes?" I ask, feeling a tingling in my neck.

"Yes, the one with the sleeping bag and dirty shoes. Let's go meet him."

I look up at her briefly. "What if he is dangerous?"

"He's not."

"What if he'll hurt us?"

"He won't."

"How do you know?"

"I don't."

CHAPTER 2

The Homeless Man

I watch Annabelle approach the dirty looking man. What is she doing??

The voices in my head tell me to stop going after her. To slow down and change course, fast. After all, this is nuts. I only just met her! Why on earth did I follow her in the unknown?!

Was it curiosity..? Boredom? The need for something exciting to happen in my life? Truth was, I'd grown tired of life these past few years… Something I remembered just before I signed the contract. A distant memory popped in my head, a thought that had kept me awake for more than just one night. *If this is what life is… I don't want it.*

Yet, what got me here was suddenly urging me to stop going further, putting brakes on my feet as Annabelle marched on, determined.

A second memory. The night I was attacked by a gypsy in the middle of an otherwise empty road. I was still more trusting back then. Before he beat the living crap out of me, and any remaining confidence I still possessed.

I stopped next to a tree to the right of them, a few metres out, watching from a distance. I recognised his smell... a mix of dirt, sweat and alcohol. The hair on my neck stood up as a shiver washed across my body. My body remembered too... Not sure how long he'd been lying here, but his last shower was a looong time ago.

"Hello," she said, as if it is the most natural thing in the world.

He looked confused.

I did too... I'm sure.

Did he hear her? A big frown marked his forehead as he looked down at the bottles surrounding him.

Annabelle looked back at me and waved me over.

This is dangerous, my mind reminded me. As if I needed that reminder. *You need to get out of here.*

"Excuse me please?" She went again.

He looked around and I panicked. He saw us... he saw her... did he see *me*? Frozen to that tree I cannot move.

He looked at her, confusion written all over his face, making Annabelle giggle.

What's with that giggle?? And how can she giggle right now? Seriously, this girl is insane!!

She moved closer to him, her steps deliberate and took him in slowly, head to toe.

He shifted, releasing an angry grunt, before he looked back my way and locked eyes with me.

A shudder washed all over me when he did. He saw me... He knew I was there yet there I stood glued to the ground unable to move. My legs felt heavy, as if made of brick. Annabelle on the other hand, didn't even flinch. How could she be so calm? He was at least five times taller than her and about ten times bigger... *and faster*, my brain reminded me of the situation with my feet. Geez, thanks for that.

What happened next was one big blur. I could see Annabelle talking to him, but she was talking quietly and I was too far removed to make out what she said. Glued to that tree I stood and watched on.

At first, he seemed wary. Unsure of what to make of her, his eyes scanning his surroundings every so often. He stayed silent for the most part, moving his head slightly here or there, making me wonder if he was listening or lost in his own thoughts. But when he looked up at her, there was something in his face I didn't recognise. It washed over him within seconds, before he caught it.

Annabelle continued as she was, purposefully or unaware. He looked at her again, more closely this time. Surprised, then thoughtful... and then his shoulders dropped. That's when I saw an expression I recognised only too well. *Pain...* written all over his face. Raw, deep, and vulnerable. Whatever memory just came up for him, came deep from within. One he must have been trying to avoid for a while, considering his struggle with it.

Annabelle watched him patiently as if waiting for something. And all of a sudden, as if turned on by a switch, he broke his silence and started talking. Slowly at first, then faster and faster, his chest moving quickly as he did. He must have been waiting for this moment for a long time, everything just seemed to blur out of him.

I wanted to move closer, understand what was going on, but it felt wrong to interfere with what was happening before me. He gestured his hands, speaking so fast, he gasped up for air between words as he continued, releasing whatever he was holding onto.

There was a brief pause before a big cry left his mouth.

It sounded like defeat.

This big and scary man didn't look so scary anymore all of a sudden. On the contrary.. he looked broken, exposed... lost.

I was glad I didn't come over when Annabelle wanted me to.

Didn't interrupt the moment building before my eyes. I felt like an intruder as is, watching this personal moment from afar. And yet seeing him crumble like this, stirred something within me too.

I watched him sit in shame and regret as he was going deep, reality hitting him hard. Yet unlike me, who moved these thoughts aside as quickly as they came, he seemed to have surrendered to them, embracing the storm he could no longer control.

Tears were rolling down his cheeks as he lifted his legs and hugged them to his chest, looking as if he would otherwise break apart.

I had to look away. The pain written on his face was eating him alive, making him unrecognisable to the man we saw just moments earlier. He looked like a little boy sitting like this...

Regardless of what he did and without knowing his circumstances, I caught myself feeling sorry for him. Wanting to go over and comfort him. Tell him, whatever it was, it was going to be ok. Almost, that was... I thought, remembering the way he looked at me just moments ago.

Annabelle took his hand and whispered something in his ear.

He released another big cry, followed by a big sigh, and nodded slowly, wiping his tears from his cheeks.

They sat quietly for a while, his eyes now closed, Annabelle still holding his hand.

I caught her whisper something into his ear from time to time, before the lines on his face softened. His breath deepened, his mouth fell open, his body relaxed.

Annabelle laid him down gently.

I waited another moment before making my way over slowly, as not to wake him.

Smiling at me broadly, Annabelle took my hand.

"Time to go my friend, he will be ok.

Luke

Ring beep beep ring beep ring ring.... the sound of the alarm clock tore him brutally from his dream. Geez, already? Luke sighed half asleep and rubbed his eyes. He turned to the other side and hit the "off" button. *5min more minutes* his body begged, but that wasn't going to happen today, and he knew it. Scratching his head, he lazily swung one leg over the bed and then the other and made his way to the bathroom in boxers and slippers. He threw some cold water at his face, jumping back as his body shivered against the cold.

Now he was awake. He brushed his teeth and hit his morning playlist, jumped into the shower and let the water run across his body and thoughts. Tuesday, here we come. This would kick him into gear.

Whistling alongside the music, Luke found himself in a very good mood today. He felt good too, Luke thought, when he felt a little nag. He ignored it. Turning off the water, Luke grabbed a towel and dried his blonde hair.

Looking up at the mirror, his green eyes and freckles stared cheerfully back at him. Luke formed a gun on both hands and pointed it at his reflection, pretending to shoot one after the other, before giving his reflection the biggest smile and a cheeky wink. Something he heard a chick talk about on the radio the other day apparently was good for one's self-esteem. It sounded so weird, he just had to try it and after it made him laugh, he decided to stick with it.

He put on his jeans and threw on a t-shirt, styled his hair and plucked his air pods in his ears. "Highway to hell" came screaming towards his ear drum. Life was just so much better with tunes, he thought.

Tug. The nagging continued.

He moved to the kitchen, grabbed a piece of toast, and stuffed it inside his mouth. The oven clock showed ten past nine, he was already late. He promised his friend Seb to help fix his Kawasaki today, or "Kwaka" as he liked to call it. Seb thought it was a piece of junk, but Luke knew a thing or two about bikes and this one was still more than solid.

He wondered if Seb ever saw what junk truly looked like, having grown up on the East End and all… But since Luke thought that machine was pretty rad, he couldn't wait to put his hands on it and give it a go. He grabbed his denim jacket, threw his backpack over his shoulder and made his way towards the bus stop.

Tug.

Tug.

Tug.

Luke ignored the feeling. Instead, he turned up the volume on his headphones and put his hands in his pockets.

The bus stop was only a few steps away and the bus rolled up the moment he got there. *Sweet!* He thought and jumped on, making his way to the middle. It was only three stops till Seb's house, so he didn't bother sitting down.

Seb and Luke had been 'almost neighbours' ever since he arrived here three years ago, when he was just fourteen.

He looked out the window as they passed the rugby field where they first met. It was also where they had their first fist fight, smoked their first pot and puked half the day after. Turned out they hadn't gone to 'the right place' to get 'the good stuff' but took whatever was offered first before running back to the park as fast as they could, freedom behind them, hearts beating fast. Luke smiled at the memory, they were mates ever since.

He hit the stop button and jumped off at Marks Park. It was quiet here today, he observed looking around. Few people walking their dogs, two boys chasing after a ball, a girl cartwheeling across the field and a tired looking elderly couple fearfully following their grandchild on his bike, clinging onto each other and their coffees.

Luke took in a deep breath and exhaled out filled with gratitude. He loved this place. Had done ever since he first set foot here.

Tug.

Yes… Something told him this wasn't going to be an ordinary day.

He moved past the "closed path" sign and took a sharp right.

There Seb was, leaning across his bike, his back to Luke. Luke chuckled watching him rumble around his bike. They both knew Seb didn't have a technical bone in his body, and yet he was already covered in dirt.

"There she is," Seb exclaimed cheerfully, spotting Luke through the rear mirror. "Sleeping beauty finally came out to play."

Luke laughed out loud. "Sleeping beauty won't be much help here," he countered. "You'll need the frickin` fairy godmother herself to fix up the mess you already made"

He paused for a moment. "Let's see how much damage you added, shall we?" He added with a grin.

Seb flipped a towel at him, grinning back. "Is that so?" He replied. "Well I'm glad you finally made it, Tinks." Wiping his hands, he passed the tools to Luke. "Show us how it's done then, your majesty."

Luke slid out of his jacket and got to work. His granddad, or "Gramps" as he used to call him when he was little, was a mechanic, so that's what they did most of the time. Whilst most kids climbed trees and swam in lakes all summer, Luke spent his time fixing all sorts of stuff. He didn't mind though. He loved his Gramps and that was much better than what waited at home for him. He looked up to the sky for a minute before turning his focus back to the bike. "This will be a piece of cake."

Tug

CHAPTER 3

Sometimes a moment, that comes from nowhere,

All of a sudden makes it so clear.

A moment, that triggered a deja-vu

The memory of someone I used to be

Careless and free, now so hard to see

A shadow of it looking back at me.

Nate

Annabelle and I didn't speak much since we left the lake twenty minutes ago and started walking in the opposite direction to the city. I didn't mind… I had a lot to think about.

I watched Annabelle from the corner of my eye, expecting her to say something, but she seemed deep in thoughts. Part of me was glad… I was also still processing what just happened. Has the homeless man been another test? And if so… did I just fail?

I wondered if she knew this was going to happen and made a mental note to ask her later. First, I had to make sense of it myself. And everything else. But where to start? Small talk was the last thing on my mind. It always had been, but even more since it became the only way people could connect with me. After my wife left me. The year our little boy died. When the world stopped making sense. When *I* stopped making sense…

So we just walked on in silence. Truth was, I was embarrassed. Questions started popping in my head I never asked myself before: Would I have talked to him if she wasn't there? *Probably not.* Would I have even acknowledged him? I already knew the answer to that one too. I wouldn't have.

My mind jumped in to defend me, listing several reasons why that was the case: Articles I had read, crime rates amongst homeless people, the probability of drugs being involved, my childhood… pictures and facts flickered in front of my eyes frantically.

All true, yet it made no difference.

What if it was me? I suddenly thought. I considered myself a fairly decent human being. For what it was worth, I had always worked hard, always paid my taxes and always did my part in society… but we all know life changes on a dime. Was I just lucky mine had taken a different turn?

I looked up and found Annabelle smiling at me. Has she been watching me?

She stopped in her tracks, beaming at me.

Was she reading my mind?

My inner critic laughed at me. Don't be ridiculous, it mocked me.

Was I?

My stomach rumbled, interrupting my thoughts. I needed food, fast. The last thing I ate would have been hours ago. I motioned food to Annabelle and looked around.

Standing in the middle of a residential area, I turned back to where we came from and saw the city outskirts far in the distance. I was so distracted with what had happened, I didn't notice we wandered further and further in the opposite direction. I had no idea where we were.

"Shall we go a little further and look for something to eat on the way?" Annabelle offered.

"There's nowhere to eat until 'The Baxter Inn'," a voice suddenly came from behind.

I jumped back, turning around quickly, my arms out in front of me, expecting to find the homeless guy behind us. Instead, I was met with a cheeky grin and sparkling green eyes.

"I'm Luke," green eyes told us, tipping his imaginary hat. "At your service." He grinned broadly. "Couldn't help eavesdrop. You're not from around here, huh?"

"Well observed Sherlock," I mumbled, unimpressed.

"If you need a place to eat, a friend of mine lives just half an hour away," he continued, ignoring me and pointed towards the valley.

Annabelle nodded.

"You can crash there tonight and continue tomorrow if you like. It'll be a few hours to Central from there." He added, waiting for a response.

I eyed him from the side before locking eyes with Annabelle to align. He looked friendly alright, but this felt too much of a coincidence. After all, he doesn't know us. Who was this friend we were meant to just crash at and why did that kid care where we slept anyway?

"You won't get to the village before dark," Luke continued into the silence. "And by then no one will let you in. They're not as friendly down there," he added with a wink. "What do you say?"

I was about to politely decline, when I heard Annabelle squeal behind me.

"Yes! Haha! YES, thank you. Yes, yes!

Luke smiled at her and gave me a quick look to confirm. Noticing my expression, he hesitated for a moment but nodded eventually and turned his attention back to Annabelle.

They walked ahead of me cheerfully as I followed slowly, kicking a rock in front of me. I really needed to talk to this girl. This wasn't how I imagined our adventure at all. And the rate we were going, we would never make it to Central. If that was where we were heading in the first place. Was I missing the point??

I observed them from behind. Where had this kid come from all of a sudden and how long had he been following us? Was I meant to believe he just happened to come by, sensing we needed a place to stay? Magically having one to offer? Too many coincidences for my liking…

How was Annabelle so trusting? *And when did you become so risk-avert?* My mind jumped in, reminding me of the time I brought half the pub back to my dorm.

I chuckled at the memory. Those were the days. Carefree days…
What happened to me?

It felt so foreign these days, I almost forgot they existed. It was the same year I went hitchhiking across the Himalayas with nothing but my backpack. The year I spent a night under a bridge after a truck caught my backpack with its side mirror and dragged me half across the pavement. Whilst it wasn't the zen trip I had imagined, it was a hell of an adventure. Come think of it, I must have been Luke's age at the time. Had time turned me into a bitter old man?

"Hardly old," I heard a soft voice reply.

I paused for a moment looking around, finding Luke and Annabelle chatting as they were.

"I feel old…" I replied into the nothing.

Luke, Nate and Annabelle marched on for another ten minutes before they came across a big opening in the road. Luke stopped abruptly, looked left, right, then waved Nate and Annabe over. As they came closer, they found a little path to their left, hidden behind a fallen tree. Luke climbed over it with ease and gestured to Nate and Annabelle to follow.

"We're not breaking in, are we?" Nate asked half-jokingly, lending Annabelle a hand.

"Nah," Luke laughed, wiping his hands on his jeans. "Just making sure it's just us."

Nate looked up surprised before stepping over the tree himself.

"We've had a few rowdy complaints here lately," Luke explained, "causing a bit of trouble. Sue asked me to take care of her place while she's away, that's all." He shrugged his shoulders.

"Which you do by inviting strangers to her house?" Nate asked sceptically, catching a look from Annabelle.

Luke just smirked. "I figured the tree will keep those away who shouldn't be here.. and those in, who don't behave." He added with a wink, making Annabelle giggle whilst Nate inwardly rolled his eyes.

The path in front of them had trees on either side, like the alleys Nate would see on the national geographics channel. Sue had an eye for beauty, he observed as they reached a clearing and found her white cottage behind it. To its left was a big purple Rhododendron, several golden yellow flora hostas, a few burgundy rex begonia as well as bright pink and lime green fantasia plants. Amongst it, Nate spotted one single white calla lily. It was hidden away between all the other flowers, but once he saw it, he could not unsee it. Very good eye indeed, he noted, acknowledging.

He had always been fascinated by plants.

Three white steps lead to the front door and patio, a wrought iron black fence stretched all the way to the overhang and two big wooden rocking chairs stood in the corner, completing the European look.

Luke appeared from the back of the garden with a set of keys. "There's a shed behind the main house" he pointed towards the back. "You can stay there tonight." He handed Nate the keys. "Meet at the back when you're all settled? I'll throw in some logs and get our food sorted in the meantime."

Annabelle nodded in agreement and followed Nate out back.

The "shed" as he called it, was a mix between a garage and a granny flat, Nate observed stepping inside. It would do for the night and was probably a lot better than any alternative, he concluded. He looked around searching for something that could be turned into a bed when he found Annabelle quietly in the corner.

"You ok?" He asked softly, kneeling next to her. She looked up at him, her big brown eyes filled with wonder and nodded slowly.

"Can you believe how lucky we are?" She asked. "Who would have thought we would make a new friend this quickly… and now we have a home for the night."

She beamed at him as Nate looked around slowly. This was everything but *a home*, he thought. Unless you lived in a dungeon. Tools and cables were spread across the table, a rusty lamp hanging from the ceiling, a wheelbarrow in the corner, a dustpan on the floor… which was ironic considering the windows and floors were covered in webs.. some working gloves and paint cans in one corner, and a garden hose and radio casually sitting on a wooden shelf. Nate looked back at Annabelle searching for the right words when she continued.

"I wonder where Bobby will sleep tonight." She watched Nate for a moment.

"You mean Luke?" He replied absently. "He'll stay in the house."

"No, silly," Annabelle giggled, "our friend."

It took Nate a moment to follow. "The homeless guy?" He asked surprised.

Annabelle nodded and got up slowly.

"He would probably call this a jackpot." She squeezed Nate's hand softly and walked out of the door, leaving him pondering behind.

Luke - Earlier that day

Three hours, a coke, burger and fries later, his job was done. Luke removed his finger prints from the rig when Seb appeared behind him and whistled through his teeth.

"Looks sick," he noted appreciatively. "Nice one brother."

Luke grinned and felt quite pleased. It turned out even better than expected. That wasn't the only reason he was glad it was done though. The tugging continued as he started working on the machine and got stronger and stronger as the day progressed. The more he ignored it, the more persistent it became.

There was a reason he was ignoring it. This wasn't the first time he had felt this. He recalled two separate occasions, even though they were a number of years apart. The first time he was barely out of his nappies, the second time he remembered only too well. His life turned upside down after. So, when it happened again that morning, he knew it was going to be big.

He grabbed his jacket and bag and swallowed hard. This next part wouldn't be easy.

"What's up?" Seb asked, sensing a change.

"Nothin'," he replied, earning a frown. Seb knew him long enough to see right through him and whilst he didn't understand what was going on, he could see something brewing in his friend.

"See ya at the track tomorrow?" he asked instead. He also knew him well enough to know when to leave it be.

"I guess..." Luke replied slowly, already knowing it was a lie. He gulped, walked around and gave Seb a big hug.

Surprised, Seb laughed into his embrace. "Dude, you alright?" He eyed him curiously. Luke wasn't exactly the hugging kinda guy.

Except for that very drunken night, when he leaned on Seb to walk in a somewhat straight line, this was the first time he ever hugged him.

Luke cleared his throat, nodded, and swung his backpack over his shoulder, getting ready to leave. "Love you brother," he whispered, lifted his hand to wish farewell and left the garage without looking back. As soon as he turned the corner, he took a deep breath.

Luke knew this was the last time he would see his friend and this their last goodbye.

"Fine," he growled. "Now that you have my attention, where to now?" His legs moved automatically, shifting him towards the lake. The opposite direction he had come from.

He sighed one more time and went on his way. He would miss his friend. But today was as good as any to leave this place behind, he told himself.

Some people needed to stay where they were, surrounded by everything they knew. Luke was never one of them. Or never had that luxury either, one could argue. Maybe that is why he could never understand how people holidayed in the same places, ate the same food or, in his mind even worse, 'staycationed'.

The first time he had heard about it, he didn't make many friends, calling it the dumbest thing he ever heard. He then made it worse by asking the group if they were afraid to like it so much that they wouldn't be able to come back and fit in the same parameters anymore. Like once you crossed a line, he tried arguing his point to the horrified faces staring back at him before he gave up. Luckily Seb came to his rescue back then, whilst Luke understood that conversation was pointless with some.

But not him. He'd never been one to choose the easy path, even though it was also likely the easy path never chose him. His mother a drug addict, he lived with his granddad for the most part.

Luke connected the dots very quickly, even at his young age. He understood things got too hard for his mother, when people were always up in her business. She needed that escape... and always looked so peaceful after she would get her hit. At least for a while, before the shakes and come downs started.

But he wasn't scared of it back then. Not until *he* arrived.

"Dad" as he made him call him, even though everyone knew he wasn't his real dad of course. Just showed up one day and never left. It wasn't all bad though, Luke thought. When Ma wasn't high, she was quite the storyteller.

Her adventurers he always loved the most. She told him it was in his blood too and he believed her. A flashback of him sitting on her knees in his nappies came to mind. He was way too old for nappies by then and it was way too late for him to still be up, but there he was listening to another one of her adventures. This one was his favourite. It was about the gift inside him, he recalled eagerly, waiting for it to be claimed. She'd lower her voice at that part and look at him in a seriousness he didn't know, before her imagination would melt into his.

He'd tell Gramps about it the next day, imitating an ordinary, determined sailor defeating a crew of pirates or a long-lost explorer stumbling across un-imaginary treasure.

Gramps would watch him for a while, sometimes disappear in the attic for a moment and re-emerge with old maps and binoculars in hand ready to join his adventure.

Luke used to squeal in excitement and couldn't wait to tell Ma all about it next time he was around. She'd always get the same look on her face. One that said, amongst all bad she had done, something good came out of her after all. That was if *dad* wasn't around of course. Luke scoffed at the thought and clenched his fists. Before Ma's adventures ended in hospital…

Back then he thought she was defeated by a monster or got tired of fighting it. Which was partly true. He just didn't realise the monster was living inside their house.

Either way things weren't the same after that.

He tried telling Gramps some of Ma's stories, but now Gramps face would turn blank and stare into nothing. The monster had come and taken some of Gramps too, he thought, wondering when it would come for him.

Then dad got into trouble with the wrong people again, and since they couldn't get anything from Ma anymore, they came knocking at Gramps' door. Gramps didn't say anything, but they both knew Luke couldn't stay there anymore.

That's when the monster came for him.

Tug.

～

At the core we are all lonely… at the core we're all afraid.
That one day we will awaken, and by then it's all too late.
Looking back at life so simple, yet so complicated made…

When all needed was some passion, laughter, friends and to be held
And to know that one's life mattered… to another, which was felt

～

TATJANA GENYS

CHAPTER 4

Luke walked into the shed minutes after Annabelle left Nate to himself, carrying two big sleeping bags.

"Hope it's alright for you guys," he started apologetically, handing one of them to Nate. "I promised Sue not to let anyone in the house anymore... after the last time." He shifted from one foot to another before continuing. "Party got a little outta hand." He shrugged his shoulders. "Or '*a lot out of hand*' according to that copper." His fingers formed quotation marks as he emphasized each word. Straightening his shoulders, he made a stern face before continuing in a strict voice:

"What you did was *very* disrespectful and caused a lot of damage. I should bring you in... that's what I should do. You're lucky Sue isn't pressing charges."

Pointing his finger at Nate, he continued.

"So this time, you're getting away with a warning. Next time I won't be this kind."

Luke rolled his eyes dramatically and let his shoulders drop, making Nate laugh. He used to be just like Luke when he was younger.

"It'll do," he replied smiling as Luke moved towards the door.

"I'll grab the mattress and our food," he shouted in passing and was gone before Nate had a chance to thank him.

Thinking of ways to make himself useful, he walked outside to light the fire. He placed two handfuls of tinder in the centre and added some paper he found in the garage. On the way back to the fire pit, he collected a few twigs and pine needles and placed them on top of the tinder, trying to form a tepee.

"Whoa, you some kinda boy scout?" Luke exclaimed from behind him, whistling through his teeth.

"Something like that," Nate replied amused. "I lived off the land for a few months. No technology, no reception, nothing but trees, bushes, and freedom. Survival skills 1-1000," he laughed reminiscing.

"No reception?" Luke asked mortified, clutching onto his phone in his back pocket.

"Hard to imagine these days, ey?" Nate laughed.

"Kinda," Luke agreed. "We'd be lost without it I reckon." He paused for a moment allowing his thoughts to form. "That'd be a pretty wild experience though. Probably show us how dependent we are on it and how disconnected from the real world."

"Interesting thought," Nate replied, surprised by the depth he heard in this young boy.

"I didn't feel lost back then but guess that's just how I grew up. Always liked exploring places, going somewhere." He told him about the time he quit his job and went travelling across South America, his adventures hiking the Andes ancient trails and his experience sitting in ceremony with a shaman. "You've got to follow whatever makes you happy" Nate concluded, seeing Luke's eyes light up before he jumped onto his feet in excitement.

"That's what Ma always said!" Luke noted proudly.

"Sounds like a smart woman," Nate replied, noticing a shift in Luke.

"What's for dinner?" Annabelle jumped in from behind, her hands filled with berries.

"It's a surprise" Luke grinned and got up, wiping his hands on his jeans. Rummaging in his backpack, he pulled out a blanket, laid it out in front of them and opened the cooling box next to him. A Baguette, slices of ham and cheese, eggs, tomatoes and butter followed.

Nate's mouth began to water at the sight of food, as he realised how long it had been since he'd last eaten. *I could eat a horse,* he thought, before Bobby crossed his mind. *Will he get anything to eat today?* he wondered, watching Luke break the baguette in three big pieces. He handed Nate a plate, which he took only too gladly and swallowed his pieces in three big gulps. Annabelle on the other side was still holding most of hers in her hand. Knowing she hadn't eaten anything since they got here either, he nudged her softly and pointed at her food. She took a small bite, chewed it slowly and smiled at him happily before turning back to Luke.

"Do you live in the village?" she asked after her second bite.

"Nah, I live on the other side of the lake," Luke replied matter-of-factly, swallowing his food. He picked the crumbs from his plate with his finger.

"What brought you to us today?" Nate asked, surprised.

"Curiosity? maybe." Luke replied after a short pause. "You?"

Annabelle and Nate looked at each other.

"Time will tell," they replied out of one mouth and laughed.

Luke gave Nate a long look, making him wonder if he was thinking the same. Something had brought them together for a reason. What it was was too soon to be said, but one thing was sure… This was no coincidence.

They sat and ate until their tummies were full, watching the sun go down behind the fields, turning the horizon orange.

Nate looked at Annabelle, grateful for the moment. She was right, he thought, they were lucky to be here. He imagined them wandering around in the dark, looking for a place to stay if they hadn't taken up Luke's offer.

Instead, he found himself nicely fed and surrounded by good people. It had been a while since he last sat like that, he suddenly realised. Or made time for people, really. He mostly kept to himself these days, filling his days with work from morning till night.

Often he finished so late, he barely had energy for dinner, and the few times he tried reaching out to his friends, they had already made plans. Whilst he was busy working, they were building their families… and whilst he was happy for them of course and didn't mind time on his own, he couldn't help feeling lonely every so often, realising how much he wanted what they had. The problem was, he was slowly but steadily moving further and further inside his shell. Until he woke up one morning and accepted the reality that maybe it was his fate to be alone for the rest of his life.

Watching Luke and Annabelle around the fire, he admired their ease of conversation, as they exchanged stories and laughed at each other's jokes. He thought of the unspoken beauty within friendships. Especially the unexpected ones, where judgement didn't reside. And how for some reason it often felt easier to share things with a complete stranger, then those near and dear to us.

He listened to Luke's stories with great envy, realising how he missed being this carefree and living for the day, like the "old" Nate had done.

He glanced up at the stars and made a wish. To no longer let life pass him by. To start enjoying life again. Living it.

When he finished his plea, the sky felt like it was sucking him in. The stars shone brighter, and the moon felt lighter as it painted a path across the shimmering pond, leading right towards them. He got lost in its flicker and closed his eyes for that brief moment, trying to take it all in and carve it into his mind. A promise for a brighter future he wanted to be able to recall at any time.

A scream brought him back to reality. When he opened his eyes, everything around him was dark. He had fallen asleep.

It took him a while to adjust to the surroundings. The fire was almost gone and Luke and Annabelle were nowhere to be seen. He looked down at his body and found a blanket covering him.

Looking out into the dark where he last saw the path illuminated by the moon, he was met by a pair of wide eyes staring back at him. Instinctively, he grabbed some firewood from the pit and lifted it in the air quickly to see who was there, but by the time he did the eyes were gone. He twirled around a few times, trying to find where they went, when he heard a door push open behind him. Annabelle was standing barefoot on the doorstep, holding up a little light.

"Come inside," she said softly, "you'll catch a cold out there."

"Did you hear anything?" Nate asked, nodding slowly, listening out into the distance. "See anything?" He probed again, when she didn't reply.

"The deer, you mean?" She asked, her voice sleepily. "Luke said there are plenty around. Wish I would have seen it", she added, yawning.

Nate nodded slowly. It was just a deer. He must have imagined the scream. Maybe had another one of his night terrors. He sighed deeply. There is nothing to worry about, he told himself following Annabelle inside the castle he once called a dungeon.

~

An unexpected encounter

Nate woke up to the sunlight shining through the window. When he glanced at his watch, it was barely seven am. Annabelle was deep asleep.

Anxious to get going but not wanting to wake her, he decided to go for a run to clear his head. He was used to a certain structure in his day, a routine he needed to keep his dark thoughts at bay. Maybe he could spot that deer, he thought, trying to distract himself.

Expecting Luke to sleep until midday, he was surprised to find a note by the door. Luke, unlike anyone else his age, wasn't still in bed, he'd already left.

Nate walked back into the room scratching his forehead. He had assumed Luke would join them this morning. Where did he go that early? He couldn't recall Luke mentioning it last night unless it happened after he dozed off.

The note itself was very vague: A promise to meet them in Central with the ask to leave the place as they found it. Next to the note, a piece of paper instructing them where to go and a plate of leftover f] ood from last night.

Kids… Nate thought, wondering what Sue would make of this. Over time he had become good at ignoring his own inner state, by focusing his attention on others.

"Did he mention anything to you?" He asked Annabelle after she got up an hour later, packing away his mattress and sleeping bag. Annabelle just shrugged her shoulders.

They ate in silence and continued on their way an hour later. Luke's directions turned out to be *directionally* correct, so by the time they arrived in Central, it was already past midday. The market was in full swing.

At first, it felt strange to be surrounded by so many people again but they quickly adjusted. As Nate and Annabelle mingled their way through the crowd from stand to stand, they were surprised by the selection of Lamps, candles, carpets, jewellery, food, spices... in every colour and flavour imaginable. Handlers were shouting, haggling, trading on top of each other from every side, trying to convince their potential buyers to stop as often as possible.

Annabelle's eyes lit up the second she got there, and her fascination kept growing as she moved from stand to stand, her little hands touching their goods with growing appreciation.

Much to Nate's dismay, as she stopped next to every handler and curiously listened to their story. Yet even he found it hard not to notice the effect she had on people. Her joy was infectious, as her face lit up like it was Christmas morning. Nate on the other hand, looked like Grinch himself trying to rid himself from one handler after the other.

By the time they reached the twelfth stand, he gave up. Frustrated, he sat down on a stool behind one of the hagglers and watched Annabelle approach the next. As he observed her, his anger evaporated. The more he watched Annabelle, the more he realised how people changed around her. Their whole demeanour shifted as soon as she connected with them. *It must be the way she makes one feel*, he thought. As if nothing else mattered and as if they just had the most precious gift on earth for her.

He thought of the time he first met her and how quickly he felt comfortable in her presence and seeing her so joyous now, he couldn't help getting a little excited himself. It was the way she looked at each item, as if it was the first time she ever saw them. It also made him realise how little attention he paid to any of them and how quickly he moved from one thing to another. Maybe they were just bodies moving past him… he wondered, remembering Annabelle's first questions, recognising how little time he had spent with those who were near.

Annabelle meanwhile, sat on a Persian cushion next to one handler, a spiced tea in hand and watched him transform into a fabler. Speaking of his quests within the deepest jungles of the Maharaja, he was waving his hands around frantically, pointing to the garments next to him, the 'treasures' he found along the way.

Nate rolled his eyes, ready to jump in and ask how they found electricity in those deepest jungles to connect those lamps, when another handler stepped in, boasting of his adventures in the desert.

He spoke of animals never seen before and stories too scary to repeat, lowering his voice whilst looking around suspiciously. He kneeled next to Annabelle and whispered in her ear how he had to promise to never mention the name of that place again, or he would never see another day. Told her of the shadows appearing in the middle of the night, out of nowhere, to keep an eye on him, so he wouldn't break his promise and disappear again as quickly as they came. Because if he did… the handler looked expectantly at Nate and Annabelle when he paused, there would be fatal consequences. No trace of him would be found the following morning. He lifted his hand and traced it across his neck to demonstrate, before opening his coat to reveal a selection of ancient looking bracelets.

Annabelle squealed in excitement, touching the gold chain carefully, the few items he had left to remind him of the place he once visited. She seemed engrossed in his story.

Nate wasn't sure if she believed him, but could see her fully immersed by what he shared. Especially when he told her about the queen of Tibutai, her majesty herself. As beautiful as one could only imagine, who personally saw to his release.

Nate sighed and turned to watch the handler more closely. What was going through his mind? He wondered. Was he tired of performing every day or did he crave the attention? He would easily be able to tell Nate and Annabelle weren't the big shoppers or change the outcome of his day, so why go through with this charade? Did he also crave the distraction?

Whatever it was, Annabelle seemed to motivate him to continue. His adventures grew bigger and more colourful by the minute, each story more fascinating than the one before. They started attracting a crowd.

"For the last time, leave me alone!" Nate suddenly heard faintly in the distance. He turned his head to see where it came from, when he spotted a woman in a long green dress on the other side of the street.

Three children were surrounding her as she tried to push them out of her way, each jumping onto her path not letting her through. Frustrated, she took off one shoe and pretended to throw it at them. Squeaking, the kids ran away in search of hiding, recovering quickly moments later. They moved closer again, jumping around her giggly, forming the letter L with their little fingers, holding them up against their foreheads.

The lady stepped back inside her shoe, fixed her oval shaped hat and turned the corner. As she did, Nate caught her expression. One he didn't expect. Her frustration had changed into sadness. There only for a split second and easily lost with everything happening around her, but he was sure of what he saw. Whatever caused her reaction didn't stem from hate, he concluded.

Annabelle grabbed his hand and started pulling him behind her. Puzzled, Nate followed her fast pace through the crowd. He tried asking her why they left so abruptly, but his voice got lost in the crowd as Annabelle marched on determinedly, until she stopped so abruptly, he nearly crashed into her.

"There," she said.

"There?" he repeated, two big question marks in his eyes.

"There," she confirmed as if it is the most obvious thing.

What's there? And where 'there'? Not wanting to lose face, Nate looked right, left, left again, and then back to Annabelle trying to find something out of the ordinary.

"Stop," she said softly, watching him. "You have eyes my friend, but you don't see. Try seeing with your heart instead."

Nate wanted to protest, tell her about the women he was watching just a moment ago and the details he noticed, but something told him this wasn't the time. Instead, he paused, closed his eyes and took a long deep breath. He listened to his heartbeat for a few seconds, before he re-opened them, tilted his head to the left and looked around one more time. Taking in every detail, he waited for his heart to give him a clue.

That's when he saw her. Leaning against a wall between the candle maker and sculptor, wearing a light blue dress and the biggest smile. His heart skipped a beat when she looked up, her dark blue eyes taking his breath away. He looked back at Annabelle, to confirm he was looking in the right direction, but realised there and then it made no difference. His eyes moved back to the young woman automatically.

"Who is she?" he asked, wondering how he missed her the first time.

"Why don't you go and find out?" Annabelle replied softly.

It took a moment for her words to travel from Nate's ears to his brain. "Come again?" He noted slowly, releasing an awkward laugh.

He would never go up to her. Not after he had sworn off relationships after his last attempt failed so miserably.

"What are you waiting for?" Annabelle nudged again.

Courage, shot through his mind, *or your insanity, whatever comes first.*

"You just need to take the first step" Annabelle tried again. "The rest will happen automatically."

Nate's heart started to pound loudly in his chest. For a moment he was convinced the whole market could hear it. He knew what would happen automatically. Last time his words got stuck in his throat, he rambled something unrecognisable and then went completely blank, whilst the girl just kept staring at him, her brow rising higher and higher as the minutes passed. He disappeared as soon as he was able to regain himself again.

"Get Luke to do it." Nate replied dismissively. "Where is he anyway??"

"If you won't do it, somebody else will," Annabelle countered softly.

And as if on cue, somebody did. It played out in front of Nate's eyes in slow motion, causing a sharp pang in his heart. Dark hair, green shirt, three buttons undone, a young man made confident strides towards her, his eyes fixated on her like she was prey. Nate hated him already. 'His girl" meanwhile, oblivious to it all, kept re-arranging the clothes on her stand. She didn't see him until the very last moment and gasped in surprise when she did. Taking a hesitant step backwards as the young man moved closer, she caught herself quickly and smiled. PANG, made Nate's heart again.

"I've seen enough." He muttered angrily and turned away. Why did she bring me here?? I didn't sign up for this. Don't *need* this...

Why didn't we just stay where we were?? His disappointment was hitting him hard.

"Let's get something to eat," Annabelle interfered with his mental monologue. "You must be starving, how inconsiderate of me. I could never do this hungry either. Come, my friend, I know just the place."

As they turned to leave, Nate took one final glimpse towards the young woman and regretted it momentarily. She looked in his direction and blushed when the man in front of her brushed a strand of hair from her pretty face. Urgh, Nate sighed angrily... that guy knows exactly what he's doing.

If only I had taken that damn first step, he thought, turning away for good.

~

Nate

Annabelle was sitting cross-legged on the grass next to me. Her eyes closed, she was bathing in sunshine, a smile playing on her face. I admired her peace of mind. Craved for mine to be just as peaceful.

My inner calm went away a few years ago, and this morning especially it was at high alert. For many reasons. I knew I had to get back to the market. Had to get back to her. Lucy…

I let the name roll off my tongue. L-U-C-Y. That's what he called her yesterday, at lunch. I couldn't believe my luck. I mean, what are the chances!

First Annabelle couldn't decide where we would eat. We went to five different places before she finally made up her mind. I really couldn't care less. Where we went, what we ate… made no difference. We settled in the *Garden café* and sank into their big brown leather chairs around a wooden table. Annabelle kept going on and on about how rustic the place was, how much character the fireplace gave and how she loved the vintage style festoon lights. *Made no difference.* I know she was trying to lighten the mood, but it didn't matter. I was angry. Angry at myself for missing the opportunity. Angry at Annabelle for putting me in that situation. Angry at Mr 'no button' for showing up when he did. I zoned out.

The waiter came over and introduced himself as Dan, passing our menus. I tossed mine to the side without looking. I couldn't believe I had missed this opportunity and was kicking myself for not walking over to her. There are other girls, I tried telling myself. *It didn't help.* Something about her felt different. Familiar. I couldn't put my finger on it but it was there behind her smile.

Dan gave up on my order and turned to Annabelle for support. She smiled and ordered on our behalf. Twirling the wooden spoon between my fingers, I shrugged my shoulders at her apologetically. I felt ridiculous. Why did this bother me so much? I had sworn off relationships five years ago. Accepted my situation and settled on staying alone. Why was this just a big deal?

I was content, wasn't I? And what was so special about her anyway? After all, I was hardly sixteen anymore to fall in love with a pretty face.

As the spoon kept turning inside my hand, so did my perspective. He might have gotten there first, but that didn't mean anything yet. Was he even her type? Surely, she wouldn't fall for a peacock like that.

"Don't judge him," Annabelle interfered softly, reading my mind. "It's written all over your face," she explained, shrugging her shoulders.

I knew she was right, but it didn't matter. I wanted to hate him. Put my anger towards him, so I didn't have to address what was eating me at my core.

"Fine," I replied, grinding my teeth. "But I know people *like* him, and she deserves better"

Dan came round with the food, and it smelled delicious. Annabelle was right, I was hungry. Spoonful after spoonful landed on my plate, and in my mouth.

Dan looked from me to Annabelle raising a surprised eyebrow, clearly having a hard time keeping up with me.

"Girl problems," she explained.

"Aah," Dan replied knowingly. "Do I know the lucky girl?"

"The lady at the market," Annabelle replied before I could stop her.

"A local, I see. You have good taste lad. I must know her then... I know everyone in this town." Dan told us proudly.

"Doubt it." I countered, giving Annabelle a stern look.

TATJANA GENYS

"It's the lady with the beauuuutiful scarfs," she continued, ignoring me.

Dan paused for a moment. "Luce?"

Annabelle and I exchanged a quick look.

"I see," Dan continued, his face unreadable. "Lucy is pretty extraordinary, I give you that." His voice changed. "But you'll have to go through me first."

Great... An angry boyfriend. Just what I need right now, shot through my mind. *Thanks Annabelle.* I swallowed the rest of the food, ignoring the throbbing in my hand.

"That your girl?" I asked as coolly as possible, throwing Annabelle a look.

"Nah" he replied and chuckled. "Lucy and I are sort of family. She's Jamie's little sister. But since he left, I've kinda taken over." He looked at us proudly lifting his belt.

"Pretty sure she can look after herself by now," I replied, relieved.

"You don't know her like I do," Dan countered. "She might seem like she's got it all together, but she doesn't. And I won't let anyone just Waltz in here and hurt her, she's been through enough." His tone got serious... too serious for someone who was serving our food.

"What happened?" I asked curiously.

"Nothing that should trouble you," he replied quickly. "Especially during dinner." He turned to leave, but I stopped him.

"Please."

Dan looked around, hesitating.

"I'll throw in a good word with the boss," I added, pointing to the kitchen door. "Just tell me."

Dan chuckled and grabbed a chair. "Guess I can stay for a moment," he added. He eyed me for six Mississippi's before he began. I counted them silently, so I wouldn't back down.

"My Intentions are good," I added, realizing how corny I sounded the second it left my mouth.

He looked at Annabelle, who nodded in agreement.

"Very well," he finally began. Her parents died in a trailer accident when she was little, she keeps mostly to herself ever since. Especially after losing her brother."

"Her brother's dead too?" Annabelle asked horrified, her words nearly a whisper.

"No, it's not like that," Dan corrected himself. "Actually, we don't know, but we assume he's still alive. He just disappeared one day and that was that." He shook his head. "Didn't even tell me where he went and everyone kept looking for him here first of course. My best friend, he was... probably knew I would've talked him out of it. Neighbours said she still cries at night. Never recovered from it. Weeks she spent waiting by that window after he left... Just couldn't believe he'd leave her like that. Still thinks he'll just show up at her doorstep, the same way he disappeared. Like he just stepped out for milk and eggs or something. Neighbours don't think it's good for her, but she told them where to go." He chuckled. "That's our Luce... Stubborn as that girl, but as good as gold."

He got up from his chair and cleared Annabelle's empty plates.

"There's no getting through to her when she's made up her mind. Now every time someone just as much as mentions his name, she shuts off. Probably heard enough of the gossip. Some say they saw him gambling, mixing with the wrong crowd. You know, small town gossip. Broke her heart. So, she's just keeping to herself now, her head always thinking up new designs. You're lucky you caught her here, she's only just got back."

He took my empty plate. "How was the food?" He asked.

"So good!" Annabelle replied, rubbing her belly in delight.

Dan laughed. "I'll let the chef know. He'll be happy to hear it."

"How long will she stay?" I interrupted.

Dan turned back to me. "What do you want from her, lad?"

I scraped my brain for an answer, which was difficult under his stare.

"You better be nice to her boy, or you'll have me to answer to."

I mirrored his look, half amused/ half intimidated, simulating crossing my heart with my fingers. They have a funny way with their customers here, I thought.

Dan sighed before continuing. "She'll be here for a few more days. Your best bet is to find her at the farmers market in the morning or the library cafe in the afternoon." He looked at us for a reaction and found two blank faces looking back at him.

"The bakery off the little creek?" He tried again, pulling out a napkin and pen. He drew big lines for the Main Street, the station and post office, marking a big "X" for the market and his café. "She also comes here most days." He straightens his back.

"They used to come here together, you know?" he added after a little while. "Every Sunday. Would sit right by that table." He pointed to the spot two tables away from us. "She'd be sitting on his shoulders when they'd come in, she'd order tea for him and a hot chocolate for herself with extra sprinkles, marshmallows and three of our house finest. Pink they had to be or you'd be in trouble." He laughed fondly at the memory, wiping his eye. "Knew exactly what she wanted and how she wanted it. Princess he used to call her."

Annabelle shifted in her seat.

"Spoil her like there was no tomorrow. Couldn't believe it when he just packed up and left."

"Hey Dan, where do you want this?" a male voice came from

behind. We turned our heads to find a delivery guy wheeling in some boxes.

"Leave them in the kitchen next to the counter, Jimmy. And next time I'll need 4 more veggie boxes and six more leg ham. It's been selling like mad lately"

Jimmy nodded and marked something on his piece of paper. "You got it boss. Just need your signature here and here." He pointed to his invoice.

"Boss?" I repeated, raising an eyebrow.

"Oh yeah…" Dan chuckled. "Don't forget to put in a good word for me." He got up and followed Jimmy inside the kitchen, wiping his hands on his apron.

Way to go Nate…

I shifted anxiously in the grass. "Isn't it time to go yet?" I asked impatiently.

"One more minute," Annabelle replied. "This is too good."

I snapped pieces of grass between my fingers. I couldn't wait any longer. Not after I decided to finally speak to her today. I would go over to her, cool as a cucumber, just like he did.

You? Cool?? My inner voice mocked me.

I shut it down. NOT TODAY. I won't let it stop me today.

Annabelle opened her eyes, her smile widely.

"Let's go."

CHAPTER 5

Lucy's Rules

It was a busy day at the market today. Anxious excitement was filling the air. They hadn't been here in a few weeks, so everything felt fresh and exciting.

Onlookers were pacing from stand-to-stand admiring what they brought, and they weren't disappointed. Lucy laid her fabrics out carefully.

Rule #1, you must stand out. Brightest colours at the front followed by the most luxurious items, the cheaper garments in the back. Checking the little mirror in front of her, she re-adjusted her satin ribbon and pulled her silver clip with little blue Rhinestones tighter. She knew this would emphasize the colour of her eyes. She smiled.

Rule # 2 always keep smiling. People buy 'happy'. Now that everything was in position, she checked her range one final time. How pretty everything looked in the sunshine, she thought. She put her heart and soul in each garment, not one was the same as the other.

This was especially important for the gemstone décor. She wanted her clients to feel unique. Rule # 3 Make the buyer feel something. People also buy feelings, regardless how short-lived they are. Now that rule was a little harder to follow and often required real attention. Did the client want to feel beautiful? Powerful? Glamorous? Some of them simply wanted to be adored, others become somebody else for the day. Misreading the client's intentions would see the opportunity dissolve in front of one's eyes like quicksand. Yet get it right and get substantially rewarded. Lucy always viewed it like a dance. Every new buyer a new partner, and their exchange, their choreography.

As in any good dance, they would start off slow, circling around each other to the rhythm of the beat. Testing each other, teasing… Until they got bolder, their moves more aggressive, mirroring each other as their tempo increased, and with it, the flow of their negotiation. Yet before she would know it, the music would come to a halt… goods were exchanged against credit before they would bow to each other in recognition of their performance and move on to their next partner and dance.

This morning, Lucy danced two tangoes, one flamenco and one foxtrot before it hit eleven, selling two scarfs, one headband, two ribbons and three pieces of jewellery.

The afternoon, in comparison, was off to a slow start. It happened occasionally on sunny days like this, and Lucy didn't mind. It gave her a moment to breathe and observe the remaining buyers.

Her trained eyes were able to spot the sensible buyers from the overthinkers, the "buying-for-the-sake-of-buying-byers" as well as the "want to but can't" buyers very quickly. Most of the handlers called the last category time wasters and didn't want them anywhere near their stock, but Lucy didn't mind. On the contrary, she loved watching their eyes light up as they admired her fabrics. Some would drift into a different world for a few moments as their hands slid across her material. She loved watching them, and often wondered what reality they tried to escape from.

She could relate. Knew how important these moments of release were, even if only momentarily. So, whilst others shooed them along, she did the opposite and welcomed them. Sometimes even slid a piece of fabric into their pocket for them to hold onto later. They usually snapped back to reality quite quickly, embarrassed by their daydream, glancing around anxiously to see if anyone witnessed what they'd done, disappearing as quickly as they came, heads tucked in deep. Lucy meanwhile often wished they knew the gift they gave her in those same moments. It was these faces she remembered, when creating something new. That expression she called upon for inspiration and that exact feeling she tried to recreate. For anyone, rich or poor. And when another face would light up in delight the same way the others did in the past, she knew her work was done.

She often wondered if that was how a musician felt just before the applause, or an Olympian at an event before the whistle blew. It fueled her. Sometimes it felt so addictive, she didn't know how to contain it. Couldn't wait to share this gift with others.

So, when someone approached her stand, she watched them very carefully. Did they need to feel energised? Then she would add some colour to the mix and brighten their day. Did they want to feel powerful? A fitting suit would not only make them feel important, but the way others would treat them would do it too. Those who wanted to feel sensual, she would cover in silk, sometimes add a pair of stilettos, and watch them march off, ready to conquer the world. *This* was the power of clothing and the impact she could leave.

But what she loved about it the most, was that clothes accepted anyone as they were. Even those who didn't remember who they were. Clothes didn't judge... even when we made some rather peculiar choices at times, she thought, giggling at the picture of her in her purple high waist corduroy extra flared leg pants and yellow checkered shirt, she once thought was *the bomb*. Rainbow, he had called her... She sighed deeply. He was still with her most days, but this wasn't the time or place, so she moved that thought aside. Except for some of these moments, Lucy genuinely believed clothes could change your life, one day at a time.

She started re-arranging her stock and topped up the remaining pieces. Lost in that thought, she didn't notice him approaching at first.

That's when she made her first mistake. Rule #4 always stay in control.

~

Lucy, remembering

Lucy had been lonely for longer than she cared to admit. She often wondered if one could get used to being lonely, over time... Maybe she would find out some day.

First, it was Jamie she waited on, hoping for him to return and tell her it was all one big misunderstanding. As she grew older, she hoped somebody else would take his place, but since she had a hard time trusting people, that idea faded pretty quickly too.

She knew what everyone was thinking, Central wasn't exactly discreet about it. It was one of the many reasons she said yes to any opportunity to go away, even if it was just for a few days. And yet she was never able to outrun her reality. Because as soon as she got back, after all her work at the market was done, she found herself staring at the same bleak four walls again. She thought of moving for a while. Somewhere, where she wasn't "the sad Lucy, who lost her family." But she didn't. Couldn't. Because deep down inside, there was this little part that still hadn't given up. That still believed he would come back. *Someday...* when he was ready.

She started seeing Dr Jones more often again trying to move past the pain. He was the doctor, who treated her first after her parents died. And the one who introduced her to the rules, so she could learn to celebrate the small wins at the end of the day.

He couldn't have known that the day was the least of her worries. Whilst she was using the rules he had given her, she was doing so to keep her mind free from thinking about everything else. The house in particular. It felt empty all by herself, as if it too had lost its soul. Even the plants looked sad.

Josie, her neighbour, took them away eventually. She told Lucy she was going to look after them, but Lucy knew she just didn't have the heart to tell her they were dead. Dead-dead. Deader than dead. *Like my parents…* Lucy thought. She wished there would have been one final goodbye. A kiss on the cheek maybe, or even a "see you later." Instead, they were just gone. Disappeared as if they never existed. She had a hard time dealing with that reality, knowing there wasn't a single thing she could do to change that. What also didn't help, was that the town started treating her and Jamie, her brother, differently after the event. Instead of asking about their day, where they were headed or tickling her like they used to do, they were now met with big sad eyes, telling them how tragic it was that their parents were taken away from them so soon.

Dr Jones said, it's because no one really knows how to deal with loss. Lucy didn't understand that back then, but what she did understand was that she needed a hug from time to time and for somebody to tell her it was going to be okay. Even if it wasn't, and never would be.

Luckily, Jamie was still around back then… at least at first, and in body. He became quieter and quieter, slimmer and slimmer and more sombre than Lucy had ever seen him. As if someone had flipped a switch and taken his spirit. He went silent for most of the day and seemed absent a lot of the time, the circles underneath his eyes growing darker and darker. Lucy later guessed the responsibility felt too much to handle. After all, he was just a kid himself. He never mentioned it to Lucy of course, but he was petrified. Tried to pretend he had it all under control. He wasn't very good at it. Lucy saw him flinch every time someone knocked on the door and found him covered in sweat in the morning. She knew he didn't sleep, didn't eat, and later wished she told him she never expected anything from him. That all she ever wanted was to be with him.

She tried talking to him about mum and dad from time to time, trying to remember the good times, but he just couldn't go there. Went dark every time she tried and cut her off. He had never cut her off before. Dr Jones guessed it was too painful for him to remember, and Lucy believed him. He couldn't have known the real reason, since Jamie stopped visiting him after the first session.

Lucy often wished she didn't push him so hard back then, wondering if he would still be around if she didn't. But she was just a kid herself then too and didn't know when to stop and leave it be. And then one day, he too just left. She heard him close the door behind him that morning and ran to the window to watch him leave. By the time she reached the window frame, all she could see was his silhouette grow smaller and smaller, before it disappeared in the distance.

He didn't turn around, not even once. Maybe Jamie had to go somewhere, she thought, running barefoot down the stairs as quickly as her little legs would carry her. Why was he wearing his big coat? He never wore his big coat. Or his backpack... The one he usually only took on big adventures. Like the time he went on the school excursion with Dan.

She opened the door and called out his name. *"Jamie!"* No reply. *"JAMIE... wait for me!"* Nothing. *"JAAAAAMMMMMIIIIEEE!"* She screamed his name again and again from the top of her lungs. There was no reply. Maybe he went camping with Dan... she thought.

Yes, that will be it. He'll be back in a week, like last time, she told herself, closing the door quietly behind her.

That was seven-hundred-thirty weeks ago. I don't think he's coming back.

CHAPTER 6

Doors closing… windows opening.
When to know which to walk through and when?

Temptations, around each corner,
Teasing you to abandon your plan

Be patient. You know you want to. To see through
what of you has meanwhile become
Soon will close, that cycle, your journey
back home has already begun

Nate, confused

I paced across the market, my feet moving fast, eyes scanning each side quickly. Annabelle, behind me, was trying to keep up with me.

Not here... not there... not here either. Where was she?? I spotted the candle maker and sculptor, yet her stall was nowhere to be seen. Did they usually move about? If so, why would those two still be next to each other? It didn't make sense. From a business point of view, obviously.

Two more rounds across the market and Annabelle's tired face told me it was time to accept defeat. She tried telling me after the first round that Lucy wasn't here, but I ignored her. *I knew we should have left earlier...* Determined, I marched towards the candle maker.

"Where's Lucy?" I asked, trying to keep it simple.

He looked up at me and didn't reply.

"Lady with the scarves?" I tried again.

He rolled his eyes. "How should I know?" He grunted. "If you're not here to buy, make room for those who will." He shooed me away.

Geez... take it, it wasn't a good day for business. I sighed and turned to leave, when the shoe handler stopped me in my tracks.

"You won't find her here today," he told me. "She never works on this day." He gave me a long look to emphasize, waiting for me to click.

"Oh..." I replied, scramming my brain for ideas, Dan words echoing in my ears. "Her birthday or something?" I tried.

He sighed. "Something like that..." he turned to leave.

That conversation was over, he caught my bluff. Why wasn't she here today? It didn't take long before another thought creeped in. *Was she with him?*

"That's it," Annabelle chimed in, "we're going to Dan's. That'll cheer you up."

She pretty much dragged me to Dan's. I could see she was trying to be extra cheerful, and I was trying to go along with it for her sake. Meanwhile my head was all over the place.

I just didn't get it. This was meant to be an adventure.

Save the world, Annabelle had told me in the beginning, and I stupidly followed, thinking I'd be the one fighting the bad guys. Yet the only person I've been fighting so far, is myself. And for that, I could well have stayed where I was.

You? My inner voice mocked me.

Can't just be anyone, I growled back at it, unconvinced. Was this all part of the plan? And where did Lucy fit in with all of this? We stepped inside the garden café and sat down by the window. I don't know why this bugged me so much. Nor, why I was suddenly acting like a bloody teenager. Why now? I ordered a hot chocolate for Annabelle and a latte for myself.

"Dan not around today?" I asked, not looking up.

"Why? Am I still not good enough for you?" Shot back sarcastically.

I glanced up and found Luke grinning back at me. It took a moment for the penny to drop. "Luke!" I jumped onto my feet. "What are you doing here? You work here now? Thought you're going south?" Question after question poured out of me.

Luke just shrugged his shoulders. "I was... but little Miss Annabelle here convinced me to stay."

"You knew about this?" I asked Annabelle but she just smiled. "How did she convince you?" I asked, praying he didn't also think he was the chosen one saving the world.

He looked at her fondly. "Said something about my time hasn't come yet. Whatever *that* means." He shrugged his shoulders again, making me laugh.

"Welcome to my life buddy. Enjoy the ride."

"Anyway," Luke continued, "let me fetch your drinks. My shift is nearly over, but in future, you'll find me here Mondays and Thursdays. Oh, and don't forget to tip real kindly," he added with a wink, tipping his imaginary hat like he did when they first met and disappeared behind the counter.

"Thanks, Annabelle," I exhaled deeply. "You were right, that did help."

Annabelle gave me a knowing look. "You have seen nothing yet. I'll be right back". She jumped off her chair and followed Luke behind the counter.

I looked outside. It was likely I was jumping the gun, patience was never my strong suit. Not because I particularly liked being in control... *I had to be.* It was the only way to keep my anxiety at bay and this trip so far, did little good for it.

Luke delivered our drinks to the table together with a plate of biscuits.

"On the house," he added with a smile, removing his apron. "Right buddy, I'm off. Don't be a stranger!"

"Course not," I replied, gutted he wasn't staying a bit longer. I needed that distraction. "Where's Annabelle?" I asked, catching a funny look.

"Behind you," he grinned, slapping my shoulder on his way out. I followed his gaze and froze. There she was. Sitting at the table with... Lucy. Eating *her* biscuits...

Mortified, I watched her take one in her hand whilst shoveling the other into her mouth.

"Annabelle!" I exclaimed panicking, my voice calm but firm.

Annabelle looked up and smiled, her hand reaching for yet another biscuit.

I am going to die. I slid off my seat and moved to their table as quickly as I could.

"I am so sorry," I mumbled in Lucy's direction apologetically, pulling Annabelle's sleeve. Ignoring me, Annabelle chewed on her biscuit indulgently.

"Mmmgmmmgghh… these are *so* good!" She added. "You have to try them." Her hand reached for the plate.

"Annabelle, you can't go around eating other people's food." I tried softly.

"But you must try one!" She insisted, reaching for another.

I took a deep breath. "That may well be." I tried again, as cool and collected as I could manage. "But they are not yours."

Annabelle looked at me with big brown eyes, her hand moving a little closer to the plate. I used all my willpower not to slap it away.

"Why don't we go back to our table and order you some." I reasoned, my eyes begging when Lucy laughed out loud next to me.

"She doesn't mind," Annabelle protested. "Do you?" We both turned to Lucy and found her eyes widened in surprise. *Gosh she's pretty…*

Lucy shook her head slowly and shrugged her shoulders. "Be my guest" she told Annabelle.

"Seeeeeee," Annabelle concluded happily and grabbed the last biscuit.

"That is very kind of you" I confirmed in Lucy's direction. "Let me at least make it up to you." Relieved I spotted Dan and waved him over.

"I see you finally met!" Dan noted, approaching us smiling.

Oh geez… not him too.

"We only got here a few weeks ago," Annabelle explained to Lucy between mouthfuls. "Nate and I." She pointed to me and I smiled, giving Lucy a small wave. Turning back to Dan, I locked eyes with him and shook my head slightly, hoping Lucy didn't catch it.

Dan gave me an equally long look back; one that loosely translated into good luck, and 'I am watching you.' Emphasis on the latter. My palms started sweating as I turned back to Lucy, finding her smile at me curiously. She's even prettier when she smiles…

"What can I get you all?" Dan asked into the group.

"Another plate of biscuits," I started, "or best make it two. Unless…" I paused and looked at Lucy for guidance.

"Lucy," Annabelle jumped in to help me, making Dan chuckle behind me.

Very funny guys… hardy har har. The two of them were enjoying this far too much.

"Unless Lucy prefers something else?" I continued, unimpressed.

"Biscuits would be great," she confirmed softly, taking her cup of tea.

"Biscuits it is," I validated, grinning like a little schoolboy. She looked directly into my eyes when she said it.

Dan's gaze lingered on Lucy for a moment. She caught his eye and lowered her gaze immediately. *Did I just see her blush?*

"You know what? He told us. "Today is a pretty big day. I reckon this calls for something different." He watched Lucy closely as he spoke, the handlers' words lingering in my ears in the meantime. Why was today so important?

Dan, sensing my next questions, quickly added "How often do new friends meet one of my oldest and dearest? Grab a chair Nate, a plate of Dan's finest coming right up."

Annabelle clapped her hands and beamed at Dan delightedly, as he disappeared in the kitchen whistling cheerfully. "I hope we're not interrupting anything." I started carefully. "We don't usually impose ourselves like that." I gave Annabelle a long look that said "thank you" more than "you shouldn't have."

"Not at all," Lucy replied quickly.

I hoped she didn't just say it to be polite.

"You know Dan well?" she asked, and Annabelle told her about our first encounter, when I downgraded him to a waiter. Leaving the part about her out of course. Lucy laughed out so wholeheartedly when she finished, I regretted it a little less.

"Well, if it helps, I've known Dan my whole life and he's not one to hold grudges." She smiled at me. "You'll be alright. He seems to like you"

"What makes you think that?" I asked, trying not to gloat.

"Just a hunch," she replied.

Dan called me over before I had a chance to probe any further. *Great timing dude…* maybe he doesn't like me as much as she thought. "Let's just hope that feeling is mutual, by the end of our catch-up." I replied, winking at Lucy. "Excuse me, ladies. I'm needed elsewhere." I walked off casually, trying to hide the little swagger in my step. Not sure where that just came from but I felt pretty good it did. *Still got it…* came from the little voice inside me.

"Can you give me a hand with those chairs?" Dan asked, oblivious to my mental victory dance. "Sorry to ask, but Luke already left, and we just got a big crowd confirmed for seven." He looked at me. "And wipe that grin off your face, will ya?"

I grinned even wider. "Happy to help with the chairs," I replied. "Can't promise anything else."

He nudged my side playfully. "Go easy on her today, will ya? It's a big day for her."

"How come?" I asked, glad I finally had a chance to find out more.

"It's the day Jamie disappeared." I nodded slowly.

"Should we leave her be?" I asked, praying Annabelle will go easy on her in the meantime.

"Nah," Dan replied. "The distraction seems to do her good. Now grab this table over there and you're free to head back to them."

Lifting the table, I briefly glanced in their direction. *Did I just catch her looking at me?* I couldn't be sure, but my heart made a somersaults either way. "Oh boy," Dan exclaimed, catching my expression. "I'll manage from here. Go. Don't mess this up too bad, will ya?"

Laughing I got back to the table, making Annabelle and Lucy stop mid sentence.

"Am I interrupting?" I asked, finding both shaking their heads. *Good start...* Luckily Dan showed up with the food minutes later and placed the platter in front of us. It was loaded with different cheeses, antipasti, cured meats, smoked salmon, crackers, dips, cut veggies, nuts and dried fruits and looked amazing. My mouth watered at its sight. I didn't realize how hungry I was. Annabelle seemed to feel the same, forgetting about the plate of biscuits she had just a moment ago. Eagerly she loaded her plate. Lucy followed slowly, picking her food out carefully and I followed suit.

The conversation flew easily, until the door opened and a big group walked in. Was it seven o'clock already? Dan moved towards his guest, guiding them to their seats. I caught Lucy checking her watch and saw her facial expression change. She shifted in her seat nervously, hanging her bag over her shoulder. *She's leaving...* I looked up and found her looking at me tentatively.

Annabelle, next to me, was signaling something at me I didn't understand. She rolled her eyes at me. Was I meant to say something? We already barged in on her and Dan told me not to go slowly.

"This was fun," Annabelle jumped in.

Lucy smiles back at her. "It really was." She pauses for a moment. "I'm glad you came over," she added, briefly glancing in my direction.

"We should do this again," Annabelle continued. "Say, next Wednesday? Same time?" Annabelle's eyes wandered to me expectedly as Lucy nodded softly. She kicked me under the table.

"Would love to," I managed through gritted teeth, rubbing my thigh.

"Terrific!" Annabelle confirmed, pleased with herself. "See you on Wednesday."

Mirror, mirror on the wall
Look who's back here, standing tall!

Is it really? Could it be?
That I truly get to see

No more sorrow, no more fright
Those same eyes now sparkling bright?

Maybe it was the energy from brunch with Annabelle and Nate, or forgetting what day it was for a few hours, by the time Lucy got home, she was on fire. Even her walls didn't feel so bleak all of a sudden. New ideas started floating from her mind onto paper, designs and color combinations creating a life of its own.

She thought of Annabelle's joyful composition and started creating her first piece with her in mind. She thought about her innocence and yet how she made her laugh one moment and think the other. Annabelle was unexpected and her design should be just that. Vibrant, noticeable. She started big swirls in neon green before adding strokes of orange. The brush literally flew across the fabric. Big loops, small loops, light loops, and bright loops took over the garment until she came to a halt. It was good, but it wasn't enough. Lucy drew a big butterfly in the middle and two triangles around it, before adding a bit of sparkle next to each wing. *There.* She put it aside.

Nate popped into her head next. His design was harder to begin with, since he was much harder to read. He seemed thoughtful and quiet, even reserved at first, yet also had kindness in his eyes she didn't expect. It threw her, even more so when Dan picked up on it. Like he did with everything. She watched them from a distance after he called Nate over, intrigued. Especially when Dan put his arm around Nate's shoulder. He never did that… the only time she'd ever seen him do that, was with Jamie. He whispered something in Nate's ear and Nate laughed out so loud, his whole face lit up. His laugh was deep and wholeheartedly and very different to what she had expected from him at first, drawing a small dimple on each cheek. Her hands started painting intuitively with that thought in mind, mixing deep blue for his big belly laugh and blue earth pastel colors for the warmth in his expression. She looked at the drawing. It was missing something. Something else she had picked up in his eyes. Something unresolved. She picked up another brush. Hard violent red strokes were added to the design.

She took a step back. What lay before her was challenging, daring, and exhilarating. Liberating too, surrendering to it like that and just letting it move through her. Was she playing it safe before? She took out more fabric and got to work. A piece for Jamie, one for mum, another for dad… as memories started mixing with emotions, so did the colors and designs. Panting hard she took a step back a few hours later.

Exhausted, she looked at the result, her pain painted away across ten different pieces. It felt therapeutic. She didn't know how these would land at the market, but for the first time she also didn't care. She felt more connected to her family right now than she had in years. And to herself. In her mind, this was her best work. Happy, she put those items aside and got ready to bed, falling asleep with nothing but a smile for the first time in years.

Lucy sold four of the new designs the very next morning and another two the following day.

She could have sold them all that sam]e afternoon, but somehow couldn't get herself to sell the remaining four. Not even when a buyer offered to pay her double the price for it. To her surprise she found herself telling him they were already taken.

As a result, her evenings were now filled with more new creations. She didn't try to replicate what she knew worked in the past anymore or waited for someone to come along for inspiration. It was as if something unlocked within her, that had now come through her.

Minutes became hours and some days she got so lost in it, she only remembered the beginning and end.

By Wednesday, she sold another five garments within the first two hours. That was starting to attract attention and the occasional snide comment from her fellow handlers. Lucy didn't mind. Tonight, she was going to celebrate this new beginning with her new friends over a glass of wine, she thought giddy. Treat Annabelle to an extra-large hot chocolate. She couldn't wait to see them both. A feeling she hadn't had in a long while.

Wearing her long, black sheer skirt and a matching black top and silver necklace, she slid into her white sneakers and added a little perfume. When she turned the corner to the garden café, she found Nate sitting by the window seat. He hadn't spotted her yet, so Lucy allowed herself to take a closer look.

Wearing a white T-shirt, Nate had swung his light brown jacket casually over his chair. He looked different today.

'Look *beneath*,' a little voice whispered from inside her, making her stop in her tracks. Flustered, she stood as she was, when Nate spotted her and smiled at her widely. He got up and gave her the longest embrace as she entered. It felt familiar somehow... People don't hug like this anymore, crossed Lucy's mind, wondering when she was hugged like this before.

"Where is Annabelle?" She asked.

"Not sure," Nate replied. "She told me to go ahead and said she'll meet us here shortly, so guessing she'll be here any minute." He handed Lucy the menu. "You hungry?."

They ordered a plate of buffalo cheese, prosciutto, rocket salad and Artisan breads. Whilst they waited when Lucy started telling Nate about her week. He beamed from ear to ear when she told him about her new designs and how well they were perceived at the market.

"This calls for a celebration," he concluded, waving Dan over "Wine?"

Lucy nodded happily. She was surprised how easy she found it to talk to him and found herself opening up to him quickly. Long before the food and wine arrived.

They talked about their hobbies and families and how they had shaped who they became. Nate listened intently as she spoke, asked questions every time she paused, and later shared the places he visited and friends he made along the way, before surprising himself by telling Lucy he felt something was missing in his life lately. Even more so when he felt Lucy was able to relate.

So, they ate and drank like old friends not newly-meets, an honesty between them one doesn't see every day.

"What are you looking for now?" Nate asked between mouthfuls. The words were out of Lucy's mouth before she could stop them.

"A soul connection," she replied, taking both by surprise. Neither of them said anything for a while after that, so when Dan appeared at their table, Lucy was glad. Unable to read Nate's expression, she has no idea what he was thinking. Nate meanwhile, was lost for words. How does one respond to a sentence like that? He wondered. He never met anyone like Lucy before. Not that he met many people lately, but few people he met had her level of depth. So he just kept looking at her, in awe. Way too obvious for his liking.

Dan, shifted from one foot to another. "Sorry to interrupt," he started slowly. Lucy's color rose in her cheeks when she realized where this was going. All chairs and tables were already stacked up, they were the last ones left at the restaurant.

"I'm so sorry Dan," she muttered, jumping to her feet. Nate, slightly slower on the uptake, gave her a bewildered look.

"We lost track of time," she continued, signing him to get up.

"Have you heard from Annabelle," Nate suddenly asked sobered, catching up with what had happened.

"I did," Dan replied, grinning. "She got held up by Judy Baker. You didn't seem to miss her too much, so I didn't intervene." He added winking at Nate.

"What can I say, time flies when you're having fun," Nate countered, smiling broadly. Lucy turned crimson and walked out of the door, hearing Dan's loud laugh behind her.

I will never hear the end of this, she thought.

"Oh by the way" Dan called out after Nate as he hurried after Lucy, "Judy asked if you're still good for tomorrow?"

Nate nodded. They've been staying with the Bakers for the past few weeks, so he tried to help out as much as he could.

"I'll tell her," Dan confirmed, "just in case you forget, amongst other things." He closed the door behind him laughing even harder. Never hear the end of it, Lucy confirmed silently.

"Can I walk you home?" Nate asked, noticing her shiver. Her home was in the opposite direction to the Baker's family and they both knew it.

"How about we walk towards city hall together and go our separate ways from there?" She offered. From there it would be easy for him to catch a bus back home and it meant they didn't have to say goodbye quite yet.

Nate nodded and disappeared back inside, returning with two brewing teas moments later.

As they walked, they talked about dreams they had. Lucy shared how she always dreamed of owning a little boutique somewhere in

Europe. "Paris maybe…" she started, her eyes sparkling bright. "Wake up by the Eiffel tower and stuff my face with Croissants all day."

Nate smiled at the thought. He could easily imagine her there and wondered what it would be like to walk alongside the Seine with her. He dismissed the thought very quickly.

When it was his turn to share, he suddenly struggled. The image he once had about his future… a wife, a little Nathaniel or Natalie on each hand… a little cabana sunset bar for the locals playing live music has disappeared after his wife had left him.

"I don't dare to dream anymore," he told her honestly.

"Maybe you just need to remember how to," Lucy offered lighthearted and playful. "I am not giving up on you!" She added cheerfully. "Come, visualize with me." She closed her eyes to demonstrate. "Close your eyes," she told him, giggling.

Nate looked amused, but did as he was told. At least for a second, before he opened his eyes again. Unaware of this, immersed herself in the experience, throwing herself fully into the exercise.

"Where are you? What do you see…? How does it look? Smell… taste…?"

Smiling from ear to ear, she continued eagerly.

"Are you by the ocean? Can you feel the sand underneath your feet or sun shining on your face? Are you in the city? Surrounded by city lights and park alleys?"

Nate stood in front of her in admiration. Who was this woman? Where did she appear from all of a sudden and where had she been all his life? That thought scared him, as a ray of sunlight brought up all these warm feelings in his chest. He wanted to see life through her eyes. Live it, exactly as she described.

Excited Lucy opened her eyes and found herself staring directly into Nate's. His look was so intense, it caught her off-guard. Feeling as if his eyes pierced right through her.

She turned crimson, realizing he had been watching her this entire time. Looking down at her feet, she tried to collect herself, her heart beating fast.

No one had ever looked at her like that before... itt made her nervous.

They continued walking in silence, Nate wondered what she was thinking. He knew she had caught him staring, but just get himself to look away. Especially once he sank deeper into her beautiful blue eyes. Was he coming off too strong? *Get a grip*, he told himself.

They walked past city hall, where he was meant to wish her goodnight, neither of them mentioning it. A few streets further, they sat down for a while, exchanging quick glances as they continued drinking their tea. The air felt electric.

Up until George Webster made an appearance, stumbled out of the Royal Oak, looking worse for wear.

"Coo cooo," he mouthed at the pigeons. "Off you go, you little rats." He located Nate and Lucy and slurred his way over. Lucy cringed inwardly. George wasn't the best of people sober, let alone drunk. He came to an abrupt halt in front of them, his body swaying dangerously from side to side, before pointing at the sky, reciting slogans from the recent election campaign. Remembering the audience in front of him, he turned back to Nate.

"Awwwwww," he slurred. "You two are sooo adddoorabbble." He pointed at Nate, his eyes zig-zagging on his face. "Youuuu shhhouldd put aaaaaa ring on her fingerrr."

Nate laughed out loud. "We only just met," he replied politely.

George nodded his head a few too many times before continuing.

Contemplating his next move, he decided to give the young couple a hand.

"*Theeen youuuu should kiss herrrr.*" He concluded, perching his lips, feeling like cupid himself.

Nate shifted in his seat uncomfortably. He wanted to kiss Lucy, but this wasn't the way to do it.

"He's shy," Lucy jumped in, sensing his discomfort.

"I'm not shy," Nate protested, leveraging the opportunity to plant a soft kiss on her cheek. George, satisfied by what he saw, stumbled away in the dark.

"Now, wherrree where weee?" He mouthed back at the pigeons as he left.

Lucy looked up at Nate and found him watching her. She held his gaze for a few seconds, her heart pounding fast. She could feel the butterflies in her stomach and still felt his kiss on her cheek. She broke eye contact and looked down at her tea. She knew he was still watching her, but she couldn't face him and she knew her reaction would give it all away.

I really wanted him to kiss me, she realized, and knew it was written all over her face. Embarrassed, she just kept staring at her cup, overcome with shyness in herself she didn't recognize.

The silence lingered between them as neither of them knew what to say. Nate cleared his throat a couple of times, his mind racing.

"Can I kiss you?" He finally asked, almost in a whisper. Lucy smiled and nodded shily as he took her face in his hand and kissed her slowly.

He tastes sweet, Lucy noticed, feeling more butterflies in her stomach appear. Nate's kiss was soft and gentle, his tongue exploring her mouth slowly.

Everything a first kiss should be, she thought. And the second...

she smiled, maybe even the third. She couldn't recall how many times Nate kissed her that night. All she remembered was coming home on a cloud and falling asleep with the biggest smile on her face. One even bigger than the time before. Even liking George a little bit better.

Lucy's world changing..

A memory from the past

She could still hear their voices… warm, kind and loving. Standing on the patio in her white nightdress, she was clutching onto her teddy. 'Snuggle' went everywhere she went. He only had one eye left and a button in place of the other after Jamie's friends got to it with his scissors, but he was still her favourite.

She could see Mum waving at her, calling her name. She was meant to stay with them tonight, in the trailer, but she fell asleep so peacefully, mum didn't have the heart to wake her. Jamie, her brother, was meant to stay in the house with her.

"Lucy-Lou," she heard her voice, "Come here angel." Mummy sounds different, she noticed, wondering why she was calling her through the window. She moved towards her, her bare little feet running quickly across the cement. The floor felt cold, yet the closer she got, the warmer it felt.

It always started that way. Before she could hear the screams. Lucy started running faster instinctively, trying to get closer. Her eyes itching from the smoke. It smelled funny too, she thought pushing her little legs harder, hoping this time, she would make it in time.

They were meant to go away that morning. Mum was beside herself when dad rolled up in the trailer. She always wanted one of these and didn't care that it was old and rusty.

"Think of all the memories we will be able to create in them," she told dad beaming, pulling him tight. "We'll have the best time, you'll see."

Dad had parked it out in the driveway, so it was ready to go in the morning. He suggested trying it out that night, to see if anything was missing.

Lucy came too late… She always did. Pulling the door handle frantically, she tried opening it, but the door didn't budge. She needed to get there before the fire did, but the door was jammed and her little hands too weak.

Her face got hotter and hotter, the smoke making her cough. She could hear mommy coughing too, as she was hitting the window screen trying to break free from inside.

Lucy saw Daddy lying on the bed. "Help!" She screamed. "Daddy, help!"

He didn't move.

"Mooommyyyy, daaaaddyyyy!" she snuffled.

It didn't matter how hard she tried, she just couldn't do it. Strong manly hands grabbed her from behind and pulled her away with force.

"No! NOOO!!! MOOOOOOOOOOMMYYYYYY!!" She screamed from the top of her lungs, her arms and legs kicking against him violently. Snuggle fell to the ground as she tried freeing herself from the man's grip. He sat her down next to her neighbour, Valerie.

"Val, thank god you're here," the man exclaimed. "Look after her."

"You," he turned to Lucy, "stay where you are" and ran back to the van.

Val, pale as a ghost, sat down next to Lucy. "Come here sweetheart," she whispered, "you must have had quite the fright." She tried hugging her with her bony fingers. "It's all good now, John is here. He will take care of it." As soon as those words left her mouth, Lucy heard a loud noise and her mum's agonizing scream. The trailer turned into a big flame as a wave of heat washed over them.

Covered in sweat, Lucy sat up in bed, heart pounding fast, her throat tight. Mums scream still ringing in her ear. *Not again…* She tried to remember what Dr Jones told her. *Take a deep breath and count backwards*. Ten, ten, ten.... nine, nine, nine... eight, eight, eight... she tried slowing her breath and clearing her mind. seven, seven, seven... six, six, six... five, five, five... She got out of bed, her fingers trembling, her hands searching for a box underneath it four, four, four... three, three, three... two, two, two... She opened the box and took Snuggles out quickly. He lost his arm and ear that night too, but John did what he could to save whatever was left of him. Lucy cried into him, hugging him tight.

She didn't remember much else of that night, apart from the big flame becoming fuzzy behind her tears.

For a while, it was all she dreamt about. She'd wake up from her own screams, covered in tears, hugging her pillow. Her brother Jamie would climb into bed with her those nights and hold her tight. Laying with her until she calmed, whispering to her it was just a nightmare. She sighed. It was just a nightmare, she whispered to herself.

Her phone beeped on the bedside table next to her and she grabbed it absent-minded.

> **Just wanted to say thank you for your great company last night. I thoroughly enjoyed your company... and the drunk chap :D Still buzzing and feeling really good.**
>
> **What are you up to?**

Lucy smiled and put Snuggles to the side. She climbed back into bed hugging her phone tight. Just a nightmare.

Susie Brewar & Edwina Rose

Lucy and Nate texted all week and agreed to go on another date on Saturday. Meanwhile Nate was organising Annabelle's birthday surprise for the following week.

Lucy was surprised how much thought and effort he put into the preparations, wondering if that was what families did for each other. He even asked Dan for help, who agreed to put several flyers up in his café, which he quickly removed every time Annabelle was in sight.

As a result, her birthday became the talk of the town. With all that planning, it was surprising that by midweek, Annabelle was still blissfully unaware of any of it. She came to visit Lucy at the market on Wednesday, or hopped towards her rather, her little ponytails bouncing each step along the way.

Every handler stopped to talk to her and even Suzie Brewar and her bestie Edwina Rose paused mid-sentence. Now *that* caused quite the stir. Everyone knew not to interrupt Suzie Brewar, to an extent some handlers even held their breath as she passed.

As head of high society, she was something like royalty here, known for her extravagant taste and soirees, within 200 miles.

Her events were the highlight of the year and the talk for another, passed on by those who heard it from the kitchen staff, beamingly sharing how they managed to catch a glimpse of their favourite actors, artists and people of wealth or high society.

The unspoken rule between the handlers was not to speak to Suzie Brewar unless spoken to. Especially after the new guy at the market broke that rule in his first week, which quickly made it his last week thereafter. His punishment was to vacate his stall immediately.

So when Annabelle approached Suzie Brewar with an ease and familiarity, it didn't go unnoticed. Especially when Suzie Brewar broke etiquette and laughed out wholeheartedly at something Annabelle said, taking even Edwina by surprise.

Lucy was proud of her new friend. She had seen a good amount of people pass through Central over the years, several settling happily in the community, but not once did she see someone break through to Suzie Brewar. Lucy herself wasn't too bothered about Suzie, she rather spent her evenings curled up on her couch with a good book than at an event where one tried to outshine the other, but seeing Annabelle break through to her made her happy.

"Can you believe it Lucy?" Annabelle beamed excited when she made it to her stand. "SUZIE BREWAR invited me to her farm!" She squeezed her hand gently. "They have horses and animals and grapes... and a barn. A barn!!!" She couldn't contain her excitement. "And, and... when the sun goes down, the moon is thiiiiiiiis big." She held her arms out as wide as she could. "And there are *a million* stars," she continued pointing to the sky.

Lucy smiled. She knew exactly what Annabelle was referring to. Dan delivered food there once before after one of their chefs got an order wrong, and brought her along for it. Safe to say he saved that guy that day.

Their estate was unlike anything Lucy had ever seen before, or since.

"It's a Vineyard," she corrected Annabelle laughing, "not a farm. And the animals you will get to see are all exotic, you'll love it!"

Annabelle's smile grew even bigger. "I knew you'd say yes!" she expressed eagerly. "That's why I said we'll come Monday afternoon. So, you don't miss too much work," she added proudly, gloating a little.

"Is that so?" Lucy replied laughing, unsure if Annabelle was joking or not. "What if I don't want to go?" Annabelle tilted her head to the side, considering this for a moment.

"But of course you do," she concluded confidently. Lucy shook her head softly, making her pause. "Plleeeeeeeease?" she then begged instead.

Lucy sighed, resigning to her friend. "Of course, I do," she replied. "If Mrs Brewar doesn't mind me coming along, that is."

Annabelle squealed beside her. "Not at all," she replied, smiling wide. "Especially after I told her about your 'hush hush' new collection, which you will bring" she added with a wink.

"You didn't." Lucy muttered astounded, as Annabelle grinned and nodded. "Annabelle! I've never done anything for someone like her... she's the biggest deal in town.. And one week... that's nothing!"

Annabelle looked at her calmly. "Just do your thing."

"My thing??" Lucy repeated horrified. "I don't know what 'my thing' is." Questioning she looked at Annabelle.

"You'll know what to do," Annabelle concluded confidently. "Just promise me we'll go and put it in your calendar thingy," she added, sensing Lucy's despair. She looked like she was about to faint.

Lucy knew her new friend had her best intentions at heart. She also knew Annabelle genuinely thought everything was possible. *What if it was?* The timid voice came from within. Lucy took a deep breath.

"I promise," she finally said. Annabelle's mind meanwhile, was already elsewhere.

"Lucy... what's this?" she asked, clapping her hands. Lucy followed her gaze as she moved past her towards her new drawings.

"When did you make these?" her eyes sparkled bright.

"Just recently," Lucy replied. "It was just a little fun... and then I got a little carried away," she smiled. "You should have seen the others, they sold in a day! Which reminds me" she added slowly, crouching by the table, digging inside the boxes beneath it. "I've got something for you."

"For meeee?" Annabelle's ears perked up.

"Yes," Lucy replied smiling, dragging the box out from underneath. "An early..." she caught herself just in time, "gift for our farm getaway." Watching Annabelle's expression, she hoped she didn't just give away the surprise.

"For me?" Annabelle repeated untethered and moved closer. Nodding, Lucy took the headband she designed after the dinner with Nate out of the box and passed it to Annabelle. She added a big bow on one side and a few flowers on the other.

"For you," she confirmed.

Annabelle fingers followed the outline of the design carefully as she took it all in slowly.

"I love it..." she whispered, lost for words. Lucy moved the mirror in front of her and placed the headband in her hair. "It fits perfectly, Lucy" she said, hugging her tight before turning back to the mirror.

"I look so CUTE!" She squealed towards her reflection. Twisting and turning in front of the mirror, Annabelle started singing loudly. "Cute, cute, I'm so cuuuute!" Her hands were clutching the hem of her dress, as she swayed her hips back and forth.

"Winnie, look!" she half screamed at Edwina Rose spotting her through the mirror. "Look how cute I look!!" Lucy froze to her spot as Edwina's face dropped. No one had called her Winnie in years. Startled Edwina looked from Lucy to Annabelle.

Lucy shrugged her shoulders apologetically, her mind frantically looking for a way to rescue the situation.

"It fits you perfectly," Edwina finally managed, regaining her composure. She turned to Lucy.

"I see you made quite a few changes" she remarked approvingly. "Dolores was wearing one of your scarves the other day, the girls just wouldn't stop talking about it. 'Parisian chic' I think they called it."

Lucy's heart jumped a cord when she heard the name.. Dolores was one of the most popular girls in town. Her brain started listing every buyer she had this week. Who was secretly buying for Dolores and how could she have missed them?

"Anyway," Edwina jumped in, "I'm hosting a Sunday brunch for the Winton High School lady's week after next. "Why don't you swing by with some of your new designs? Say twelve-ish?" She didn't wait for her response. "I'll get my assistant to send you the details." She didn't wait for a reply, no one ever said no to her invites either.

"So long ladies," she nodded and disappeared into the crowd.

Annabelle turned away from the mirror and gave Lucy a big hug.

"Thank you" she nuzzled into her hair. "I love my gift very much."

Lucy stopped her. Didn't Annabelle understand what she just did for her?

"I need to be thanking *You*," Lucy replied. "You don't know what this means to me Annabelle… I've never been invited to a Winton High brunch before. Let alone to present my work to Suzie Brewar. This is *beyond* big for me."

Humbled, her words were stumbling out of her mouth.

"I mean… we are talking elite here… They're usually off limits for people like me. If I only sell one of my items there… if only one of those girls likes my designs… I mean… it would be life changing!" She paused trying to let it sink in.

"Parisian chic," Annabelle repeated mimicking Edwina's impression. Lucy laughed.

"Which reminds me… Winnie? Where did that come from?" She asked.

Annabelle grinned before replying.

"She loves honey," she simply stated. "Almost as much as Winnie the pooh, so her mum nicknamed her Winnie." Lucy was astounded.

"How do you even..." she began but Annabelle stopped her.

"More importantly, how was your date with Nate?" Lucy couldn't help her grin. She bit her right cheek to pull back the smile.

"Good," she replied coolly. "We're grabbing ice cream on Saturday."

She paused for a moment, conflicting thoughts crossing her head and heart. "Want to come?" she finally asked, her heart protesting loudly.

Annabelle clasped her hands. "I'm glad," she said and giggled. "I'm going to see Elenore on Saturday, would've had to drag him along with me otherwise, but I know he'll enjoy your company a lot more." She paused grinning. "Should have seen his face the next day. Couldn't wipe his smile off his face either... and his was even bigger than yours!" She laughed heartily. "You are both equally bad at trying to hide it, you know that?"

Lucy flustered, happy and embarrassed at the same time.

"Have a big scoop for me though, will you?" Annabelle asked, before shaking her head. "No, have two for me. One chocolate and the other Nutella."

"Aren't both the same?" Lucy laughed.

"Nooooo," Annabelle replied, shaking her head vehemently. "Totally different. Promise me you'll try them both."

Lucy nodded her head slowly. "Sure," she promised.

As Annabelle turned to leave, she paused for a moment, hesitating.

"Hey Luce..." she started slowly. "Be gentle with him, will you?"

Lucy looked up surprised, noticing her serious expression.

"Of course," she nodded, "why do you say that?"

"He's been through a lot," Annabelle replied. "Doesn't talk about it much, but I know it sits deep. Bigger than he lets on. Be kind to his heart, will you?"

And with that, she was gone, leaving Lucy pondering behind.

CHAPTER 7

Lost

Lucy woke up in a great mood on Saturday. Giddy with excitement, she didn't know what to do with herself. Since it was still a few hours until her date with Nate, she decided to clean her house to pass the time.

She started stacking the dishes in the kitchen, humming along to her favorite songs, organised and sorted out her clothes cupboard, belting her heart out to Adele, cleaned her bathroom mirrors and found herself smiling at her reflection. Her cheeks glowing rosy, her eyes sparkling bright, she hardly recognized herself.

She opened the bathroom window and let in some fresh air. How symbolic, she thought, like turning over a new leaf. Or in her case, a whole tree.

The prospect of a new beginning was exciting. No more 'sad Lucy,' she thought. Today was an opportunity to recreate herself and that made her feel on top of the world. So much so, she almost texted Dr Jones.

Instead, she plugged in her ear pods, picked up the mop and danced with it across the living room to the 'dirty dancing' soundtrack. When was the last time she felt that way? She wondered.

Her phone beeping interrupted her thoughts. She saw Nate's name pop up and smiled. Until she read his message. The mop dropped to the floor.

Had an accident, on the way to the hospital.
Won't be able to meet today, sorry.

Lucy shook her head in disbelief. Hospital... that was serious. She spent enough time in hospitals after the trailer incident to know what it meant. *Was he ok??* She picked up the mop and placed it on the kitchen counter, concern washing all over her.

Disappointment followed next, hitting her hard. *Told you,* her brain chimed in. No! She shook her head firmly. But it was too late, the thought had already formed.

Maybe he changed his mind? Surely this wouldn't be the way to tell me, she countered. *Maybe you just imagined it all.* No! she repeated. Nate isn't the guy to just pick up and leave.

You said the same about Jamie, her brain reminded her. Oh, how she hated her brain sometimes. She moved that thought aside, trying to recall their last date and the honesty she saw in his eyes. He *isn't* like *that,* she repeated firmly, cutting off the next thought before it entered her mind. She whispered a little prayer for him. *Please be okay!*

The next few hours were agony. Minutes feel like hours and not knowing if he was okay or not was eating her up alive. The energy from this morning, gone like the stale air in her bathroom.

She tried calling Annabelle but didn't get through, switched on the news for a mention of an accident... nothing. After pacing around the house for another twenty minutes, she decided to go for a walk to calm her mind. That's when the phone rang.

Recognizing his number on her speed dial, she threw her jacket back in the closet. *He's ok!* She thought as she picked up the phone, her heart jumping a beat.

"Helloooo," Nate sang into the phone. *Gosh, was it good to hear his voice.*

"How are you?"

His reply was joyful. "I am walking down Walker Street… the sun is out, the birds are chirping, Life is good, rainbows and unicorns."

Lucy started laughing, realizing what was going on. Whilst he sounded carefree at first, he was drifting in and out of the conversation, his voice trailing off as they spoke.

"What did they give you?" She finally asked.

"Opiates, acetaminophen, naproxen…" Nate started listing them off one by one.

"That's quite the cocktail…" she observed. "What happened?"

"Funny story," Nate replied. "Judy," his landlady, "was helping me with Annabelle's cake. It was nearly ready, so Judy started on the cinnamon scrolls."

Lucy's ears perked up when she heard the beeping sound in the background. It was the sound of a pedestrian light, she thought.

"Nate, where are you?" she interrupted gently.

"Walking to my car," he replied cheerfully.

"Your car?" She asked carefully "Should you be driving right now?" She was trying to keep her voice calm, picturing him walking the streets high on painkillers.

"Doc didn't say," he simply replied, his voice detached.

"How about I come get you?" Lucy offered, but Nate declined momentarily, a lot more somber. He didn't want Lucy to see him like this.

"I'll be alright," he replied quickly.

"I just want you safe, that's all…" Lucy added softer.

Only then did Nate agree to continue on foot.

"Anyway," he started again. "She must have put the hot pot back on the stove when I wasn't looking, and as I lifted the cake from the oven, my hoodie got stuck. I tried pulling myself free thinking my hood got stuck somehow until I felt something hot pouring all over me." Lucy shuddered at the thought.

"Nate... that's *awful!* Are you ok??" She asked, horrified.

"Yeah, he replied. Burns are pretty bad and I reckon I've had enough chili con carne for life." Lucy sighed at his attempt to stay positive.

"Doc put me under cold water for thirty minutes," he continued "and ordered to stay out of the sun for a week."

Lucy's heart sank at the thought. "How bad is it?" she asked.

"Hard to say" Nate replied. "Need to come back next week to scrub off the crust." Lucy's stomach knotted, the thought alone made her sick.

"Doc said I was lucky Judy put cold water over me when it happened. Might reduce the scarring a bit."

Her heart clenched... this was a lot worse than she imagined and far more painful than she had hoped.

"Know what I thought about in that tub?" Nate asked, interrupting her thoughts. Lucy shook her head.

"Our date tonight. I'm bummed we didn't get to do our ice cream date."

"Me too, Lucy whispered. "me too... But we will. Once you're all better."

Told you he's different, her heart whispered, opening a little wider for him.

Claire

Dan arrived at her house just before dawn, ready to take Lucy to Pereira, a village ninety minutes west. It was the first Saturday of the month and usually the busiest weekend at the market. Whilst Pereira itself wasn't big, its location by the harbor made it not only popular, but easily accessible and usually attracted people from all over the state.

Lucy didn't usually travel this far with her garments, but Dan insisted on taking her this morning. He was convinced this was the place to be for Lucy's new designs and since the garden café was closed in preparation for Annabelle's birthday, he knew he would be back in time before it all began.

Lucy protested about missing Annabelle's birthday at first, but eventually agreed this was an opportunity she couldn't miss, though her thoughts were neither with the party, nor with the market that day. All she could think of was the agony in Nate's voice the night before.

"You're very quiet this morning," Dan noted in the car. "You nervous or somethin'?" Lucy shook her head and smiled. Knowing him, he was ready to give her a pep talk. She was grateful he was always there for her, pushing her to go after her dreams.

"I was just thinking about life, you know?" she replied. "And how it changes on a dime." Dan gave her a side look, reaching for his coffee.

"Blimey, bit early for them kinda thoughts, don't you think?" He asked, making Lucy laugh. She told him about the luncheon for Winton High and the invitation from Suzie Brewar. His face lit up momentarily, his chest growing a little bigger.

"My little Lucy..." he said, overcome with pride. "Look at you! Why didn't you say so straight way?"

Lucy shrugged her shoulders. "Guess I wanted it to be a surprise."

They reached Pereira just in time for Lucy to find a good spot and before Dan had to head back. Lucy handed him Annabelle's gift, a rose gold pendant with her name engraved on it and matching chain. She had placed it in a little pink box, tied a pink bow around it and put it inside a little pink bag. Annabelle's favorite color.

Dan took the bag carefully and waved goodbye. He was nearly in his car when she called him back. Passing him a piece of ripped paper from her notebook, she handed him a note.

"For Nate," she told him, unable to look at him.

He eyed her for a moment, not saying a word. Nodding, he placed it inside his side breast pocket and gave it a good tap.

"It is safe with me," he told her fatherly and set off for good.

Lucy set up her table, Nate's voice echoing in her ear. He was in so much pain last night, she just couldn't shake it. His meds had started to fade, replacing his soft and warm voice with a somber sounding tone.

"Good morning!" Lucy called cheerfully into the crowd. "Please come closer, don't be shy!" She had tried to cheer him up any way she could think of, even send him a little video of herself wiggling her ears, but reality hit harder and harder the longer they spoke.

"Are you looking for anything in particular?" She asked, smiling into the crowd, wondering how he felt this morning. It was such a big day for him.

"Great choice!" she told one buyer. "Try this one, it will emphasize the color of your eyes." How would I feel in his position? She wondered. Not knowing the damage his injuries were going to leave on his body or face.

"That's 25 rupees for one, 40 rupees for two or for 60 rupees I'll add in another sarong." She picked up a piece of fabric from behind her without looking and passed it to the lady in front of her.

"This will highlight your daughter's complexion."

She glanced at her watch briefly, seeing it was nine am. He would be getting ready now, preparing himself to host the party, dreading to be the center of attention.

Was he in pain? She wondered. She knew he was worried about how people would react to his face, since this was the first time he'd step out of house after his walk down Walker Street and the doctor had strictly implied to add an extra layer of cream.

Lucy placed sixty rupees inside her wallet and stuffed it in her back pocket.

"Thank you!" She said, giving the customer her biggest smile. "Have a great day!" She pinched herself inside her pocket. *Pull yourself together Lucy*, she told herself, *we are here for business*. She knew this one was a lucky sale and that they wouldn't all come that easy.

She straightened her jacket and took a few deep breaths, watching more and more people stroll towards her stand. No time for daydreaming, let's do this Pereira.

Half an hour later, the place was unrecognizable. It got so busy; she could barely see through the crowd and had to keep track of her designs as they went from hand to hand with the buyers. One even nearly ripped it off the other!

By the time the sun reached the highest point, she had sold six of her old designs and all but one of her new designs. It would have taken her days to sell all of these items in Central, she thought, placing the money in a little black box.

But what she was most excited about, was the connection she made to Claire, a seamstress from Bairu. She noticed her straight away the first time she came to her stand and recognized her instantly again the second. Maybe it was the way she was observing her new designs. This was a knowing look, not a simple buyer, she thought.

Nothing about Claire was simple in the first place. Claire was tall, slim, and beautiful. Whilst already of age, she was gracefuller than many, wearing her head high as she confidently marched towards Lucy, a big boa swung around her neck.

"Did you make these?" She asked, handing Lucy her card.

Lucy nodded curiously.

"You have talent," she told Lucy knowingly. "Are you free for lunch? I have something to share that might be of interest to you"

Lucy nodded slowly, finalizing another sale.

"Good," Claire replied, "I'll wait."

And so she did, for forty five minutes. She didn't just wait though, she monitored Lucy's every move, noting her professionalism and devotion to her craft.

During lunch, she told Lucy she was from São Paulo, but settled in Bairu many years ago, where she opened her own atelier a few years back. Most recently she had been assigned to a project that was growing too big for herself and had an opportunity to expand much beyond Bairu.

Lucy was intrigued. Bairu was four times bigger than Central, breaking through there was like making it in Paris.

"What do you say?" Claire asked, her amber eyes piercing into Lucy's. "Will you come to my studio and see for yourself?"

Lucy nodded. She didn't know why, but she knew she wanted to do this. A project like this had a lot of potential, not only financially. There was also something about Claire, she felt drawn to straight away.

"Great," Claire replied. "Oh, and don't even think about bringing those." She pointed towards Lucy's older designs. "It's *this* I'm after," she said, pointing at the last scarf from her latest collection.

"Then it is yours," Lucy replied, placing it inside her hand. Claire took the garment, watching her closely.

"You sure?" She asked.

"As sure as I'll ever be," Lucy replied, already thinking about the next patterns she would do this weekend. This whole experience gave her many new ideas she couldn't wait to put them in place. Claire nodded appreciatively and placed it in her bag.

"Until we meet again, darling heart," she said and waved Lucy goodbye. Her heels clicking alongside the pavement, she disappeared in the crowd.

Few hours later, Lucy packed up her garments and got ready to leave, when she heard a familiar voice behind her.

"Not so fast little one, where do you think you're going?"

She stopped in her tracks. *Jamie!* Shot through her mind. She turned around and found Dan standing behind her, smiling broadly. *Will I ever stop looking for him everywhere?* She wondered, trying to hide her disappointment. *He used to call me little one too...*

"Didn't think I'd just leave you here, did ya?" Dan asked with a grin.

"Shouldn't you be at the party?" Lucy asked, giving him the biggest embrace.

"Nah," he said, "they are fine without me for a bit. I can finish everything off once I'm back. Couldn't just leave you here now, could I? Amongst this *wild lot.*"

He looked around protectively, making her laugh. Sometimes he took his self-proclaimed role of 'adopted brother' way too seriously.

"*This* lot?" She asked, looking around. "They're harmless." Dan shrugged his shoulders.

"Or so they seem," he replied with a wink. "At the heart we're all bit wicked."

He paused for a moment.

"What's family for, ey?" It was then Lucy realized she was as much family to him as he was to her. His family had moved overseas a few years back. *Did he stay for me?* she wondered, hoping he didn't regret his decision. He passed her a flask

"Sencha green tea, 3 minutes brewed, just the way you like it." Lucy took it only too gladly.

"Mmmhmmm," she replied. "Brewed to perfection," his expecting face turned into a smile. "Hit just the right spot."

They packed up the remaining items and marched back to the car elbows hooked. On the way back, she was grilling Dan about the party and Annabelle's reaction. He talked about it at great length, telling her about the people, the gifts, the food… everything he could think of except for mentioning Nate.

Lucy wondered if that was on purpose but she wasn't ready for his questions yet. Instead, she told him about her meeting with Claire and the successful day of sales.

"Something tells me Claire and I are going to be very good friends," she concluded. "Thanks Dan… this would have never happened without you. I'm glad I listened."

Dan shifted uncomfortably in his seat. He wasn't very good at taking compliments.

"You're very welcome Muppet," he replied, staring at the wheel. Things were changing and he could feel it.

The young woman sitting beside him wasn't the young girl she had been barely a few weeks ago. It made him happy and scared at the same time. Happy, because he could see her come to life in front of his eyes and find strength within herself, and scared, because he could feel her drifting away from him.

He was always her go-to, for everything, yet she hadn't mentioned

TATJANA GENYS

her date with Nate even once, nor what happened after or what she had written in the note.

It took all his strength not to read it after he sat down in his car and the entire car ride home, and especially just before he passed it on to Nate.

He was watching Nate's expression like a hawk when he opened it and saw his confused face turn into a smile and his hand moved to his heart as he read it. Whatever she told him, he received it deeply.

He turned into Lucy's street on autopilot an hour later, dropping her back at her gate.

"Hey Luce," he said, stopping her as she was about to close the door.

Lucy turned around and looked at him expectantly.

"Might wanna take a look over there." He pointed to the left. Her eyes followed his hand until they spotted a little box on the porch. She nodded, waving goodbye quickly and nearly sprinted past the gate. Glancing back at Dan, she waved him goodbye once more and watched him drive off moments later.

Inside the box was a big piece of chocolate cake and a note. The cake smelled amazing, but she had to read the note first. Her fingers fished for the piece of paper quickly, finding her name written on the outside. She smiled. *I like his handwriting*, she thought, remembering the haste she wrote her note in, blushing inwardly.

She shouldn't have worried though. Nate didn't know what to expect when Dan handed him the note, especially since he was so reluctant to let go of it. He first thought Dan was messing with him, until he opened it and found Lucy's message inside:

I hope you have the greatest time today and get to enjoy yourself.

Don't worry about your shiny face… the sun shines every day, and everyone loves it!

Nothing shines as bright as the heart anyway 😉

The last two sentences pierced through his heart without warning. To say he was surprised by Lucy these past few days was an understatement. She was more supportive and encouraging than he expected, cheering him up with her funny videos and texts whilst listening to him blabber on about the potential damages this would leave to his face and body. She didn't seem to mind. Even more so, he somehow felt she would be able to see past it. Given his past experiences, he found that initially hard to believe, but the more they spoke every day, sometimes for hours on end, the safer he felt in her company.

It had been a long time since he felt safe with a woman. Safe to share and safe to be.

So, when he first saw her note, he didn't know how to respond.

He folded it neatly inside his back pocket and found himself reaching for it again and again. Almost as if to prove to himself that it was true.

All of a sudden he didn't feel alone anymore and closer to her than ever, in a crowd full of strangers, answering the same questions repeatedly about the day his burns occurred. That's when he realized the true power of her words and when he finally knew how to reply.

Thanks for the note Lucy! My morning started off by scaring the neighbor's kid… poor little Jacklyn thought I was a monster at first but warmed up to me eventually. The rest of the day only got better from

there. And... not to sound too corny or anything, but I thought today that I'm really glad we met.

Lucy smiled at the note and held it close to her chest. Me too, she whispered. Me too...

She then grabbed the spoon and made her way for that chocolate cake.

The date

The birthday party all the town would speak of the following week. Nate had outdone himself, Annabelle's reaction was the cutest, the food mouthwatering and Dan's cake for anyone passing by the garden café, a big hit.

People from all ranks mixed and mingled at the end of it and after the official party finished a street party spontaneously erupted outside.

"It was excellent!,"

"So much fun!" and

"You missed quite the event," were sentences Lucy heard most the following few days. She didn't mind. Whilst she was gutted she couldn't be there, part of her was glad.

Big events weren't really her thing, she somehow always felt a little out of place and a lot like she didn't belong there. Yet she loved seeing everyone in such high spirits and couldn't wait to meet the birthday girl herself this morning, to hear about everything firsthand. And to find out more about Nate of course.

Annabelle, dressed in a bright orange dress, was waiting outside the library café, waving eagerly at Lucy as she approached. She was wearing the little pendant Lucy had given her, which she gently touched every so often over the next few hours.

Beaming from ear to ear, she told Lucy about the room full of banners and balloons and a mountain of wrapped gifts.

"You should have seen the cake and doughnut stand," she said gushing. "And all the pink glitter! I was so absorbed with it all, I jumped when everyone came out of hiding and screamed 'Happy birthday!'" she laughed. "When I finished saying hi to all the guest,

Suzie Brewar, surprised me with *a pony* from her estate! A PONY!!!!"
she squealed excited, making the waiter look their way.

"It was all white, and... and big and... and beautiful!" she
continued eagerly. "and had a big red ribbon around its neck. It had
been waiting there *all this time* so it could take me on a ride. Can you
believe it, Lucy?? Such a good horse... didn't even make a sound!"
Annabelle took a quick breath and continued.

"Suzie got it just that morning. She said I can ride it whenever I
want." Annabelle smiled happily. "She even let me name it, can you
believe it?" she looked at Lucy expectantly.

"...And?" Lucy asked, wondering what name she would have
given it.

"Blue," Annabelle exclaimed proudly.

"Blue?" Lucy repeated, not following. "Why blue?"

Annabelle sighed and moved a bit closer.

"I wanted to call her bounty first... or Coco or something... you
know, 'cause she's all white. But then I thought about it... I want her
to have to have all the same experiences as any other horse. With a
name like Blue..." she leaned in closer and whispered into Lucy's ear,
"she'll be able to compete in all competitions too and have all the
same chances as a stallion."

Pleased with herself, she moved back in her chair. Lucy opened
her mouth to tell her they'll still know she's not a stallion, but decided
against it. She didn't have the heart to tell Annabelle.

Annabelle, meanwhile, had already moved on from that topic and
was eagerly telling her about the big water slide the Baker's family had
waiting for her in their backyard upon her return.

"Everybody joined in," she told Lucy happily, "even the grown-
ups! Sometimes they do remember they're just big kids in big suits,"
she added smiling.

Lucy loved seeing her friend so happy. She knew the moment they met there was depth within her way beyond her years and looking at her now Lucy couldn't help but wonder what had happened for her to become like this.

She also noticed how humbled Annabelle was by all the gestures. That's when she realized how little she knew about her new friend and yet how much Annabelle knew about everyone else.

"How did you celebrate your birthdays in the past?" she queried as Annabelle loaded a piece of cake from the waiter's tray onto her plate, and then another. Noticing Lucy's surprised expression, Annabelle shrugged her shoulders.

"What?" She asked. "It's still my birthday somewhere. Probably..." She grinned.

They chatted away, soaking in the last bit of sunshine. Lucy loved coming here. This place was so peculiar, it was amazing. Sitting next to a water fountain carved from stone, underneath a chandelier dangling from the ceiling, feet on a Persian rug, she was looking out at a picture of three pugs hanging off a dark wooden wall. One of the pugs was wearing sunglasses, the other a crown and the third was sticking its tongue out.

In the middle of the garden was a big red leather couch and next to it a rusty old bathtub filled with pots and plants. To their left were big white wooden chairs underneath a mountain of oriental pillows, whilst multiple iron figures decorated the ground next to a suitcase that looked like it came from the fifties.

Not one thing seemed to belong to the other and yet somehow everything fit perfectly well together. Maybe that's why she liked it so much, Lucy thought.

She never felt out of place here either.

"He doesn't want you to see him that way," Annabelle muffled, ignoring Lucy's earlier question.

"How bad is it?" she asked, putting down her fork. She knew Nate had to stay out of the sunlight for a little longer but didn't know much else.

"Pretty bad…" Annabelle replied. "He's seeing the doctor again today to get more scrubbed off."

Lucy's stomach churned at the thought, her appetite dissolving momentarily. Annabelle didn't seem to face that problem, loading her second piece of cake onto her fork.

"Is he ok?" Lucy asked. He sounded so upbeat when they spoke last night. Why didn't he tell her?

"He's getting there," Annabelle continued shoveling a piece of cinnamon apple cake into her mouth. "After all, he has good motivation to get better."

"He does?" Lucy asked, wondering what else he didn't tell her.

"Your ice-cream date, silly. Wednesday night, right?" Annabelle probed, smiling.

Lucy's heart started to race a little faster. She nodded happily.

They agreed to meet just before sunset to be on the safe side, and she couldn't wait. Nate let her pick where they would meet and Lucy had chosen Vito's, a new ice cream parlor close to her house. It was a tiny place and looked very cozy. Whilst she'd never been inside, she always saw a long queue of people there during the day, and yet hardly anyone at night, which made it the perfect for the occasion. This would make it intimate enough to give them privacy and ensure people wouldn't be staring at Nate, giving him a break from it all.

"He doesn't need to worry, you know?" Lucy told Annabelle, and meant it. She had looked up fourth degree burns in the library and was prepared for pretty much anything. Eventually she would tell Nate about it during their date, taking him aback in the most wonderful way, but for now she was just surprised by how much closer she already felt to him. Not being able to see him had its advantages.

She had gotten used to the sound of his voice and to having him on the other end of the line each day. Every conversation felt more familiar than the other, the tone of his voice more comforting and his laughter what she looked forward to each day. Whilst distance tried keeping them apart, these conversations brought them closer together.

By the time Wednesday arrived, Lucy wasn't nervous at all. Unlike the first time she didn't feel the need to distract herself. She felt calm, strong… safe. And very much herself.

The only thing she worried about was how others would perceive him. She knew her neighbors wouldn't be subtle and since she couldn't control their reactions, she decided to focus on hers. So whilst getting ready for their date, she contemplated all sorts of possible responses to make Nate feel as comfortable as possible, if needed.

She put on her red maxi dress and walked up and down in front of the mirror to see how it fit. She always liked how she felt in this dress. It looked cheerful and cute at first sight, covered in white flowers and hugging her body in just the right places, but became playful when she walked and the cut below the knee showed off her legs with every step she took. Especially when the spaghetti straps occasionally slipped off her shoulder.

It was unexpected, that's what she liked about it the most.

Lucy looked outside the window. It was way too cold for this dress, but she didn't care. Considering her options, she added a black little cardigan. It would still be too cold, but it would have to do.

She slipped inside her favorite sneakers, applied a bit of mascara, added a touch of lip gloss and tied her hair up. Not bad, she thought, checking herself in the mirror, before adding a few drops of her favorite perfume. Lucy liked the simple look.

Checking her phone, it was 4:35pm. Nate texted fifteen minutes ago to let her know he was on his way, meaning he would be here any minute.

They agreed he would meet her at her place and walk to Vito's together. Lucy could have told him she lived in a block of buildings which all looked the same, much to the dismay of the postman most days, since her building was at the end of the driveway, but since he was so confident, he could find her easily, she opted to have a bit of fun with him instead.

"Where am I, Sherlock?" she teased when he arrived on her street. Giddy and playful, she closed the door behind her and went to greet him, her heart skipping a beat.

The first thing she noticed as he walked up her driveway was his warm woolen knitted blue jumper. *Do people still wear these?* She wondered and couldn't help but smile. It was endearing. Unlike her, he had clearly opted for the more sensible look tonight.

He gave her a quick kiss on the lips and said hello.

"Can I take a closer look?" she asked cautiously and moved a little closer. There was some dried-up crust above his left eye and forehead, but the rest had healed pretty well in the meantime. Except for his arm and shoulder, she would later find out.

His face was still shiny from the layers of cream, which they joked about as they walked alongside the promenade before they watched the sun go down together.

Nate put his arm around her shoulder as they walked, whilst Lucy kept hers clutched onto her handbag, unsure where to put hers hands… What seemed to come at such an ease to him, was all very new to her. Her last relationship was a while back, if one could even call it that, so today, she felt like a fish out of water.

They walked into Vito's and ordered their ice cream. As promised, Lucy ordered chocolate and Nutella whilst Nate opted for hazelnut. She took a big spoonful of her chocolate scoop and cringed her face. Wow… can ice cream go bad? she thought. Surely that wasn't how it was supposed to taste, was it? She looked at Nate trying to read his expression. He didn't say anything, but she knew he was thinking it too.

In a few weeks she would pass Vito's again and find it turned into a shoe shop, explaining why it tasted like feet, and they would joke about it after, wondering if their imaginary 'bad' review had caused it to close. But tonight, they didn't care. They felt young and carefree and happy to be in each other's company.

They left Vito's and walked around the block, so Lucy could show him her neighborhood. Since it wasn't very big, they kept walking around in circles to spend more time together.

High on coffee and sugar, Lucy's heart was racing as she found herself talking for a living. And since Nate seemed so calm and collected, then some.

She told Nate the story of a young woman who discovered her life after her forties, a movie she watched with her mum when she was little. That story had always resonated with her somehow, but since she was so nervous, she forgot half of the story.

The important half, she realized when Nate asked her about the main point of the story.

They laughed so hard their bellies hurt. By the time Nate walked her to her gate, it had already turned dark. Nate pointed to the sky.

"Look, there is Orion!" he said excitedly. Lucy followed his gaze looking around. "And over there is Ursa Minor so you see?" She concentrated on the spot he was pointing at before he added "and here are Cygnus and Cassiopeia."

Lucy nodded slowly, taking it all in. It all looked pretty, but she had no idea what she was looking at. They all looked exactly the same to her.

"Can you see?" Nate asked, moving a little closer. She shook her head.

Honesty was more important to her than making a good impression. Plus, looking at the sky with him whilst listening to his stories was good enough for her today.

Nate took out his phone and opened an app.

"Look," he said, turning it side to side. With this app, you'll be able to see all the planets and star signs. "What month is your birthday?"

"March," she replied as he started his search. She glanced over his shoulder as he located Virgo, Gemini, Libra, Pisces, Taurus and Sagittarius... he searched on determined. Lucy had no words for what she felt that moment, all she knew was that out here in her front yard, watching him screen the sky almost frantically by now, she felt something she hadn't in a long while. Cared for... the way one wishes to be cared for by another.

Everything felt right, she thought.

"There you are!" Nate exclaimed cheerfully, pointing to his screen. Lucy moved closer to take a better look.

"Here I am," she replied softly, looking at the star constellation for Aries in front of her eyes. Just as he leaned in and kissed her. Stars, Planets, Ursa, Orion and Jupiter, all disappeared from her mind. There was just him and her and her and him, underneath the universe and its vast complexity. She forgot about her neighbors and their curious eyes, the horrific ice cream they had earlier and the early start she had the next day.

She would even have forgotten her own name when he deepened his kiss as his hands moved up and down her back slowly, if he didn't suddenly wince underneath her touch. She had come across an area that was still healing. Lucy jumped back mortified.

Nate assured her it was nothing, trying to pull her back into his arms, but as much as she tried all Lucy could think of from then on was chickpeas and beans, and was even more unsure of where to place her hands.

Coriander

Lucy and Nate agreed to go on a hike on Friday. It had only been two days since their ice cream date but since Nate's landlord had insisted Nate doesn't return to the bakery until he fully recovered, Nate only too gladly took him up on the offer, giving him an opportunity to spend more time with Lucy. Neither of them could wait to see each other again.

Nate wasn't a big hiker per se, but enjoyed the outdoors and was told that just twenty minutes from Lucy's place was a stunning bushwalk, nestled between greens and stunning water views. It took knowing how to get there and reaching the top and wasn't for the faint hearted, but the views were well worth the climb since each section offered a new and unique sight of the city.

To get onto the right path, one had to cross a bridge, leading to a stairway. The first hurdle and missed by many since it was hidden behind a bush seemingly leading nowhere.

Those who descended down the stairs, oftentimes celebrated too early, finishing after the first section. The second part of the trail was made of rocks and timber and led to the first hidden beach, where the water was turquoise blue and crystal clear. Those who continued on their journey from there, learned it only got better.

A steep staircase led into a rainforest looking area, where big leaves shielded from the sunlight and a waterfall provided cooling. Last, came the part Lucy considered tricky with Nate, having to climb higher alongside the stone wall, holding onto nothing but a metal chain. Since Nate was prone to injury, she first wondered if it was smart taking him there, but decided that the views and water merging with the horizon as well as the path of native flowers were worth a little risk.

The way down would be equally beautiful, descending on a rocky path alongside the coast, the final and most relaxing part of the hike before reaching Shelly, a tiny village by the sea. Since it didn't offer much but little treats, people rarely made it all the way, but that only made it only more attractive to Lucy. It became her hidden gem.

Her phone beeped. Lazily, her hand felt for it alongside the bed as she turned over sleepily. She had already hit the snooze button twice and since there was still a little time, she allowed herself a few more minutes in bed. She brought her phone to her face.

Morning sunshine. Do you eat coriander?

Nate was standing in the kitchen finalising their lunch. He had prepared most of it yesterday, listening to music sipping a cold beer, convinced his good mood would translate into the dishes. He was excited to see Lucy again since last night when he lay awake thinking about their date. Unlike Lucy, he woke up just before dawn, giddy with excitement.

He packed their food inside his backpack and set off towards Lucy. This time, he didn't need help finding her house and when Lucy stepped outside minutes later, she found Nate in the biggest hat he'd ever seen and an even bigger smile on his face.

They set off early to get to the top before the sun hit, which also meant they had most of the path to themselves. Both dressed in white T-shirts and dark trousers, they went on their way. From the side, it was easily assumed they had known each other for a long time and not just because their clothes were matching, their energy and mood was too.

By the end of the day, they would feel it too and talk about it many times after but for now they walked and talked grinning like two teenagers, teasing each other along the way. Nate surprised Lucy a few times that day. She had always enjoyed the fun times between them, but that day got to see a more thoughtful side of him. Attentive and curious, he was asking a lot of questions and whilst the mood was mostly light and fun, he also didn't shy away from topics others felt were usually too deep. As a result, she shared more with him that day, than she had with anyone else in a long time. He made her nervous too, she noticed, in the best kind of way.

Nate on the other hand, was surprised by how down to earth Lucy was and how willingly she shared what was on her mind. Her thoughts seemed to run at a million miles per hour, yet out there in the forest, away from all distractions, she seemed more gentle and relaxed.

He liked the way she teased him, giggling wholeheartedly, her cheeks turning pink.

Her laugh was so infectious, he found himself grinning half the time and wondering when it was appropriate to kiss her, the other.

They stopped at the top of the hill and took in the view. Lucy was right, Nate thought, the view here *was* breathtaking. Then again, he would have also just as happily stared at a brick wall with her, he then realised.

He moved closer to the edge and saw Lucy flinch behind him. Taking him on this path was one thing, she thought, standing near a cliff another. That's when Nate had an idea. Stepping closer to the edge, well aware Lucy was watching him closely, he pretended to wobble.

"Nate," Lucy started, trying to sound calm.

"What?" He asked sheepishly, swaying his body back and forth, waving his arms around in search for balance. She reached out for him without hesitating before Nate caught her wide eyed, surprised expression as he pulled her in close and kissed her passionately.

It didn't take long for Lucy to understand what just happened, and by the time she did, he only pulled her in closer. When she finally managed to untangle herself from his embrace, panting hard, all she could manage was "Please be careful."

Lightheaded and slightly weak in their knees they continued on their way. They were meant to sit down at the top of the hill and enjoy their food over the most magnificent view, but since Nate kept stopping every few seconds just meters away from it, Lucy quickly came up with plan B. Unsure about the hurry, Nate couldn't understand why Lucy was pulling him away from all these beautiful spots.

Wasn't he giving her enough attention? he wondered, grabbing his camera. He tried snapping a few pictures of her, as Lucy vehemently tried to outrun them all. She squealed when he pulled her in close and snapped a picture of the two of them. Bright eyed and rosy cheeked she smiled at the camera wholeheartedly. It would be the first of many pictures of them and one they would carefully observe back at home many days from now. Dan would come across it eventually, surprised by how familiar they looked, afraid he was losing Lucy once and for all.

Meanwhile Nate started to wish he had listened to Lucy. Not just because the views there were breathtaking, but also because he was starting to get *really* hungry and the bag on his shoulders heavier and heavier as they went on. Lucy, oblivious to it all, didn't mind their little detour in the slightest. Seeing how much Nate was enjoying the surroundings, she thought it much more important to let him indulge in it, then find the perfect spot, so was in no hurry to sit down and make camp from then on.

They marched on for another thirty minutes, before they,

according to Nate *finally,* reached a secluded little bay by the water, one of the many hidden gems along the way.

The sun had gotten stronger by then and worried about his burns, Lucy was glad they had already started their descent.

She located a shady spot alongside the sandy beach of the lagoon and stopped midway underneath the leafy trees. This was the perfect spot.

"Here," Lucy nodded pleased. "How about this for our lunch spot?" She turned around and found Nate unpacking his bag. She didn't have to tell him twice.

Nate laid out his picnic blanket on the sand, a big grey elephant covering its front. *This was going to be a proper picnic!* Lucy thought, watching him closely. She usually just sat on the rocks and had a bite to eat whilst listening to the sounds of the ocean, so thought it was cute of Nate to bring it along. That's when she also noticed everything else he had brought.

Nate didn't just pack a sandwich for them as she assumed: out came a whole set-up!

She watched in disbelief as three salads, two kinds of bread and multiple spreads landed on the blanket, followed by metal plates and cutlery.

"Tea?" He asked, pouring her a cup of freshly made chai. It was at that moment, another layer melted around Lucy's heart. She looked at the man in front of her, unsure what to say. This must be what it feels like being taken care of, she thought, taken aback by his gesture. Nate could feel a shift in Lucy and see the change in the way she looked at him. This moment didn't require words. As they glanced at each other, neither of them breaking eye contact, their silence said it all. A bubble of appreciation surrounding them, booth recognised the significance of this event and the purity of their connection.

It was there and then they both knew this was something special and Nate later only too glad he followed through with his idea.

They sat long after they finished eating, indulging in the moment a little longer, reminiscing in the past. Every so often they would smile at each other shyly and once they continued on their walk, find little excuse to brush up on one another ever so slightly.

By the time they reached the little village, there was little keeping them apart.

Light-hearted and with a heart full of joy Lucy arrived at her house that evening and found a message from Nate moments later.

If you are not too tired of me or ice-cream yet,
Can I take you out for some tomorrow?

∼

Beauty by the lake

Nate offered to take Lucy to a place he kindly nicknamed 'Little Italy.' He came across it accidently, taking a wrong turn one night, and planned to show it to Lucy ever since he learned how much she loved Italy. They agreed to meet by the white chapel next to city hall and take the bus from there, so when Nate turned up on a white scooter, Lucy couldn't believe her eyes. Beeping as he drove towards her he stopping next to her with a loud

"Ciao, Bella! Need a ride?" grinning he handed her a second helmet as she climbed on behind him eagerly.

"Where to, Signorina?" He asked.

"Napoli!" Lucy exclaimed beyond excited and quickly forgave he was nearly forty minutes late. "Where did you get this??" she asked him, beaming.

"Let's just say I pulled a few strings," he replied. He would have to clean John's gutter for a week for it, but he wasn't thinking about that just yet.

They arrived at the big piazza about twenty minutes later, adding a few speedy circles around the roundabout, so Lucy would have to hold onto him tightly. Hearing her laugh from behind him, Nate felt joyful and carefree.

The piazza was deserted. It must have been busy at some point, seeing the deserted cafes and restaurant signs but all that was left now was a simple big square. To Lucy, who had nothing to compare it with, it felt like the real thing. The little balconies surrounded by flower pots as well as the tables beneath big patio umbrellas all came to life in front of her.

She imagined a waiter running past them with a tray of pasta, calamari and wine, the buzzing square filled with families and laughter, 'Felicita' blazing through the big speakers above them.

"Una insalta mista ma senze chipolla prego," she heard herself say, smiling fondly.

It was a sentence she memorized from a library book, where she first fell in love with Italy and their people, culture, and architecture. She twirled around in delight. Italy was her Paris.

When she opened her eyes she found Nate looking at her curiously, wondering what was going through her mind. She seemed so happy, making him want to learn to appreciate the little things as much as she did. *Had he become complacent?* Seeing her so excited, he couldn't help but smile too.

They strolled alongside the little promenade and stopped for some gelato, before continuing their walk alongside the canal. Little ducklings swam hastily behind their mother duck as the wind picked up a little.

It was colder than expected and as usual Lucy wasn't dressed for the occasion, but she didn't care. Today felt perfect. Especially when Nate opened up about his family for the first time. She listened intently, not wanting to miss a beat.

They reached the halfway point of the lake just as the sun began to set and watched it go down in the distance. The sight was so beautiful, Lucy didn't realize Nate taking a few pictures of her looking out at the lake, her long hair glimmering softly in the sunshine.

He would send them to her the following day, dubbing them "beauty by the lake," but for now, he just took her in his arms and kissed her fondly, pulling her closer into his embrace as he did. Conscious of their very public display, Lucy was hesitant at first when he pulled her closer. But when Nate sensed it and pulled her even closer, signalling to her that nothing else mattered, she allowed it. Until they stood so close, a needle wouldn't fit between them.

He was right. Wherever they were, whoever was around them, didn't matter. It was just him and her, and the bubble they had built between them. At least back then.

They found a little wine bar that looked as if it came carved out of a cave. It was tiny inside and only had space for a handful of people, so they moved further to the back for some extra privacy.

The waitress brought them their menus and lit a candle as they ordered baked cheese with walnut & pear, a mushroom bruschetta, and a salad to share with two glasses of Chianti.

The food was delicious, but Lucy wasn't hungry. Sitting next to Nate in dim lighting, she felt closer to him than ever. She was overcome by a feeling she didn't recognise in herself. She wanted to be with him. All of him. Give herself to him in every single way and be closer to him than ever. Maybe it was the atmosphere or maybe it was the wine, the air between them became thinner and thinner as they looked at each other, their gaze lingering and deepening each time.

They finished their food and went back outside. It was colder than before, an icy wind howling around them. Nate opened his jacket and welcomed Lucy inside as they ran back to the vespa arm in arm, one of her hands around his waist and the other inside the arm of his jacket, Lucy's hair blowing freely in the wind. Lucy nestled against Nate's chest.

"Would you like to come back to mine?" She whispered trying to hide her red cheeks. A wave of warmth hit Nate as he wondered if she could hear his heart beating faster when she did.

"Yes…" he replied slowly. "I would like that very much."

They ran down the street and jumped back onto the scooter, Nate squeezing Lucy's hand gently before they head back. Lucy didn't need a reason to hold onto him tight this time as she leaned her head against his body and hugged him tight. Nate, meanwhile, had a hard time concentrating on the road.

It was a while since he was intimate with a woman, and this wasn't just any woman he was talking about. Was this what Lucy implied when she invited him to her house? Feeling her body pressed against his would indicate so but he couldn't be sure.

Lucy, meanwhile, remembered the dishes she left in the sink and washing she left next to the washing machine. She froze, starting to regret her offer. Not because she had changed her mind, that part she was still very certain of, but because this would be the first time a man would step inside her house. Other than Dan.

What would he make of it? She wondered. What will he think? She decided to run inside and clear everything whilst he was parking the scooter, trying to calm her nerves. Nate touched her hand gently at the next red light. He had noticed Lucy freeze behind him. Did she change her mind? He knew he wouldn't do anything, she wasn't ready for and decided to be decent enough to ask. His lower part of the body scolded him for that suggestion.

The scooter stopped at her gate and Lucy climbed off quickly. Nate tried reading her face as she took off her helmet, but she handed it to him so quickly and literally darted towards the door, leaving him confused behind her, her helmet still in hand.

Was he meant to follow her? Or leave her be? What happened at the back of the scooter? Had he done something to upset her? Everything seemed so perfect up until then. He switched off the engine and packed away her helmet, doing it very slowly, to buy himself time. Debating what to do next, he couldn't decide what was more appropriate.

Following her inside could make things better, but seeing how quickly she ran away, could also make things a lot worse.

The door opened and Lucy's face appeared behind it slowly.

"Everything alright?" He asked carefully.

"You coming?" she replied. Nate's groin jolted in response.

"Yeah, just putting away my gloves," he lied.

Relieved, he followed her up the footpath and inside the house. It was a simple duplex with wooden floor panels, a spacious lounge and kitchen area downstairs, her bedroom, bathroom, and balcony on another level.

Everywhere he looked Nate found books, fabrics and candles. Her old guitar was leaning in one corner, a set of drums in the other. Paintings and mirrors decorated the walls and shells she collected at the beach, her windows. A big couch, scattered with her latest designs and materials was standing in the middle of the living room and a matching sparkling vase on the wooden table completed the look. Her house was filled with character, he thought, leaning in closer to kiss her at the top of the staircase.

This kiss was slow and gentle at first, giving her a chance to respond as she pleased but soon became hungry and urging as his mouth took over hers, his arms moving up and down the back of her neck strongly, whilst pressing her close to his chest.

His body flexed underneath her touch as she returned his kiss passionately, sucking on his lower lip, pulling it gently between her teeth, challenging him back with her tongue. His hands moved up and down her body more eagerly, playing with the hem of her blouse, wandering underneath it slowly.

Lucy pulled herself away from Nate, panting hard.

"Tea?" She asked, trying to control her breath.

"Sure," Nate replied equally flustered. He couldn't care less about the tea. Lucy didn't either but she didn't want to be rude. And she needed a moment to collect herself.

She made it as far as the kitchen table before Nate caught up with her again. They never made it to their tea. Clothes fell to the ground quickly, their bodies mingling as they stumbled towards her bedroom door.

It was everything both hoped it would be... connected and close, passionate, and strong, and yet tender and loving as their bodies found each other again and again between kisses, melting into one. They rocked against each other, with each other and towards each other, feeling their connection and intimacy long after the event.

This was the first, and second time they made love to each other. The second time they almost missed the pizza delivery they ordered in-between. Laughing, they sat and ate the pizza half naked on top of her bed.

Lucy's chest expanded and filled with a feeling she could only describe as a mix of content, peace and warmth all in one, coming straight from the area of her heart.

Everything felt right. *That's usually when things go wrong,* her brain whispered.

She pushed that thought aside.

⌒

CHAPTER 8

Dialogue between Head & Heart

Dear heart,

I don't get you. I simply cannot get my head around you.

You never listen, never learn.

Keep telling me to trust you, to have faith... every time I try to protect you

I couldn't believe it when you whispered your wish for true love when we are still trying to put all the pieces back together. Are you insane??

I vehemently disagreed of course. There was no way I was going to let you do this.

You have to understand, you can be quite foolish sometimes... protecting you becomes a full time job these days.

So for the love of all of us, can you please stop breaking down the walls I so firmly built and finally start working *with* me?

Sincerely, the brain

Dear brain,

Thank you! I know you mean well and I get it. Logically, I often don't make any sense.

But a heart doesn't follow logic.

I am so full of feeling! Happy, excited, sad… sometimes I'm afraid I will overflow.

Yes, I was foolish in the past, naive maybe and too trusting at times… and I too am afraid. But remember all the good times! The highest heights… sunrises and sunsets.

I will die for love. Or the possibility for it alone! Because I only need to be right once.

So don't try to tame me. Don't ignore me. Take my hand and come on the journey with me! Find the energy *once* more. Because I only need to be right once.

and one day we will be loved the way we love.

> With all my heart,
> Your heart ♥

Dan

Nate went back to see Dan a few days later, like he did most days lately. They'd become pretty good friends since he first got here, but today he needed to make sure Dan was cool about the whole Lucy thing.

Dan was leaning against a bar stool when Nate entered.

"Hey bud!" He greeted him cheerfully from across the room and pointed to a table by the entrance. "Place yourself there, I'll be over in a minute."

Whilst he waited, Nate dropped a quick text to Lucy

My day was good. No sunshine, wind in my hair or gentle sounds of the ocean like yours but hoping to live vicariously through your messages. What are you up to?

He put a smiley at the end of the message and then removed it. *What am I, five?* He thought. His day was actually everything but great, but Lucy didn't need to know that.

Some days Nate's brain worked against him, and today was definitely one of them.

A run would sort him out later, he figured, when Dan popped over with his coffee. "Cappuccino, no milk, no sugar, no nothing," he said smiling, placing a black coffee in front of Nate. Nate didn't know how he did it, but Dan always got his drink right. According to Dan it was written all over his face, but Nate didn't buy it.

"You do it with others too and it's not like we're a walking drinks catalogue," he told Dan. "You're just wired that way." He liked coming here this time of day, when lunch already finished, and dinner hadn't yet begun. It was peaceful… and peace was exactly what he needed today. He had barely slept again last night.

Annabelle and Nate had been here for a couple of weeks now and the unknown was getting more and more unsettling to him. It made him uneasy. John Baker, his landlord, had offered him a job at the bakery after one of his staff fell through and whilst Nate knew this was only short term it threw him when Johasked him about it yesterday morning. He couldn't know that John asked because he was impressed with Nate's work and his attention to detail. Because Nate was used to giving everything his two hundred percent and yet still feel it was never good enough at the end of day.

How long *are* we staying? Circled in his mind. Annabelle was always vague in her responses and the longer he waited, the more nervous it made him. *A year or a day, what difference would it make now?* His skin started to prickle at the thought.

A bigger one day by day.

Dan re-appeared behind him, clapping him on Nate's shoulder. *Tell me again, you don't have a sixth sense,* Nate thought.

"You're quite the chameleon, you know?" He told Dan instead. Dan looked at him equally puzzled and amused.

"A chameleon?" he queried.

"Yeah," Nate continued, "you know everyone by name, what they need, when to say what at exactly the right moment."

Dan also knew when to disappear and let them be, but that was beside the point. "Like a chameleon," Nate concluded. Dan knew he could switch between being professional and light and fun within seconds, but to him it was just part of the job.

"Can't everyone?" He asked.

"Reading someone like that? Nah…" Nate replied, "that's pretty epic. Like the guy who can read minds… what was his name again?

The one all girls got mad for, for a while?" He raked his brain for a name.

"Imposter?" Dan tried with a smile, before it hit him. "Hang on, you're not comparing me to that vampire dude… are you?!" he asked, raising his eyebrow, his nostrils flaring up.

"You read Vampire chick flicks?" Nate countered matching his eyebrow. Dan laughed out loud.

"That's all Lucy talked about for weeks." He shrugged his shoulders. "Kinda had to." He cleared his throat.

"Anyway," Nate continued holding back a grin. "With a radar like yours, you should be making millions, not coffee." Dan chuckled.

"I happen to like making coffee," he told him. "Don't think I'd be doing anything else, even with those millions. Speaking of which, I should probably head back to my beans… they'll be missing me." He winked and straightened his jacket, turning to leave.

"Before you go," Nate stopped him. "I must ask… that thing with Lucy and me… you cool with it?"

"That thing?" Dan repeated and Nate shrugged his shoulders apologetically. He didn't know how else to call it or how much Lucy had shared.

"Will it change anything if I'm not?" He asked.

"Probably not," Nate replied, smirking. He didn't expect that question and decided to be honest.

"Thought so," Dan countered. "Yeah, I'm cool with it. As long as you treat her well that is," he added. "Just wipe that smile off ya face, will ya?" Nate grinned at him broadly.

"I'll work on that," he replied.

Dan gave Nate a pat on his shoulder and disappeared inside the kitchen.

He liked this time of day too. Once most clients left he was able to let his guard down and relax a little too. He usually did this on his own, but today in the kitchen, he had a change of heart. Since Jamie left, he hasn't really grown close to anyone else. One of the reasons he was so protective over Lucy. So Nate asking him about dating Lucy, meant a lot to him.

He noticed Nate visiting more often these days, with or without Annabelle, and whilst he initially thought he kept coming back for Lucy, he soon realised he wasn't.

Nate wasn't his only regular of course, yet Dan noticed very quickly that whilst everyone else came for coffee, their favorite dish or a quick catch-up on the latest, Nate came to catch-up with him.

What Dan didn't know was how highly Nate thought of him. He understood very quickly how much Dan cared for everyone, but what cemented it for him was Annabelle's birthday party. It wasn't just that he offered his café basically free of charge or that he moved all his reservations to another day to accommodate for it, offering his booked client's free wine, starters, or deserts… and even half price dining for the most stubborn guests. When Nate called him in the evening after coming across another big box of decorations, he didn't hesitate for a second to help him set it all up. Which also meant that by the time he picked Lucy to drive her to Bairu, he barely slept an hour.

To Dan's surprise, he didn't mind. For the first time in a long time, he felt needed again. Ever since Lucy told him with a stubborn look, both hands in fists, at the innocent age of twelve that she was old enough to look after herself now 'thank you very much'.

She wasn't. And he wasn't ready to stop looking after her, but since it was her wish, he had no choice but to accept it. On the outside, at least.

So, he kept checking on her from a safe distance. It was his

TATJANA GENYS

brotherly duty after all, he told himself, but deep down he knew he needed it as much as she did. Once he saw, she arrived at school safely, he turned back momentarily and got back to work.

Up until the time he caught a few teenagers teasing her, that was. He asked her about her day when she returned from school, but too proud to admit it, she never mentioned a word. It became one of those defining moments between them, where she wanted to prove herself and he didn't want to probe.

So he waited and waited, painfully watching her being teased day after day, until he saw red one morning, when she cycled right past him, eyes filled with tears, nearly blowing his cover.

He got out of the car casually, looked left then right, marched over to those kids and pinned them against the wall. Since he was more than two heads taller than them and of strong build, he looked intimidating enough not to need to do much more than raise his voice to achieve the intended effect. Wide eyed, they promised to leave her alone and never speak of this. He shook them one more time to be on the safe side and told them 'he'll be watching them' from now, which he thought was very 'Terminator like' of him, before he finally let them go.

So, when Lucy turned up at the café unexpectedly that same afternoon, his first thought was 'one-of-them-had-leaked'. Until she gave him the biggest hug, unaware of what had happened that morning and too ashamed to admit she didn't know how to handle things herself. She nuzzled her head into his beard and squeezed him tight. Something she hadn't done since she was little.

Dan, overwhelmed with all sorts of emotions that moment, just held her tight. And so, they sat like this, for fifteen, maybe thirty minutes… in silence and a close embrace. Equally afraid the other would find out the truth someday, relishing the moment in the meantime.

A moment at Annabelle's party reminded him of that. He could see Nate surrounded by a bunch of people he recognized instantly. It was the same nosy lot that wanted to know all about Jamie back then and later spread the news all around the city.

He saw Nate cornered just like Lucy was back then and moved in. Needless to say, they disappeared very quickly. Turns out one of those teenagers had eventually leaked, and ever since Dan's reputation became 'the one not to be messed with'.

Nate grabbed a newspaper and leaned back in his chair. He was glad he brought Lucy up with Dan and happy about how he had responded. It had been weighing on his mind ever since their last kiss.

"You have got to try this," Dan told him, returning from the kitchen with a big smile, putting a hot beverage in front of him. "This one is a game changer." Nate looked at the white liquid in front of him.

"Chocolate?" He asked, judging by the smell.

"Try it!" Dan encouraged him. Nate didn't have a sweet bone in his body and couldn't remember the last time he ordered something sweet, apart from their ice cream date a few weeks back, which didn't exactly leave him begging for more. He shuddered at the thought.

"Go on," Dan nudged. "You won't want anything else in future."

"Highly doubt that," Nate muttered quietly, taking the cup in his hands. "Big promise," he said instead.

"It's made with coconut milk," Dan told him proudly, "like a hot bounty"

When Nate didn't respond, he added:

"Not as sweet and heavy as normal hot chocolate, but with all its flavors and more!"

"Hot bounty, hey?" Nate chuckled and took a small sip. "Mhmmmhh… not bad, not bad at all." The sugar hit him instantly, clearing the fog in his head.

"Told ya," Dan confirmed knowingly and disappeared back in the kitchen. Nate put his cup to the side and moved his attention back to the paper. The headline was still the same:

'Police continue to be on the lookout for burglars killing a local man outside of Central'

Nate's eyes skimmed the page quickly. Poor guy, he thought. Murdered in his own house. Why didn't they just take what they need? *Unless he knew them,* he concluded. Apparently over half the crimes happen by someone known to the victim. No wonder people stopped trusting, he thought. Maybe he surprised them.

He kept scanning the article for new information, surprised by how little seemed to be missing from the house. At least according to his only son, who was said to be distraught. *Course he would be,* Nate thought, reading on to learn he was adopted at a very young age. A nurse had to tell him during a visit to his mother, who had been in a coma for the past eighteen months. *Poor kid,* Nate thought.

His eyes landed on a sentence that made him stop abruptly.

"Refill?" Dan asked cheerfully at his puzzled face.

"What?" Nate asked bewildered.

"Want another one of those?" Dan asked again, trying to read his expression. He must have downed the first cup without noticing.

"Sure," Nate replied absently, his eyes back on the article. "Hey Dan," he asked, counting backwards. "What date is it today?" But Dan was already gone.

He squinted his eyes searching the page for the last sentence, re-reading it a few times before reaching the end of the page. 'Article continues on page seventeen.'

His gut clenched instinctively. *Tell me I'm wrong*, he whispered, flipping the pages. He wasn't.

There he was, smiling at Nate from a photo that covered a quarter of the page, holding the hand of a tall and beautiful woman, his mother presumably.

He got her looks, he thought, as he watched the picture more closely. The woman, standing next to a tall and strong man, was smiling at the little boy fondly.

He couldn't have been older than six in that picture, but Nate recognized him instantly. Even before he saw the second picture.

Sitting on the same spot presumably just a few days ago, his face gloomy as he looked directly at the camera. There was a quote underneath his picture:

'Whoever you are, justice will find you. You have taken an innocent, kind, and loving man far too early from this planet." Next to it a highlighted section in big, big bold letters

'If anyone saw or heard anything related to the crime, please come forward immediately. A reward will be given to anyone who can help capture the suspects.'

"Bill please," Nate called out to Dan. He didn't know what he was going to do, but he had to do something. Help somehow.

He turned the paper and checked the date. Twenty-fifth of June. His mind was counting backwards. These past few weeks had flown by and with the accident, Nate had completely lost track of time. How long had they been here?

He scanned the pages again. With what he could remember, this would have been around the time they arrived in Central.

Nate sat up straight in his chair. *Impossible...* he whispered. *It couldn't be.* As he moved his chair back to stand up, memories started flooding his brain. *That night. Those eyes. The scream.* What if he didn't dream it after all? he wondered. Followed by 'How long had he known?' 'And why didn't he say anything?'

The restaurant doorbell rang announcing a new customer.

"I'll be right there," Dan noted from the kitchen. Nate's head followed the noise as a young woman dressed in high waisted blue jeans and beige blouse entered cautiously, scanning the café as she did. She chose a table in the corner, on the other side of the room.

Nate folded the paper in half as she pulled out her chair, placing her bag neatly on the other. She took her hat off and placed it on the table and before putting her long blonde hair up in a bun with two swift moves with her fingers.

Fascinated, Nate watched her movements, when the woman turned around and caught his gaze. He looked away quickly, focusing on the paper in front of him, counted to ten.

By the time he looked back up again, she had turned her back to him.

Dan came out of the kitchen and stopped in his tracks. *Did he just see his friend blush?* Nate narrowed his eyes. Well butter my butt and call me a biscuit... Dan had a crush! The woman brushed stray hair from her face unaware Dan's eyes were following her every move. He couldn't help but chuckle.

When she looked up and saw Dan, she looked away shyly. *She liked him too,* he noted. He felt bad for watching this, but he couldn't help himself. Especially once everything started unfolding in front of his eyes the way it did.

The woman, looking for something in her bag, didn't see Dan lean in to move the flowers out of her way. When she turned around abruptly, landing inches away from his face, she jumped back reflexively knocking her handbag over the chair.

All contents went flying in the air landing on the ground with a loud thud.

Dan, clearly uncomfortable, shifted from one foot to the other, scratching his head helplessly.

Nate cleared his throat, signaling him to give her a hand as she kneeled to collect her belongings. Kneeling beside her, Dan started handing her the spilled belongings, observing them casually as he passed them. Mortified, the young woman collected her pen, tampons, and her lipstick from his hands, before putting them in her bag quickly, mouthing an apology.

When they tried to get up at the same time, their heads collided. Nate couldn't help but laugh. He tried to disguise it as a cough quickly and with no success, making both of them turn his way, still rubbing their foreheads.

Dan jumped to his feet as if hit by lightning, mumbled something about checking the oven and disappeared inside the kitchen. He shut the door firmly behind him and leaned his head against the door. *What a nightmare*, Dan thought. She'll think I'm a joke.

Inside the cafe, arms dropped and shoulders hanging, the young woman kept staring at the door in the meantime, kicking herself for being so clumsy, wishing she would have chosen another day for her visit.

She knew she would be too embarrassed to come here again after what just happened, so at a loss of what else to do, she just stood there and waited, as one minute passed after the other. The door remained closed.

Nate, feeling slightly responsible, tried an apologetic smile in her direction, but she didn't register him. She didn't seem to register anything at that moment, she just looked sad. Nate paused for a moment. He remembered that look and he remembered her. But from where? He inspected her more closely as she snapped out of her haze and started packing up her belongings.

Pretty, petite, he was sure he had seen her before. She took her hat and placed it on her head. *That's it!* he thought. This was the woman we saw the day Annabelle and I arrived in Central. *Knew she looked familiar!* He was proud of himself, recognising the woman wearing the big hat and green dress. He couldn't wait to tell Annabelle.

Still facing the door Dan disappeared behind, a big frown started playing on her forehead. The door remained closed, Dan hidden behind it.

'TAKE THAT DAMN STEP,' Nate pleaded with his friend quietly, wishing he too had the ability to control minds right now. He could only imagine what Dan was going through right now. Anxiety had dictated Nate's life for years and made him second guess his every move, especially the most important ones. Watching this from the sideline, it suddenly glared on Nate, how often we stood in our own ways. He always thought it was just him… did others have it just as bad? Just not as often? He wondered, tempted to walk inside the kitchen and drag Dan out himself. She clearly liked him too and he was just unable to see it.

Maybe he should push his friend to his luck.

But was that what he wanted? He remembered how he felt when Annabelle interfered. Maybe he misread the whole situation. Maybe there's a reason he was holding back…

For all Nate knew, this woman could be married. Promised to someone else or involved in something Dan didn't want any part of.

He saw her shift from the corner of his eye and realized they were both still staring at the door in front of them, both praying for it to open. 'Common Dan,' he urged. Just in case. *Get back out here, so you won't regret it.*

The woman opened her purse and placed a few dollars on the table. Letting out out a sigh, she swung her bag over her shoulder and, with one final glance towards the kitchen door, turned to leave. The doorbell rang as she closed the door behind her.

Expecting a new customer Dan appeared from the kitchen moments later, carrying a big smile. *Chameleon,* Nate thought again, but this time even he could tell the smile was fake. Dan's trained eyes scanned the cafe quickly, screening it for any new faces before his gaze landed back at the table the young woman was sitting just a few moments ago.

He lingered there for a little while. He looked sad too.

That's when Nate knew he was right. He wanted to console his friend, but also knew there was nothing he could say right now, that would make it better. And yet he also couldn't believe how the guy who knew everyone, saw everything, helped everyone… was completely oblivious when it came to himself.

The doorbell rang again. Hopeful, Dan looked up at the door as Annabelle walked in cheerfully. She was about to approach Dan when Nate shook his head softly, signaling her to come over.

Dan straightened his jacket and started clearing her table.

"Fill me in quickly," she whispered, giving Nate a quick hug.

"Hey Dan," Nate yelled out, as Dan wiped the table and put the chairs back into place. "Can you get Annabelle one of those amazing hot chocolates?"

Dan nodded and disappeared in the kitchen. Once out of ear shot, Nate filled her in quickly.

"We have to do something," he concluded moments before Dan returned to their table.

"Something interesting in the paper?" Dan threw out casually trying to distract from what just happened.

"Yeah actually," Nate started, following his queue. "I was going to ask you earlier, have you seen…" Annabelle kicked him under the table. "Ouch!" He exclaimed, rubbing his shin. She had got to stop doing that, he thought, firing her an angry look.

Dan, confused for a second time today, looked from Annabelle to Nate.

"Dan," Annabelle cooed as if nothing happened. "Who was that young lady I bumped into on my way in?" Dan stiffened momentarily.

"Who?" He asked, clearing his throat.

"I don't know her name, but I know I've seen her before and she looked rather upset," Annabelle continued undisturbed.

"Me too," Nate jumped in. "At the market, the day we arrived. Don't you remember Annabelle?" Dan turned his way.

"You saw Ellie?" Dan asked curiously. "Where?" Annabelle didn't move.

"She was leaving the market, quite frazzled that day," Nate jumped in. "Her kids were giving her a bit of grief. I almost didn't recognize her today."

"She's very pretty," Annabelle noted.

"I hadn't noticed," Dan lied, rubbing his index finger inside his palm.

"Anyway," Nate continued, trying to help his friend. "Must have been a nice change for her, coming here today. Those kids seemed quite the handful. She almost seemed upset that day."

"Course, she'd be upset! Dan chimed in. "Those little rascals aren't hers and know exactly what they're doing." His voice was louder than usual. "I swear to God, next time I see them…"

"You know her well then?" Nate queried trying to defuse the situation.

"Like anyone else," Dan said dismissively. "Just know she's been through a lot, that's all."

"What happened?" Annabelle asked innocently.

"Had her heart broken," Dan said, debating how much he should share.

Didn't we all, Nate thought, unsure of where this was going.

"Just left her, you know?" Dan continued in a fury. "Ran off with another, a week before their wedding. She didn't believe it at first, told everyone to go to hell.

Until she saw them. I bumped into her in the flower shop just days before, she was beyond herself with excitement. Like any bride to be, I guess." He shrugged his shoulders. "Told her he was no good for her, but she wouldn't listen." He paused for a moment, deep in thought.

"Pregnant, she was, when she saw them. Nearly killed her. Tommy found her by the river, cold and soggy, said she'd fallen off the cliff, but I know that's not what happened. No footsteps up that track, checked it out meself the next day." He paused again, shaking his head. "Half frozen he found her. Clinically dead by the time she arrived at the hospital. Barely made it that day. If Tommy didn't take this route after a fight with his dad, she wouldn't be here today."

Annabelle squeezed his hand gently.

"Baby didn't make it of course. Nurse told her after she woke up. Had to give birth to it and everythin…" His voice broke as he continued. "Little girl it would've been. Little angel. Pretty like her I reckon… Elliee ssaid she felt it kicking for months after… Mind can play some cruel games on ya sometimes." He sighed. "Thing with that floozy didn't last of course. Came running back to her just a few weeks later, begging her to forgive him, and she believed him of course. Good-hearted as she is." He sighed again. "Maybe she thought it'd be easier to grief one, than two. Promised her they'd have another baby and they tried, for about a year, before he had one with another. Don't think she ever got over it."

He glanced back at the door.

"They say, he still knocks on her door every so often, but that door's firmly shut now. Literally shut it in his face last time," he chuckled, shaking his head. "Just wish he'd leave her alone, you know? I mean, it's been four years."

"If only she had someone to lean on and protect her," Annabelle offered slowly. "Someone proper," she continued. "Someone, who knows her and who she can trust."

Dan raised an eyebrow as Annabelle took the candle out of the candle holder and pulled it closer.

"Can you light it?" she asked, and Dan did as was told. "It will take that person a long time to come close to her." Her fingers drew two big circles around the candle to illustrate. "First, she would see him the same way as the flame that burned her. But over time, her fingers move to the circle closer to the candle, with a lot of patience, tenderness, and vulnerability, she would learn that this flame doesn't hurt her. Understand thta it is safe to come closer. Until one day, she placed her hands around the candle carefully, she would see that she could come close enough for the flame to warm her. Provide her with comfort. Give her everything she craves" she added almost in a whisper. "That's when she will learn she doesn't need to be afraid anymore."

Annabelle placed the candle in Dan's hands gently and got up to leave.

"If only someone could be that light for her…" she added, signaling Nate to follow her. As they closed the door behind them, Nate looked inside and found Dan in the same position they had left him in, still staring at the candle in his hands.

He gave Annabelle a quick hug, in awe of what just happened.

But this would have to wait.

"Annabelle, have you seen Luke?"

CHAPTER 9

An Opportunity of a Lifetime

The following morning Lucy set off to Bairu to meet Claire, the designer she met at the market several weeks ago. Claire had shared a few more details about the project when they spoke on the phone and Lucy got more and more excited by the minute.

They had hit it off instantly, bouncing ideas off each other easily.

It was a half day journey to Bairu and Lucy's train scheduled to arrive late afternoon, Claire offered to pick her up from the station, grab dinner together and then visit the textile store and atelier in the morning to show her the designs.

Lucy packed a handful of belongings for herself, so most of the stuff she carried were sketches and samples of her latest designs. She set off mid-morning, checking her bag several times, worrying she forgot something. That was unusual for her. She was used to traveling to the market, so usually knew what to pack.

She had promised herself not to overthink the meeting with Claire and allow the journey to unfold wherever it needed to go. That made this trip feel even more like an adventure and made her all-giddy inside.

What would she see and who would she meet? she wondered on the train.

And if they decided to work together… Would she have to move? That thought crossed her mind so quickly, it took her off balance. Would she move? Nate popped into her head the second she asked herself that question. What about him? Too soon to think about that, she concluded, moving the thought aside. She knew sooner or later, she would have to ask herself those questions and that she was only delaying the inevitable, but for now she decided to focus on what was ahead of her. One step at a time, she thought.

Get a train ticket to Bairu, check. Board the train, check. Read the paper on the train, half check… since admittedly she mostly screened the headlines and first few lines of each article, so she would be able to hold a conversation should it pop up.

Change trains in Magda, check. Get from platform eight to platform fourteen in four minutes, check. Sleep on the train from Magda, not checked, she was too nervous and way too excited by then, so replaced it with a cup of coffee on arrival. Check.

Claire arrived twenty minutes later than promised though Lucy heard her long before she saw her. Music blaring aloud, her caprio rolled up in front of Lucy. She had her sunroof down and greeted Lucy in bright sunnies, a colorful skirt, tank top and her signature red lipstick.

"How are you, my darling?" Claire greeted Lucy cheerfully, opening the passenger door from the inside. She looked fabulous.

"Good!" Lucy replied happily and climbed inside, wishing she would have made more of an effort this morning. "I brought a few new pieces," she started, opening her bag.

Claire stopped her midway.

"Plenty of time for that later," she replied. "First, I want to hear everything you've been up to. How about we grab a drink at Jimmy's and go from there?"

She put her hand out of the window instead of a blinker, missing the car behind her by an inch. "Thank you!" She called out to the driver behind her giving him a wave.

Music blasting, they went on their way. Claire was a free spirit. Tall, loud, and witty, she was a head-turner. But she was also sophisticated, smart and extremely laid back.

There was just something about her that made Lucy like her the moment she saw her.

And not just for her daringly bright lipstick. Claire was strong. Confident. Fierce. Everything Lucy wanted to be.

They sat down by the bar and ordered their drinks. Lucy took a swig from her cocktail and nearly fell off her chair. She would have to go easy on those on an empty stomach.

By her second glass, she felt like she had shared half her life with Claire, and she probably did.

Claire believed in meeting the artist behind the art and in understanding the story that had to be told. She was a woman of truth, guided by her independence and creativity. She didn't believe in 'status quo' and most of all, she didn't believe in living an ordinary life.

Smiling, she went behind the bar and grabbed a few snacks.

"Add them to my bill," she told the bartender in passing, kicking her head back as she laughed.

"You can't do that," the bartender tried, but she just touched his arm and gave him the biggest smile.

"Forgive me, doll."

Lucy, meanwhile, a little tipsy to say the least, was thinking about Nate. What was he doing right now? She wondered. Had he finished work? She hoped it wasn't too stressful of a day for him. He seemed more tense somehow lately.

Annabelle's question popped into her head. She had come to visit Lucy yesterday to give her a good luck charm for her travels. Yet Lucy could feel there was something she wanted to ask her all night.

"Do you like Nate as a friend, or more than a friend?" Annabelle finally asked, eying her curiously. Lucy paused for a moment, surprised by her question.

"More than a friend," she simply replied. "He has a good set of values and I like the way he makes me feel." Annabelle looked at her for a moment.

"I was hoping you would say that," she beamed and gave her the biggest hug.

Claire returned to the table with two glasses of wine and some more chocolates.

She put them on the table and winked.

"I'll be right back," she added and disappeared back in the crowd.

Lucy took her out phone and send Nate a quick text:

Before I get all high on wine and white chocolate, I want you to know I have a lot of 'like' for you in my heart. Thanks for brightening my life these past few weeks and look forward to catching up with you on Saturday!

She put her phone away and turned back to Claire, who arrived with the bartender in tow that same moment. Whatever this trip was going to bring, she wasn't going to miss it.

~

Decisions

Claire arrived at the hotel bright and early the next morning, wearing the bartender's shirt, heels, and a smile. Lucy wondered how she managed to still look so fabulous, when Lucy barely made it out of bed. Luckily the fresh morning breeze and ride with the roof down helped remove some of her headache.

She stretched her arm out of the window and let it dance with the wind. The atelier was only a short ride from the hotel and they arrived at Howard Avenue before the second song finished.

After parking her car, Claire rummaged in her trunk and changed into a pink top, brown boots and a colorful skirt moments later. She hooked her arm into Lucy's and steered her towards the promenade.

"Let's grab coffee first," she suggested, and Lucy nodded in agreement. She was dying for a cup of coffee. And her bed.

They sat down at a café facing the water, in a bohemian looking corner bench full of cushions. Lucy was tempted to put her head on one of those pillows, when the waitress arrived with their menus and water. She looked around.

Whilst it was still early, people were already out running, surfing, or walking their dogs. She checked her watch. At home, everyone would either still be in bed or on the way to work, grabbing breakfast on the go. There was no in-between. This felt a lot more balanced.

Claire looked at the menu and smiled. She ordered a Golden turmeric Latte with vanilla, nutmeg and cinnamon. Inspired, Lucy opted for a chaga chocolate made from raw cacao, vanilla, carob, cinnamon and chaga mushroom. It sounded so strange, she just had to try it, even though she had no idea what a chaga mushroom was.

When it arrived, she wasn't disappointed. It smelled heavenly and tasted even better and gave her that homey feeling holding the clay mug close to her heart.

The morning with Claire passed very quickly. Claire was a fascinating woman with incredible stories to tell. She grew up in a city an hour outside of Bairu, a small town that never understood her thirst for fashion or desire for the big city.

So she finally decided it was time to leave at the sweet age of seventeen, not looking back once. Claire told Lucy how she started her business, selling her clothes on the street or during a garage sale, oftentimes exchanging her own clothes against hand-me-downs she could turn into little gems of fashion.

For a while, she told her, she travelled nowhere without a pair of scissors in her pocket, so that she could randomly approach people for a spontaneous make-over on the street. And whilst she earned a few raised eyebrows during that time and wanted to throw in the towel on more than one occasion, people started seeking her out eventually.

She pulled a picture out of her wallet, showing a younger version of her in front of her atelier beaming from ear to ear.

"This was when I knew I made it," she told Lucy proudly. It was in the way Claire had described it, that Lucy could see the atelier before putting one step inside.

They finished their drinks and walked down the promenade when Claire dragged Lucy into a tiny store behind the main street.

"Yvonne, my darling, meet my wonderful friend Lucy." Claire introduced Lucy to the shop owner, Yvonne.

"She came all the way from Central to see our designs, can you believe it? And I just couldn't let her go without showing her your store."

Yvonne beamed at Lucy and shook her hand eagerly.

"Any friend of Madame Berthiers is my friend," she said politely.

"Papperlapapp Madame Berthier," Claire interrupted. "How many times do I need to remind you to call me Claire?" Yvonne smiled at her and shrugged her shoulders.

"Madame Berthier?" Lucy asked.

"Yes…" Claire sighed. "When I first got here, I was afraid people wouldn't take me seriously if I didn't have a suitable name. Berthier sounded 'French chic'… guess it stuck ever since. Especially after that horrific article."

"You got bad press?" Lucy asked surprised and Claire shook her head.

"No, the press itself was very positive. It's just that the author didn't know satin from silk." She laughed. "Everyone said I should be grateful, getting a raven review like that. Whilst I only hoped no real fashion designer would read that bloody thing." She winked at Lucy.

"I've come a long way since. Those words were forgotten nearly as quickly as they were written." Pausing, she gave Lucy a long look.

"One just can't take life too seriously my dear, or it will do the same in return. Mark my words my friend." She moved away quickly, her skirt swishing behind her as she did.

Lucy looked around. She could see why Claire brought her here. The cuts, web, tissue, and pattern were different to what she knew back home. It was like stepping out of a black canvas into color. She observed the shapes, colors and cuts in front of her, not knowing where to start. Claire on the other hand, was in her element. Taking one piece of clothing after the other, she thoroughly observed it through and through.

She seemed to make her mind up quickly, checking seams and zippers to understand what adjustments could be made. Many did not pass her test and landed back where they came from. Yet now and then she found something she approved of and her whole face lit up.

"Now we're getting somewhere," she said. "When did you get this one Yvy?"

"Just yesterday Mada… Claire." Yvonne corrected herself quickly.

"From someone we know?" Claire clarified, a frown playing on her head.

"No Madame, never saw them before. I'd remember."

"I know you would darling," Claire replied, giving her an acknowledging look. "We don't get things like these very often around here," she explained to Lucy pointing at a chiffon dress.

"Last time I saw someone wear something like this was off the coast."

She thought for a moment. "Wonder if this place is ready for it," she said out loud. "Maybe we should give it a try… shan't we my dear?"

She looked at Lucy expectantly, a wicked expression in her eyes. Not waiting for her reply, she continued.

"I think we shall." Smiling brightly, she placed it in her bag. "I know just what to do with you. Yvy, put it on my bill."

An hour later, the two women left the shop, each holding their new belongings like treasure.

"This was so much fun!" Lucy exclaimed, gushing.

"It really was," Claire confirmed. "I'm glad I finally found someone to appreciate this with," she added.

"You have a good eye for fashion Lucy, and I don't say this lightly."

Lucy smiled at the compliment, her mind already in creation mode. As soon as her hands had touched the Bengaline Suiting Fabric, it went into overdrive. Especially after she found some Eucalyptus Gum Blossom and a few pieces of Lace and Velvet to complete the set, before finally adding a few smaller items as prints to her designs. Her hand was itching to get in front of a piece of paper and let her ideas come to live.

Lucy knew she had to catch the creative wave fast before it disappeared and dot everything down in as much detail as possible. Because once gone, it disappeared just like the tide. Claire, sensing a shift in Lucy, knowingly handed her pen and paper and walked off to take care of the parking.

"You should never go without," she told Lucy as she left.

Lucy took the notebook and started drawing. By the time Claire returned, she was onto her fourth sketch.

"Woah," Claire exhaled. "How long was I gone?" She looked at Lucy and back down to her drawings.

"You've got real talent girl. Remind me again what you're doing in a place like Central?" Lucy swallowed hard. It was all she knew.

"You really think so?" She asked, placing her drafts inside her idea folder.

"I know so dear," Claire nodded. "I've been around long enough to have acquired an eye for these things. Let's go to the studio and you'll see for yourself."

She paused for a moment, turning on the ignition.

"Can you stay one more day? There is someone I want you to meet."

The studio

Lucy fell in love with the studio the second she set foot in it. It was light and spacious and had Claire written all over it. Designs, colors, and fabrics were challenging each other in every single way. Claire wasn't afraid to combine what usually wasn't combined and it showed in her designs. Her fashion was daring and overpowering, yet idle with just the right proportions to make it all work. It was her signature look, Lucy thought, impressed.

Claire grabbed her hand and pulled her over to the window.

"You have to see this," she told Lucy, excitement playing in her voice.

"Now *this* is what I wanted to show you. And I think you'll be able to appreciate it."

She pulled back the curtain and exposed a mannequin standing by the window. Lucy gasped.

Layers over layers of black sheer mesh wrapped tightly around the model. The top had a big V neck reaching just above the chin and a plunge cut and a bow around the chest leaving little to the imagination. The back was nude, the skirt sheer. Big spike-y heels elegantly wrapped themselves around the models leg, a silver snake draping around her forearm.

Lucy was astonished. New York meet Metropolitan and London meet LA, all in one. But even that didn't give it justice. It was different, in the most wonderful kind of way.

This was fashion at its finest. True fashion, like all her favorite designers combined.

"All part of my new range," Claire told her proudly "and you're the first to see it."

She disappeared behind the corner and returned a few seconds later, a big yellow folder in tow.

"Few more of my ideas. I've been asked to do a runway a few months from now. It's not enough time to get them all done." She handed Lucy the folder.

"But together, we could make this work. If you're keen."

Lucy browsed through the catalogue. Pages of sketches and ideas, cut-outs and rib-knits, puff-sleeves, and Lace-ups... each different in color and design yet with a distinct characteristic to make it unquestionably one of Claire's.

Lucy was amazed by the prospect. Was she ready for it? Probably not. Was Bairu? Central wasn't for sure.

"I know what you're thinking," Claire piped in, noticing her frown. "It's a little out there and a bit of a risk. That's where you come in. I saw what you can do and what you want to do. And I also saw you find the right balance. The way I look at it, to live the high-life, you gotta take risks sometimes." She paused for a moment.

"Don't let this chance pass you by Lucy. Fail doing what you love or die doing things you despise and call it living."

Lucy smiled at the metaphor. "I think they'll love it," she concluded. "Maybe not at first, but they will eventually. And once they do, you'll bathe in champagne." Claire laughed out loud when she said it.

"Cheers to that girlfriend! I knew you'd get it."

Nate couldn't wait to see Lucy again. She texted him two hours ago that her feet touched the ground in Central, so he worked extra hard to finish in time today.

They agreed to go dancing in the city after Nate received Lucy's text and it had played on his mind ever since. *I have a lot of 'like' for you in my heart...* that message touched him in more ways than he imagined. Before she unexpectedly extended her trip in Bairu and some blurry messages about a bartender.

What did this all mean? He felt anxiety building in his throat. He thought about the last time they spent together. It wouldn't happen tonight, he knew, after Lucy gave him a timid heads-up, letting him know all she could offer tonight was her mind, soul, and dance moves, after an unexpected visit from mother nature.

"That is good enough for me," he had told her and meant it. "We will just have a cuddle," he added, asking her if she was ok, making her heart sing aloud.

He couldn't have known what this moment meant to her. As hard as it was, Lucy had declined Claire's offer.

"Think about it," Claire had insisted before she left, but her mind was made up. The thought of leaving Nate, even just for a few months felt too big to even consider.

That's when Lucy understood she had fallen for Nate, hard.

It was playing on her mind on her train ride back home, when she sat opposite a woman with a bunch of red roses. Beautiful, she thought. Flowers always reminded her of spring and new beginnings. She smiled at the woman and thought about the prospect of seeing Nate again that evening.

On her next train, halfway through her second ride, she looked up and found another woman carrying a large bouquet of flowers on the platform.

What are the odds? Lucy thought amused. Up until she got off in Central and found a third woman crossing the street in front of her, a bunch of flowers in hand.

Why am I met with flowers wherever I go?

She wondered, taking out her phone. It wasn't mother's day, too soon for Valentine's and there was no other glaring celebration she could think of.

Because no one ever gave you any, her head replied, scolding her for her decision with Claire. Was she making a mistake? She considered walking to the florist and buying herself some flowers, just to prove a point mainly, but decided against it. She was going dancing tonight, with Nate, and that's what she would focus on.

Nate, oblivious to all of this, came home after a long and busy day and jumped in the shower. He was so tired, he could barely stand on his feet. A cold shower, jeans, and shirt later, he put on some aftershave and splashed more cold water on his face.

His reflection in the mirror looked tired too. John asked him to go to the night market unexpectedly after two extra shifts that week, before the bakery opened. And so, he did.

He got up at 3am and worked through until it was time to get ready for Lucy.

Yet he was determined to not let it interfere with their night.

Putting on a big smile, he popped his head around her door, a hand behind his back.

The first thing Lucy noticed was the effort he made. It was the first time she saw him in a shirt and smiled at the thought of him picking it out in preparation for the dance.

When she stopped daydreaming, she saw something else in his hands and stopped in her tracks. Behind his back, she caught the most vibrant bunch of flowers.

"I picked them at the market today," Nate told her, "Passing her the bouquet and giving her a quick kiss. The natives reminded me of our walk and the red lilies to match your gate and kitchen." Lucy took out her vase and filled it with water. She didn't know what to say. It was both overwhelming and overpowering. Not only did they look and smell amazing, it was the thought that really got her. She gave him a big hug, thinking back to this afternoon, suddenly very glad she didn't get herself flowers earlier.

"I missed you," she whispered, confirming to her brain she made the right decision with Claire. She didn't.

Fighting a demon or slaying a dragon,
Such an adventure, when we are small.

But what if that dragon is sitting inside us,
even when we are, double as tall?

Somebody pass me, my armour and weapons,
to face that monster, once and for all

Unlike in stories, I don't need ones saving,
I'll be the hero & the one braving
The beast deep within me, that came on too strong

Attacking in silence, the already weakened
and hurting the wounded, day after day
Showing no mercy, regardless what happened
or even a touch of dismay

So come to the light, we'll fight til the night
Or till you see, 'no more' with me
I won't need the glory of winning the fight
All I request is, you stay out of my sight

And should you return, just know from the start
There will wait a dagger, aimed right at your heart

The monster returns

Luke hadn't set foot in this place since the day he left. *Dirty pig*, he thought looking at a picture of Malcolm, his step dad. It was filthy in there. He knew it would be here somewhere, he just had to find it. It had to be. Whatever he did, he couldn't leave without it. Not in his filthy hands. Luke knew it was only time before he came back for it and he was sure *Malcolm* was too, so it wouldn't be easy to find.

Think like that prick, he told himself. *Think like that prick.*

Where could he have put it?

He went through the cupboards quickly, his eyes scanning the contents between his fingers. Not here, not there. Memories of her popped up as he did, meeting him along the way.

He gulped. Don't go there, not now. He worked himself through the wardrobe, the sock cabinet and the bathroom drawers. Fuck. Where did he put it?? He had to think fast.

And then it hit him.

The two things Malcolm loved were horror movies and crime series. Not for the plots, obviously. Luke caught him a few times leaning in closer to see where the bad guy's hid their stuff or when they explained how they got away with it.

There was one episode in particular he kept watching over and over again…

Common Luke, remember, which one was that? He raked his brain. Something about a chick boiling a rabbit. He moved to the kitchen and checked the oven, his hands gliding along both sides. Not there.

He extended his arms to reach the far end. Nothing. Pulling his hand back, his eyes fell to the sink. He closed the oven door and moved towards it slowly, charged with adrenaline. A vile smell greeted him as he opened the door underneath it, making him gag. Nasty... yet something told him he didn't just forget to take out the trash....

This was there on purpose. A trap.

He held his breath and slid his fingers past the bins carefully. His fingers followed the sink tube, avoiding any other contact. When he reached the last of its curves, he grabbed hold of something firm. Bingo. Exploring it carefully, he felt out a little box and pulled on it strongly, ripping it off the tube. The noise behind him startled him.

He's home, he thought panicking, closing the door again quickly. He stuffed the box inside his pocket and jumped to the other side of the room as fast as he could.

"There you are, you worthless little cunt," came slurring from the other side of the room. "Knew I'd find you here someday." Malcolm looked around the room, screening it quickly. His eyes landed on a half open cupboard door. He was hammered but knew exactly why Luke was here. Luke walked towards the garden door as slowly as he could.

"See you're keeping well," he told him, acting as if nothing happened. Malcolm stopped him on his way.

"Where have you been, you little bastard?" he slurred.

"Around," Luke replied casually, his heart in his throat. It didn't matter what he said. *PANG!* Malcolm's hand slapped the back of his head hard.

"Don't lie to me you little cunt. You're as bad as the little whore."

"Leave her out of it," Luke spat back through grinded teeth, his voice shaking. It always did when he brought her up.

"Oh yeah?" Malcolm replied mockingly. "Whatcha gonna do about it?"

He hit him again, in the stomach this time. Luke fell to his knees, breathing hard. This one's gonna bruise. "Didn't think so," he laughed, his tobacco-stained teeth showing.

He moved past Luke and started rumouring in the drawer.

I gotta get out of here, Luke thought. *Fast.* Crawling on all fours, he made his way towards the stairs.

"Leavin so soon again, are we? I don't think so…" came from behind, Malcolm's heavy steps and breathing following after. Luke jumped onto his feet, but he wasn't fast enough. Malcolm grabbed hold of his leg and kicked hard.

"AAARGHH…" Luke screamed, clenching his jaw. Don't make a sound, he told himself. It'll only make things worse.

Something hit his ribs. Hard. Once, twice. He winced, struggling to breathe as it hit the same place a third time. His mouth started to taste of metal.

Not again, he thought. Last time that happened he was in hospital for a month. Had to eat through a straw for a week.

"Lucky little boy," the nurse had told him after he woke up. "With a fall like that, you're fortunate to be alive! if your father wasn't there…"

Luke remembered Malcolm's face behind her and the smirk on his face. Especially after she added

"Thank the lord your dad found you when he did."

Luke was going to be that fortunate again soon, if he wasn't careful. And this time, Malcolm will be dancing at my funeral if he finds out what I have in my pocket, he thought.

He turned to face him and saw him get ready for the next punch, just in time to duck to the side. Malcolm missed him by an inch, hitting the metal instead, crying out in pain.

His face changed. He was *mad.* Luke could see the rage building and his eyes widen, saliva rolling down his chin as Malcolm grabbed Luke's head and smashed him against the wall.

Scrambling to get back on his feet, Luke felt something running down his temple. *Blood,* he realised. *Think fast Luke. You must use the seconds between the punches wisely or you're toast,* he told himself, hearing Malcolm huff against the wall.

Lucky he's fat, he thought. That'll buy me ten seconds, give or take.

He tried to get up, but Malcolm kicked him back down, past years of kickboxing serving him well. He grabbed Luke's leg and dragged him across the hallway.

Looking around quickly, Luke suddenly saw his mother's face appear in front of his eyes. *Not now,* he pleaded. *Let me get out of here first.* Blinking through one swollen eye, he spotted the bat. *Bingo.* It was as if mum pointed him there, and that was all he needed.

"Bring it on motherfucker," he whispered, grabbing hold of it quickly. He knew his changes were 50/50… make it out of here alive or eat out of a tube again, tied to a beeping machine next to hers. Or end up inside a coffin.

He swung the bat around and hit Malcolm's knee as hard as he could. Screaming, Malcolm sank to the ground. Mum's face in front of him, Luke took another swig at his head. Malcolm's body dropped to the floor like a heavy bag.

"Who's the wimp now, ha??" He screamed, hitting Malcolm again and again, getting only grunts in reply. One hit. Two hits. Three hits.

"*This* is for my mother and the mornings I found her swollen and bruised, still making excuses for you, unable to look me in the eye.

This," he gulped, "is for my baby brother, who I never got to meet because of you." "And *this,*" he took a hard blow, "is for what you did to Gramps."

He heard him murmur underneath his breath.

"What was that?! Stop??? Not so strong now, are we motherfucker??"

Luke could hear the panic in his voice, but he wasn't going to let him get away this time.

The punches felt easier and easier as he hit harder and harder, long after Malcolm stopped resisting.

When Luke snapped out of his haze, he found himself staring at a puddle of blood.

"Fuck!!!" He screamed, dropped the bat from his hands. His blood was still pumping through his veins, his arms shaking from the adrenaline. Malcolm wasn't moving.

"Fuck. FUCK. FUCK. FUCK. FUCK. FUCK!!!" Luke looked around, cold sweat running down his back. He needed to act fast. Fiddling Malcolm's phone out of his stepfather's pocket, he quickly covered the speaker phone with a towel.

"What's your Emergency?" came through on the other end. He lowered his voice and spoke as calmly as he could.

"My name is Malcolm Carray, I think someone is trying to break into my house." He took the bat and broke the glass window. "Come quickly, I think they're armed."

"Sending an officer right away," the female officer replied, before he hung up. He looked down at his stepfather.

"Keep it simple," Luke told him. "You taught me that." He wiped the phone and placed it in Malcolm's hand, stuffing the towel inside his pocket. No time to waste.

Hitting a few plants on his way out, he knocked over a table, took the bat and ran into the forest as quick as his legs carried him.

I need an alibi, he thought, hearing the sound of the sirens in the far distance.

⌒

CHAPTER 10

The Middle

Over the next six-month Nate and Lucy spend every free moment together.

One night Nate prepared dinner for her and they chatted until the early morning hours. Another they sat under the moonlight, sipping hot soup on a cold winter night, warming each other by the fire pit. They went for picnics and walks, talked about trips they would take one day, leaving each other voicemails in different languages to re-create those adventures at home in the meantime. Lucy showed Nate how Jamie used to wake her up when she was little, making him giggle all morning. And her.

They listened to podcasts they each found for the other, spiced up their days with cheeky messages to distract each other from work and spend intimate dinners over candles or take away card boxes, sharing how they both started to enjoy life again.

At night, they would find each other, their bodies intertwining like two trees. Lucy felt safe with Nate, regardless of her limited experience and when Nate held her tight after they made love to one another, she felt herself wrapped inside a bubble that became her whole world. It was in those moments she knew she finally belonged somewhere.

Few months later

There was a noticeable shift in Nate. The closer he got to Lucy, the darker his nights became. Heartache, betrayal, and grief of the past, his constant companion. He was afraid. Afraid this would end the same way his marriage did. Unable to see he was causing a big part of it. His soul started hurting, his body did too. It was at this point he listened, and finally withdrew.

Lucy could see the pain in his eyes. When she told him she loved him, he questioned her 'why?' So, she listed all reasons, none of which were a lie. Yet despite his surprise, of how much she recalled, he could not bear to receive it, causing further dismay.

When he left her that night, in the wee-morning hours, he kept wondering all morning if she would be too cold. Yet when she texted that morning, his fear came back forward, disabling all actions, stopping a reply. As he further withdrew, Lucy worked through her own fears, chose to open her heart wide and to love even more fierce. She would cherish each moment, as rare as it got, thinking he just needed time to heal his hurt broken heart.

In the meantime she bought herself roses, intended to help her to cheer herself up.

~

TATJANA GENYS

Lucy, another few months later

I knew it. KNEW IT! KNEW IT! Knew *it*. This is why I never let anyone in, she thought. *Did you really think he was different?* Her head scolded her, its tone harsh. *I told you he wasn't, but you wouldn't listen.* Lucy shook her head, her heart breaking into little pieces. Why did I listen to that little voice? She wondered. She wasn't referring to her head.

I was getting better, she thought. Why deceive me like that if you knew it wouldn't last? She dropped her shoulders, accepting defeat. Didn't I endure enough?

Tears were running down her cheeks as she asked those questions. She sobbed and sobbed, in sorrow and pity, before sobbing some more, at last in regret.

True love, it had whispered, that little voice inside her and when it had spoken, it came direct from her heart. Her head pushed it down, as fast as it could, but she'd already heard it and believed that it could.

Fool! The voice screamed. *Did you still not understand??* She shook her head slowly, whilst raising her head. *Everyone leaves you, it's just a question of time, and the longer they stay, the hurt's only greater.* Lucy whimpered and dug her head even deeper, no longer believing that Nate was a keeper.

Fighting his demons

Something felt off again. Nate couldn't explain it, but he knew it was there. He felt agitated all morning. These were the hardest days. Sometimes he could see them coming, oftentimes he didn't. Usually, they came when he least expected them. They would simply take over, in the middle of the day and not let go off, till it was very late.

His daily routine was what kept him sane, yet as soon as it slipped, he could fall off the rails. So, on days like this one, when it all came together, he had to work hard to keep all together. He missed his routine, when the delivery came in late, made plans to make up for it, but that wasn't his fate.

His supplier lost track and picked the wrong pack, returned an hour later, sending him further back. I'll adjust, Nate thought, with it all in the air, yet that same afternoon, he was full of despair. Hands on his head he stopped in the middle of the street, taking a few deep breaths staring down at his feet.

People who passed him, nudged him into his side, until everything blurred, increasing his fright. He had to get out, fight his way through the crowd. When he reached a break, he started to run, one foot faster than the other, as the world round him spun.

The pathway echoed, each step that he took. With every new building, his day off he shook. He ran past the cinema and past city hall, past Dan's cafe and past Lucy's stall.

He ran past the park and past the big diner, his lungs hurting hard, his fear getting minor.

He never told anyone how bad it could get. Always tried playing it down, left when there was a threat. Yet these past few years, it had grown out of control, it caught up with him frequently, taking him out of his flow.

He ran up the stairs, closed the door firmly shut. *Something's off*, it kept whispering, clenching his gut. He stood under the shower, trying to cut out that voice, walked back in the darkness, ignoring his phone's ringing noise.

It was Lucy who called, for the fifth time that day, wondering where she'd gone wrong and that he'd pick up, she'd pray.

Meanwhile Nate pulled his covers over his head, shut his eyes quick and firmly, soon awoke in a sweat. He tossed and he turned from one side to the other, every incoming thought giving him more of a shudder.

The waiting game

Lucy was waiting, *again*… Lately it was all she did and it felt never ending.

She told herself she wouldn't wait any longer and felt ridiculous when she still did. Tried doing something to take her mind off him yet caught herself responding every time a car passed. Even the usually 'annoying' squeaking gate didn't bother her anymore. Instead, her heart jumped every time she heard it or footsteps approaching.

It had been four days and without any sign of Nate. Not one word.

He didn't tell her where he went and didn't ask her to come along like he used to.

She kept replaying the past few days in her mind over and over for hundreds of times.

Did she upset him somehow? Misunderstand something? Was her tone off?

He said he will come back, her heart whispered.

So did her brother, her brain replied, causing an uneasy feeling in her stomach.

The thought of it made her nauseous. Very nauseous.

What if he didn't? she asked herself, her worst fear unfolding in front of her eyes.

She would be alone again, she thought, her dinner rising in her throat.

Why was this so hard? She wondered. Why couldn't he just call?

All that she needed to hear was that he hadn't forgotten her.

Or something else… Anything but this silence. Restless thoughts were swirling in her head, lingering unpredictably, waiting for a moment to strike. Opening her to the depth of her imagination and the darkness of her mind.

What now? she wondered. And where to from here? Do I move forward? Go Backwards? Yet simply frozen she remained. She tried everything she could to take her mind off him. She talked to people, read something, watched something on television.

Yet everything seemed to remind her of him. Couple of minutes into the conversations, she found herself no longer listening.

Every time she saw something funny, she wanted to share it with him. Hear his big, deep belly laugh in reply. She remembered how his head would tilt back when he did. A big smile carving his beautiful face, his white teeth shining bright.

This is torture! She thought. How is it that something so invisible, inaudible… without an expression, yet its expression so intense, could hurt you more than words ever could? Powerful yes, but equally cruel. Words at the very least, attacked from the front.

Silence on the other hand just watched you squirm, seemingly enjoying the act of despair.

Why call it silence anyway when it had so much more to say?

What was the benefit of silence and what was it out there to teach? Frustrated, she shook her head and sent a little prayer up the sky.

If he isn't coming back, please release me of those thoughts. She felt a big pang in her heart before she finished her sentence.

Fine, she corrected herself. Scratch that last thought. Tell him to hurry back.

Her heart nodded approvingly.

Yes, do that. Tell him to hurry back to me. I miss him…

Two people, two conversations -

Nate

I heard the words leave my mouth and could see how they landed. So differently to what I had in mind. Her smile dropped, her jaw followed. She looked at me with her beautiful big blue eyes, sadness written all over them.

"I just need to know you care," she had told me just a moment ago. She said it three times that night, the last time merely in a whisper.

"Of course, I do," I told her. She wasn't convinced.

"Of course, I do." I repeated, to reinforce the message. Could she not see that?

"I wouldn't be here if I didn't."

She smiled when I said that. We kept walking up and down the same street when I chose to lay myself bare.

"I question our compatibility," I told her. She stopped in her tracks and looked up at me.

"You don't think we are compatible?" She repeated slowly, shocked by my revelation.

"We like the same things, our values are the same, don't we have a great time together?"

"Yeah, I replied truthfully, we do." I was trying to tell her I know I'm not meeting her needs. I am hurting her. She doesn't always show it, but I know I am. Not intentionally of course. I hope she knows that too… And I feel guilty for it, all the time.

"I'm not giving you the attention you deserve," I tried again. "And that makes me feel bad. *Very bad*. Which, on top of my anxiety, is pushing me to my limits."

I finally told her about it today.

"You always give so much Lucy. Not just to me, to everyone… and I can't match that."

"I don't expect you to," she replied. "That's just who I am. I like making people happy."

I know she doesn't, but that doesn't make it any easier.

"What are you afraid of?" she asked.

"That I am not able to make you happy… and that I will keep upsetting you." It killed me to speak those words but they are true.

"But you *are* making me happy," she replied and stopped me.

"Look at me Nate. You are making me happy. Today we had an argument, yes, but you *are*." We kept walking.

Maybe she couldn't see it… but I could. The misery I was causing her was obvious.

Instead, she kept reminding me of the moments we spent together and how much fun we had

"…and that night, we met for a late dinner at that little Viet place, that was fun… wasn't it?" She looked at me so hopeful in that moment, it broke my heart.

Of course we did. But that was beside the point. I nodded.

"I wonder if we are on the same path," I tried again.

She let go of my hand momentarily.

"What??" she asked, running her fingers through her hair. There was a change in her voice. "You just told me you care… how can you tell me you care and then tell me we are not on the same path together?"

I could hear the frustration and agony in her voice. She took a deep breath, her body tensing.

"I will not convince you to be with me," she said, looking away.

"What if it doesn't work?" I tried again. "In the long run, I mean. Then what?" The thought of continuously hurting her is unbearable. "We would be back to square one."

"At least we would have tried," she whispered and it sounded like defeat.

"I will not convince you to stay with me."

We walked back in silence. She wasn't watching where she was going, nearly bumping into a pole. I gently moved her to the side.

"Thank you," she said and went back within.

What was going through her mind??

She asked me to wait when we reached her front gate and returned moments later, my jumper and a little bag in hand.

"I bought you a gift whilst you were away," she told me, handing me both. I took the bag.

"Keep it," I told her, handing her back my jumper. "I don't wear it very often and it suits you much better than me."

She shook her head firmly and looked at me, eyes filled with tears. Seeing her like this was killing me.

"Are you ok?" I asked and she started to cry.

"No." she replied, shaking her head. "But I don't expect myself to after what you said tonight." It broke my heart. The last thing I wanted to do was to hurt her even more. I did it *again*... I tried hugging her, but she froze in my embrace, not hugging me back.

"Can I call you tomorrow?" I asked and she shook her head again.

"Why don't you take a couple of days to think things through…"

Pain was written all over her face as she tried to control the tears.

"And let me know after," she managed and ran back inside her house.

"Call or text me… any time!" I cried after her, but she already closed the door, not looking back. *SHIT!* What just happened?? Bewildered, I walked back to my car, staring at the jumper in my hands.

Lucy

"I am resisting moving forward with you," Nate told Lucy when they finally met a week later.

"Why?" She asked and felt like someone just punched her in the gut.

"I question if we are compatible," he continued.

Lucy nearly puked.

"You don't think we are compatible?" She managed.

"And if we are on the same path," he added, confirming her worst fears.

The ground underneath her feet broke open, swallowing her whole. *He doesn't want me.*

It hit her like a slap in the face. And her stomach. With a sledgehammer.

Tears were running down her cheeks, but she didn't care. She had to get out of there.

Gagging, she ran to the bathroom. Was this really happening? Did he really just speak those words? Her stomach couldn't take it any longer. She hurled up the little food she had inside her. She couldn't eat, knowing they would talk today, sensing it was bad. But this wasn't what she expected. She gasped for air. He said he cared… Then why couldn't he see a future with her? She hurled again.

Her arms were clutched to the toilet ring, her body trembling hard, desperately trying to find something else to release. With shaking legs, she sank to the ground and wiped her mouth.

Moving to the bedroom slowly, she curled up inside her bed and pulled her covers close, his words echoing in her ears.

Not compatible… It was too early to sleep but she didn't care. Everything felt numb. Apart from her heart, that was.

She switched off her phone, then switched it back on again. What if he called?

He won't, her head replied, releasing more tears.

Not compatible… She fell into a restless sleep and woke up a few hours later.

When reality hit, she let out a sob.

When it got light, she went back to the bathroom and found her pale reflection staring back at her. Eyes red and swollen, dark circles visible below her eyes. She didn't care. Didn't care what day it was or where she was meant to be.

She switched off the light and moved back to her bedroom, pulling down the blinds. There were things she had to do and places she had to go.

Not today, she thought, hugging her pillow tight.

~

Lucy was running through the forest, her footsteps echoing underneath her feet. She was running fast, leaving footprints on the ground like many others before her.

What were they thinking as they passed? She wondered as rocks moved to the side at impact. That was the only sound there was. Apart from her breathing, and the occasional chirping of a bird. On the outside at least, their conversations echoing in her ears.

She pushed on harder, faster, sweat building on her forehead, trying to outrun her thoughts. And then she stopped, all of a sudden, right in front of a big tree. It looked like no other, standing on its own, on top of a high stone wall at the end of the park, its roots hanging down the wall instead of simply laying on the ground.

The wall was at least a metre tall, Lucy thought. The tree was massive too… its roots and branches intertwining, finding their way to the ground through the rocks, green leaves covering its trump and branches. Lucy liked it instantly. *I wish I could be like this tree,* she thought. Strong and majestic. Then she paused. Who says that's how it felt?

Maybe it felt as fragile as it stood, trying to keep it together like the rest of us. Hoping everyone would look at the top and ignore the messy bottom. She looked at the tree in admiration. At what cost came your constant adjustment to climate, circumstances, and time? She moved towards the tree and placed her hands around as much as she could reach. *You're doing just fine,* she whispered into her embrace. *Just in case you need to hear it today.*

On her way back she found a caterpillar handing off a tree. *Hang in there, little buddy,* she told it. It might feel like the end of the world right now, with everything you are going through, but you just wait. You will be more beautiful than you ever imagined soon, and it'll be worth all the misery and pain.

Those were the good days. Days she felt like she was moving forward. Unfortunately, they were followed by days she kept endlessly wandering through empty streets.

They weren't truly empty of course, but they were to her. Grey, lonely, pointless…

It didn't matter what street, what park, what avenue… to her they all look the same. It was in those moments, she thought back to the tree.

That's how I must go on too, she told herself. Silent on the outside.

Yet her soul was screaming inside of her, tearing her little body apart. Her tree had faltered, more often than not, the sadness sucking her back in fastly.

It was in those moments, her heart ached as raw and fresh as it did back then.

When will this pain finally stop? My tears finally dry? She asked. Was he suffering all the same?

Unlikely, her brain replied. After all, this was his choice…

One week later

"Maybe I give so much, because I'm afraid no one will love me otherwise," Lucy told Annabelle, after Annabelle finally managed to drag her out of the house.

"Maybe it's not as selfless as it seems. After all, it makes me feel better too, at that moment."

"It's not their love you crave," Annabelle replied, chewing a bite off her apple.

"What do you mean?" Lucy queried, confused.

"It's not their approval you crave," Annabelle clarified. When she saw Lucy's conflicted face, she elaborated.

"How long does the feeling last?" She asked. Lucy thought about it for a moment.

"A little while," she replied.

"What happens after?" Annabelle probed.

"I go back to doing what I do," she replied. Annabelle nodded knowingly.

"So, if their validation doesn't last long, maybe it's not theirs you seek?"

Lucy thought about it for a moment. What Annabelle said, made a lot of sense, so far. But if it wasn't their love and approval she craved, then who's? And why did she still feel so miserable without Nate's?

"What would happen if you didn't?" Annabelle continued.

"Didn't give?" Lucy looked at her, two question marks in her eyes. "It would feel uncomfortable," she replied.

"Initially yes," Annabelle agreed. "What else would it mean?"

"I… would have more time?" Lucy guessed.

"Right, and with more time, and energy, what could you do?" Lucy thought about helping Dan out at the café, her elderly neighbour with the groceries… when Annabelle stopped her again.

"What if you didn't do that either Lucy? At least not straight away. What if instead, you invested that time in yourself? For a little bit."

Lucy shrugged her shoulders.

"That would feel very selfish," she replied quietly after a while.

"It's not selfish to look after yourself Lucy." Annabelle looked at her warmly.

"Actually, it's the most selfless thing you can do. Think about it, the more you give to yourself, the more you have to give to others." She paused for a moment. "You don't need to earn love Lucy," she told her. "And you can't tame it. It is either given freely, or it's not."

Lucy felt a lump in her throat.

"But what you can do," Annabelle continued, "is love yourself. The way you want to be loved by another." She pointed to the flowerpot opposite them.

"These little flowers, as beautiful as they are, depend on others. Forgotten to be watered, they'll die right there in that same pot. A flower in nature, doesn't wait for the rain." She paused for a moment, giving Lucy time to consider this.

"Is it my love I crave?" Lucy clarified.

"Yes," Annabelle replied, "and your approval you seek."

"That shouldn't be too hard," Lucy thought out loud.

"Harder than you might think," Annabelle cautioned. "You can't just decide it, Lucy, that's not how it works."

"How does it work?" Lucy wondered.

"You need to embody it." Annabelle replied.

"How do I embody love and approval?" Lucy questioned. Annabelle thought about it for a moment.

"Follow your emotions," she suggested.

Lucy thought about the past few weeks and the emotional rollercoaster she'd been on and rolled her eyes.

"Think my emotions find me without much of my help," she whispered.

Annabelle smiled.

"That's not what I meant. Next time, when an emotion arises, sit with it. Sit with it like you would with your best friend. Offer it tea. Ask why it feels that way and listen. Truly listen, without judgement. Don't tell it to go away. Try to understand what's underneath it all. Is it angry? upset? That's usually a secondary emotion."

"What is the first?" Lucy asked intrigued.

"Can be many things," Annabelle replied. "Sometimes it's sadness, oftentimes it's fear. Anger, upset, and shame come as a result. Listen to it and let it move through you."

Lucy nodded slowly, taking it all in.

"You have been fighting all these years Lucy. Maybe it's time to take off your armour."

Lucy thought about what she heard. Annabelle was right in one thing, she wasn't listening and hadn't been in a long time. Not to herself and not to her body. She thought of the last moment, she wanted to be like the tree and the voice screaming inside her, as if it was going to explode. She just ignored it. What if she hadn't?

Whatever it was, maybe it was trying to show her how much life she still had inside her and how wanted to be released. Maybe this part inside her, unlike her, hadn't given up on her yet. Maybe it was coming not to fight her, but to win with her.

When she got home that afternoon, she hugged herself tight.

Forgive me, she whispered. Things will be very different from now on, I promise.

It's you and me now.

~

Nate texted Lucy a few days later. It felt strange not speaking to her and he missed her. Lucy missed him too. When they finally spoke that following night, she could hear he was still torn. Maybe it's not enough to miss someone, she thought.

Nate, meanwhile, lost between what he wanted for himself and what was right for Lucy, was struggling with the decision he had to make. He was surprised how strong Lucy sounded and happy to hear her voice, relief washing over him when she didn't push for an answer. At least at first.

After they hung up, Lucy was proud of herself. She had thought about what Annabelle told her and decided to let love come to her freely. Maybe this was what unconditional love looked like, she thought.

Nate, meanwhile, couldn't help but wonder if she was better off without him and if she was getting ready to tell him goodbye.

~

The sky was grey, but it finally stopped raining. Lucy didn't mind the rain this time. She also didn't mind staying at home any longer.

This week, she hadn't felt the urge to go anywhere. Just wanted to be. By herself, that was and in her own home. She never saw it like a home before, more like four walls fulfilling a purpose, a waiting hall, without a timeline.

But now these same four walls became her cocoon. She thought back to the little caterpillar she met the other day. What if the same was happening to her?

She pulled her hoodie over her running shorts and T-shirt and tied her runner shoes. She had never been a runner up until now, but the more she ran, the clearer her head got.

First, she ran *against* herself, fighting every moment along the way. Then she ran to forget. She returned home completely drained, yet still remembering.

Now she was running *for* herself. She was running *for purpose* and running *for joy,* running *for patience,* and running *to feel whole* again.

She took care of herself. Rested when she was tired, cooked wholesome food, just for herself and swam in the ocean, when she wanted to and didn't just because others did.

She went on long walks and bought herself new body wash, even splurged on the more expensive one, listening to her body's guidance on flavours and smell.

She stopped responding to people just because she felt she had to. Stopped herself from rushing to an event she didn't want to attend in the first place and didn't reply to Nate's messages until it felt right. Saying what she wanted to say, not what she felt she *had to. Should do.*

It felt strange and unfamiliar at first, but just as Annabelle predicted, got easier after a few days. She was starting to notice the difference. Started to reconnect with herself again, in a way she never did. With a new found level of acceptance, compassion, and care. I never knew how much I did for others, she thought. There was a real honesty in that transition, that felt more real than she did in a long time. Everything simply aligned.

That's how she met him that night.

Nate

I can't sleep… again. Tossing around in bed, I stare into the darkness. My eyes hurt, it's been days since I had a proper night sleep. I feel restless, agitated. My thoughts keep me up way beyond the sound of truck drivers in the distance… sometimes all the way until dawn. And yet I am up with the birds and before the first sun ray. Wide awake.

The same questions circling in my brain. The unknown, haunting me.

Meditation and yoga steadies my nerves, I started practising it up to three times per day lately, yet my body remains restless, my mind still alert.

They say the body knows first… if so, what is mine trying to tell me?

Two Roller Coasters, one ride

To say the following few weeks were horrendous, would have been an understatement. Lucy bounced from feeling calm and at peace, wondering if she accepted this as the end, to angry and frustrated, wanting to pull her hair out.

Nate couldn't understand how Lucy didn't see he was doing this *for* her. *Because* he cared, still fighting his restlessness at home. He missed talking to her, her laugh and the times they spent together. His mind telling him they are good together, his heart still holding him back. He knew he had to give her an answer and he was petrified. Petrified of losing her and even more so of hurting her again.

She looked just like *her,* when she looked at me last time... the thought of going through this again, eating him alive.

"What are you more afraid of?" Lucy asked when they last spoke "letting me in... or losing me?" He shuddered at the thought. Both felt unimaginable at that moment.

Truth was, he didn't know how. His family let things slide rather than address them, so he grew up living in the spaces in-between. He never met anyone so intune with their emotions and whilst he admired this about Lucy at first, confronted with it, he panicked.

The gap between them felt unimaginatively big at the time. Especially when we thought back to the moment, she told him she loved him. He froze when she did.

Couldn't believe it and couldn't receive it. How could she love him, when he loathed himself? He knew how much it hurt her that he didn't say it back, but couldn't.

Didn't understand how eight letters, three little words... ones individually, he used nearly every day, simply wouldn't roll off his tongue.

He reached out to her that night. It was late but he didn't care.

He wasn't lonely, he just had to know how she was. She didn't reply.

Hope you are well?

Lucy kept staring at the text message in front of her. Was he insane??

Of course she wasn't well, nothing about this whole situation was okay. It had been another four days without an answer, and this was what she got?

Frustrated, she paced up and down the corridor. What was she meant to reply to *that*?

'*Life's awesome!*'

'*Couldn't be better*'

She snorted. Obviously not. Did it mean he reached a conclusion? She wanted to reply before the moment passed but stopped herself.

What moment would pass? She re-read his message. Maybe he was lonely. Or sad? Did it mean that he still cared?

She still couldn't understand how he couldn't see they were good for each other, but she also wasn't going to convince him to be with her. Or anyone. Like Annabelle said, love had to come to her freely.

She thought about the text during her walk the following day, unsure of where to go from here. She could leave it without a response and close that door shut.

That would be the end of it. Finito, arrivederci, goodbye. But was that what she wanted?

Rightly or wrongly, she still cared for him. Genuinely cared for him…

She could push him to a corner and demand a response. But what good would it do?

At the same time, she couldn't just keep waiting, not knowing where she stood. Yet every time they talked, they went round and round in circles. What else could she do?

It was twelve hours since she received his message, the longest she had ever gone without replying. In the past, this would have made her nervous, but today, she wanted to wait until she knew what she wanted to say.

Something she wouldn't regret a few hours down the line. Something that felt genuinely aligned with her.

She put her phone in her pocket and sat down by the beach, enjoying the sunshine on her face, the salt on her skin and the sand underneath her feet as the sound of the ocean rang softly in her ears.

2 days later

It didn't happen very often that Lucy was at a loss for words, but today was one of these days. The consequences of each path just felt way too big all of a sudden.

She knew they couldn't stay where they were, couldn't go back to where they had been and yet couldn't see the way forward.

"What do you want?" She asked Nate, out blank. This was what it ultimately boiled down to and what was holding her back from moving forward. Make *her* choice… if there was even one left to make.

Did he still see a future with her? Wanted the trips they talked about so many times before? She knew it wouldn't come easy and how much they would have to rebuild if they tried, and that it would be much easier to leave it there and then.

But she also knew she didn't want to live in "what if's?" for the rest of her life.

She needed an answer and she needed to hear it from him.

The question was hanging heavy in the air. Nate took a deep breath. He knew it was time to give Lucy an answer.

"Can we meet this weekend and talk about it then?" He asked. Lucy nearly cried at the thought. Partly, because the thought of seeing him again was just too painful, mostly because the weekend was still a week away.

"How about I call tomorrow?" She offered instead.

"You prefer to talk over the phone?" He asked, his heart clenching at the thought she didn't want to see him.

"I don't," she replied. "But I can't continue putting a plaster over an open wound."

She understood how hard this decision was for him, but also the toll these past few weeks had taken on her.

"Let me in, or let me go Nate, but please don't keep me hanging in the air like this anymore," she told him. This was when she knew, she surrendered to the process and accepted it for what it was. Ready to get on with her life either way, and finally start seeing to her wound.

Tomorrow

It was the longest 24 hours, for both of them. Neither of them slept very much that night. *Don't leave me hanging like this,* kept echoing in Nate's ears. He wouldn't.

He knew what he had to do.

Lucy, meanwhile, felt surprisingly calm. In anticipation. Knowing she would need all her energy as soon as the phone rang. *I will be ok,* she told herself, hugging her legs into her chest. Part of her wanted it to end. The roller coaster to be over.

Her heart to finally get a break.

The other part started dreading that conversation, wondering if it was self-protection or fear of what was about to come. That's when the phone rang.

CHAPTER 11

Tim

It was months since Tim, Mr. shirt-unbuttoned, first approached Lucy at her stall. When they first met, she was friendly and warm, yet guarded and cautious.

Maybe because of the way she nearly fell into his arms that day. Yet unlike others, she didn't fall to his knees thereafter, on the contrary, nothing that worked in the past without effort, seemed to have even the slightest effect on her.

For the first time, it was Tim who had to do the chasing. *This is new...* he thought, intrigued by the challenge. *I'm sure it's just a question of time.*

So, as time progressed and he found her growing closer to Nate than him, he couldn't help wondering: *Why him, not me?*

Months later, groggy and disappointed, if not a little hurt by her dismissal, he nearly gave up pursuit. Until he noticed another change in her, when she suddenly got quieter and quieter, and even the few words she spoke, no longer connected to her eyes.

That's when he came by her stall again more frequently, more determined this time, picking the quieter times to ensure they could talk. As the weeks passed, he stopped by nearly every day: on the way to the post office, after visiting a friend… His reasons became irrelevant. To him they were just excuses, and Lucy was too absorbed in her own world to notice any different.

It doesn't matter, he told himself, reminding himself it was only a question of time.

Yet as the weeks progressed, her insecurities exaggerated. Tim could see how much she cared for Nate and it troubled him grossly. He almost became obsessed.

He too wanted to be cared for, in the same way. By her. So he started staying a little longer, caring a little greater. Helping her pack up her garments one day, carrying them to her stall another. Fixed the light on her bike one weekend, dropped her to the rail station the next. His friends started teasing him, but he didn't care. The more time he spent with her, the more he missed her when he didn't.

What has she done to me? he wondered, ignoring all others nearby. He checked in with her in the morning, and then again at night.

Lucy, unaware of all of this, didn't understand why he was so persistent.

Didn't see that every time he came to visit, he looked for another reason to come.

If nothing needed fixing, he broke something on the way out, just so he could repair it again in the morning.

To Lucy, it just felt like another strike of bad luck. To Tim, that strike of bad luck became something to look forward to, as he sat at home, studying how to fix what he had broken.

Over the weeks, Lucy got used to him being around. Brought him tea or a sandwich when he came over, and prepared for his visit. She started to share a bit more openly, things she didn't share with Nate when he wasn't around.

This is who you should want, her brain told her a few months later. Knowing fair well that her heart still belonged to Nate.

~

The letter

Weeks passed since the day Nate and Lucy last spoke, or could have been months. Lucy got on with her life. She got up in the morning, cleaned her place, repotted her plants and fed her neighbor's cat. She went shopping, cooked big pots of soup, and got on with work. Her to-do list grew longer and longer each day, focused on anything she could think of to keep herself busy and distract herself from what was happening in her heart.

It had gotten cold outside, almost as cold as it had inside her. She felt hollow inside, nonexistent… Tim tried his hardest to get through to her, hanging onto each little smile he could get, fighting the urge to pull her into his arms and kiss her. But Lucy was zipped.

Top to bottom, triple locked. Completely closed off to anyone around her.

She made a vow to herself that day, to never let anyone enter her heart again and to shield it from others, with all of her might.

"Lucy!" Lucy flinched at the sound of her name and looked up from her haze.

"Oh, hey, Annabelle." She replied, trying to sound cheerful, not convincing either of them.

It pained Annabelle to see her friend like that, a shadow from the woman she once was.

"Have you eaten?" She probed softly and Lucy nodded.

Annabelle hugged her skinny little frame. She could see Lucy was trying to put up a brave face, when getting by was all she could manage.

"Walk with me?" she offered, and Lucy nodded gently. Annabelle watched her closely, as she placed one foot in front of the other, her eyes looking ahead without direction. She would follow her to the store later and watch her mindlessly pick out her food. She didn't bother with a basket.

At the till, Lucy would walk right past her, placing an apple, a bread roll, and a packet of tea onto the counter. The lady at the register would ask her some questions, which Lucy either wouldn't hear or chose to ignore, until the lady eventually gave up.

Whilst they walked, Annabelle told her anything she could think of. Lighthearted and joyful, keeping it simple and bright. Lucy would mirror her approach, smile when she saw her smiling, nod in-between when her face wasn't clear. She didn't have the capacity for small talk and found it hard to pay attention. All she wanted to do was get home again quickly.

It wasn't that she didn't want to see Annabelle… she didn't want to be seen. Or heard. And most of all, she didn't want to answer any questions.

"How are you?" Annabelle asked, making her freeze, unable to hold back a little tear escaping from her eye. This was the question she dreaded the most.

"Please don't ask me that," she whispered, wiping the tear from her cheek. But Annabelle already had. And others soon would too. One simple question, and she was back in her pain. Back in her heartache and back in her tears.

She didn't want to go on like this… didn't want to hold onto that story.

Be sad Lucy… *again!* But everywhere she went reminded her of him, and everywhere she looked, she found his face. She knew he wouldn't just magically appear in front of her door anymore, telling her he made a mistake and yet these thoughts kept crossing her mind, nevertheless.

She was grieving, begging… negotiating. Somewhat depressed and a lot in denial.

He said he'd write her a letter. Write down the words he couldn't speak.

It had been weeks since then and she kept checking her post box ever since. When she didn't hear from him for yet another few days, she called him. It was a spur of the moment decision, her heart beating fast.

"I'm glad you called," he told her, a lump sitting in his throat. It felt good hearing her voice. These past few weeks were crazy with work, and he had just recovered from a cold.

"Will I still get that letter?" She asked out-front. She needed an explanation, something to help her make sense of it all.

"Yes," he told her, his heart skipping a beat. *She hadn't forgotten him.* More so, she still wanted to hear from him. He sat up on the couch and ran his fingers through his hair, disbelief washing over him.

"I have accepted it," she told him then, crushing those same thoughts momentarily. It was a lie, but she didn't know it yet.

"Can we meet for coffee some time?" He still asked, unaware of the tears running down her cheeks. *He sounded okay,* she thought. *Was* okay. And there she was, constantly hurting. Now even more so than before. Crying over the most basic activities, resisting accepting that this was truly the end. Acceptance sounds tranquil, she thought, yet this felt everything but. She thought about what she would tell him once they met and cried at those same thoughts. She wasn't ready to tell him goodbye and didn't want to imagine someone else by her side, not now and not even ten years from now.

It was naïve to think that way, but she couldn't help herself. As Dan once called out rightly, she was a hopeless romantic. Or used to be.

Right now, she had sworn off love completely. Put a lid on it, wrapped a chain around it, placed a big rock on top of it and drowned it in the canal.

And they lived happily ever after. She snorted at the thought and the idea she once loved so dearly.

~

Surrender

The ringing of her phone interrupted her thoughts. Lucy's first instinct was to ignore it. Answering it meant answering questions and admitting what she wasn't ready to admit.

Lucy always dealt with everything herself in the past, never showed anyone how much she struggled and always suffered in silence behind closed doors.

But today was different. For the first time, she was ready to accept help.

Annabelle's good mood came through the speaker as soon as she picked up the phone.

"Helloooo," she sang through the speaker. She told Lucy about her day and her plans to move into a tiny house. One she described in such vivid colors, Lucy couldn't help but smile. This was her first genuinely smile in a long while and wouldn't be her last.

From tomorrow, she would start smiling at strangers, her sunglasses covering her puffy eyes, and talk to people sitting by themselves on a park bench. She swore not to let anyone else feel the way she did if she could help it.

"How are you?" Came the dreaded question after a while. Lucy broke down in tears again, cursing herself for not listening to her instinct.

She wanted to end the call, but Annabelle didn't let her. Tried changing the topic, but Annabelle didn't let her do that either. Just sat there quietly and watched her through the screen.

"I'm with you," she told Lucy, holding space for her softly as she did.

Lucy wanted to run. Hide. Get away from this situation as fast as possible.

"Allow it," Annabelle almost whispered. "You are ready to go deep."

The pain and discomfort Lucy felt was excruciating, killing her slowly on the inside.

Pain she had tried to avoid so hard, was staring her right in the face. Everything in her chest ached as her heart strings pulled hard in every direction.

"Don't resist it, let the wave wash over you instead," Annabelle continued. "Or it will keep throwing you back to the shore. You got this, darling heart."

Lucy listened and dove underneath the wave, surrendering to her pain, the embarrassment, and the reality that they were over.

This wave was ginormous, grown over the past few weeks to triple its size. As it washed over her, a flood of tears escaped. It took them with it.

Lucy cracked wide open, allowing the pain to move through her as she did. Until all of a sudden, there was relief. It came as quickly as the wave, soothing the wound soon after. She took a deep breath and then another. Her chest felt lighter, softer... and at peace.

Like the rock she had placed onto love, removed from her own chest.

She put on her throw-on and hugged herself tight. Only later would she understand what Annabelle did for her that day. She taught her how to receive love.

On a day she couldn't see it elsewhere. Showed her that love hadn't given up on her, even after she had given up on love. That Love had found its way out of its chains and out of the canal and come back for her.

She showed Lucy how to accept love and let it in, instead of questioning it's intent. Showing her love didn't stay because she convinced herself it wouldn't.

Lucy thought for a long while that evening and understood that the bubble she had created for herself, wasn't serving her any longer. It became lonely… and at times even hopeless.

She climbed out of her bed and made herself a cup of tea. I don't want my bubble anymore, she concluded. I think it's time for me to leave my cocoon.

Deciding to leave her cocoon, was one thing, moving forward, yet another.

Lucy knew she needed Nate's letter or speak to him to find closure and yet the longer it took, the angrier she got. But anger was good, she thought. Anger she could work with.

She wanted to tell him how selfish it was of him to keep her waiting and how impossible it made it for her to move on, not knowing what she was moving on from.

She thought it cowardly and cruel and by far the worst way to leave someone.

That's when she came across a book about a woman who found her husband cheating on her, when he called their newborn baby the name of the one he had with another. *Fine,* she thought. *Second worst way to leave somebody.*

She wanted to scream at him, ask him how hard it could be, dotting down a few lines for someone you have meant to have cared for over the past year, but she just wasn't the screaming type.

She took her phone out and started typing. After all, what else did she have to lose?

Your dignity, maybe? Her brain offered. She ignored it. Typed out a message and deleted it. Re-wrote the message and deleted it again. Her brain scolded her for her indecisiveness, but she knew her anger wouldn't lead anywhere and deep down inside, that he was lost too. So, she finally settled on:

Ready for that coffee yet?
I'll be in the city later and can pop by on my way back.

Simple and honest. She put her phone in her bag and headed to the city, immersing herself in the day. Ordered a big warm homemade pie and a cup of hot tea and sat down in the corner of the little pie shop.

This wouldn't be something she would normally do, especially on a Saturday afternoon, and it made her feel uncomfortable, sitting there all by herself, surrounded by couples and families… highlighting she had no one to share this with.

This was only partially true of course, she had Dan and Annabelle and could ask Tim if she wanted to. She didn't.

Instead, she took out her journal and started writing. After she journaled on what was happening inside her, she became present to what was happening around her. She learned to appreciate a cup of freshly ground tea instead of the tea bag she would normally get, found joy watching a couple argue endearingly about what dessert to have before settling on both and found a stranger smiling at her at the bus stop before she got lost in several book and vintage stores. This part of the city was new and buzzing with energy. People seemed much more themselves here, and Lucy got sucked into it all. So much so, she only checked her phone every so often and found Nate's reply only an hour later:

Hey! I have a full-on day at work today and was hoping we would catch-up when we have more time. I could do Sunday a week from now, if that works?

Another week from now… Lucy swallowed. It took a moment for that message to sink in.

That was a reply you send someone you don't want to see. Her reply came fast and furious:

Never mind. I won't be able to do next weekend.

Have a nice eve!

She stuffed her phone in her bag and got back to the lights of the city, humming alongside the busker playing his saxophone. It took her a moment to recognize the song:

'*Can you feel the love tonight?*' She nearly broke down in tears. But for a different reason than she expected. Because today she could. Around her, within her and everyone beside her.

She treated herself to a neck massage and fleece jumpsuit and cuddled up in bed later, a mug of hot tea and the book about the cheating husband in hand. Something told her, she would be able to relate to the woman very well.

Onto her second cup of tea, her phone buzzed again.

I do want to catch-up with you soon though. Perhaps sometime during the week?

Or the weekend after? Let me know!

A sentence echoes through my ears
It hammers wildly at my fears
What if I didn't let my pride
Keep me away from what felt right?

What if I tried just one more time?
Would he at this point still be mine?

Reflections

Lucy was sitting in Kürtősh, a Hungarian café she had passed many times before, staring at the wall in front of her.

It was a cold Saturday afternoon, the sky grey and moody and in line with how she felt. She didn't leave the house until late, blaming the weather and now found herself not wanting to go back. Tomorrow was the day she was meeting Nate, and she wasn't ready to think about it yet. More so, she all of a sudden didn't feel ready to meet him.

It had been weeks since they last spoke and after wanting nothing more for such a long time, now that it was around the corner, she wished for nothing less.

This whole week she felt pretty flat and by yesterday she was close to cancelling it. After all, there was nothing he could say that would change what she'd been through... so really, what was the point? She thought about everything she wanted to tell him, but only landed on how cruel it was to end things that way. That he had cut her, like a piece of meat, and left her out to dry. And yet the thought of seeing him, she started to cry.

She let anger move through her body, like she did with Annabelle, breathing deeply til it was gone. She knew her body was reminding her of the pain it had been through, trying to protect her from what was about to come. She imagined what he would tell her...

Sorry? Forgive me..? and questioned if she could. Then thought about how she would greet him, her body tightening at the prospect of an embrace. No, *that* she couldn't do. After everything they'd been through, his touch she wouldn't endure.

She thought about where to meet him and didn't want him anywhere near her four walls. Meeting him at his was also no option, she'd be too distracted by *everything Nate* around her, even the thought she couldn't bear.

She considered this café for a moment. Its lights were dim, the walls of brick, a big red wooden table marking the shop floor. Small tables were scattered all around it, giving it a private and relaxing feel. As she entered, one of the workers was still kneading the dough, so she ordered a cup of coffee and one of the local dishes covered in caramelized hazelnut and sat around a big wooden table.

Next to her, a woman working on her laptop, a young girl drinking a cup half her size and a man watching something on his phone in the opposite corner.

Was this where all lonely people went? She wondered. Weekends were the hardest on days she wasn't working.

She looked around the café and spotted a love-struck couple stealing hungry kisses from each other on the other side of the café. She rolled her eyes. Nate's kiss by the lake popped into her head, she turned away.

There were two more couples behind her, one engrossed in their devices, and the other deep in conversation.

Lucy picked up a magazine from the table and screened the front cover.

'How to deal with perfectionism?' 'The barefoot therapist' and 'Mums here smile 2U'

At least it wasn't one that told you how to lose 10lb in a week, she thought.

She flipped through the pages and put it back on the pile with the others.

What if he told you he loved you? Popped into her head.

I couldn't believe it, came the reply.

This too shall pass, a little voice whispered from within her.

Lucy took another deep breath and got up from her chair. It was time to face the music. Tomorrow would come whether she was ready for it, or not. And whilst it would be painful, there was also a chance it would bring closure, understanding, a new beginning... or finally give her what she needed to move on. Surely it couldn't get worse after tomorrow, could it?

Nate

I'm in the Philippines… likely because of the book I read before sleep.

Mother is there too. She does what she always does… *preach*. How nothing I do is good enough and how I should live my life *her* way.

But not today. Today I am holding my ground. Speaking my mind. No longer intimidated by her and no longer accepting what she is pushing my way.

It feels liberating. Freeing to say the things I wanted to tell her for so long, directly to her face.

Behind her, I spot Lucy. What is Lucy doing here?? This is a private conversation, she shouldn't be here. And yet her presence gives me comfort. Beside her, I see grandma. *Grandma…* I whisper. She nudges Lucy my way, tells her it's okay and that I want to speak to her. *Of course, I want to speak to her.* I always want to speak to her. Why would she be telling her that? We walk away from my mother, what needed to be said, was said.

I look at Lucy and tell her how much I regret what happened between her and I.

Give her the letter. The letter I started over a million times and threw away even more often. Looks like I finally finished it. She looks happy when I give it to her, until she sees I typed it on my computer. Guess she expected it to be written by hand. To her I am also a constant disappointment. I apologize. For the letter and the time we last spoke, when I inappropriately laugh, not knowing what else to do. I haven't laughed since.

She looks upset. I know this isn't what she wants for me. Tells me, I don't need to punish myself, but how can I not? We move to a room with a television playing way too loud, distracting me from what's in front of me.

That's how I woke up that day.

~

Lucy

Lucy was sitting on the bus, on the way to the cafe they agreed to meet, a big lump in her throat. She felt okay in the morning, even had to rush getting ready at the end, but now she was about to see him, her emotions were playing catch-up.

Anger met her first, challenging her decision to go, urging her to reconsider for the sake of her heart. Her brain jumped in quietly, letting her know it was safe to understand other people's viewpoint and right of her to go. It was a quote she had read somewhere just a few days ago. Probably in that magazine with the smiling mums.

She could really use a smiling mum right now. Her smiling mum to be precise... She would ask her if she was making the right choices, or if this was a mistake. Ask her what *she* would do, based on her experience.

Would she wait at home for her, worrying on her behalf? Knowing all she could do was to have the biggest hug ready, if it all fell apart?

Would they watch their favorite movie together? Maybe she would cook her favorite meal... or call in for a celebration if this turned out well.

Would they sit in the kitchen, dispelling the conversation over a cup of hot chocolate? Or would she give Lucy her motherly advice?

Lucy would never know the answers to those questions. But she liked to think that, wherever her mother was, she would be beside her tonight. Even if she couldn't see her.

Because the truth was, Lucy felt torn. These past few weeks, she had marched through the worst, or so it felt. Was she knowingly marching into the cave with the enemy? Would tonight reopen her old wounds? Or help them heal faster?

She looked outside the window. It took her a moment to recognize the buildings passing by through the raindrops. The bus driver didn't seem to face that problem, speeding down his lane overtaking one car after the other.

Her gut turned and she started to feel squeamish. *Please don't let me throw up in front of him*, she silently prayed. In hindsight, that wouldn't have been the worst option.

Street after street moved past her, the bus driver seemingly in a rush to reach his destination. At this speed, they would arrive earlier than scheduled and much earlier than she expected. Which also meant, she was early. Even earlier than usual.

They turned into the final street and she pushed the red stop button in front of her, her nerves kicking in, heart racing fast. Was this going to be the end-end? Or a new beginning?

Lucy suddenly wasn't sure, if not knowing wasn't easier after all. As crazy as it sounded after what she had just been through, she was afraid of what was to come.

Was she ready to hear his answers? Her heart wasn't ready for another blow for sure. She looked at her watch… Five minutes to go and too late to turn back now.

This is happening for you, she told herself. Cheesy, yes, but it usually helped.

It didn't today. She didn't want to pump herself up this time or put her hopes up high and assume everything would be alright. Because last time she did, the crash hit even harder.

Nate was waiting outside the café when Lucy arrived. Her heart jumped a beat when she saw him. There he was… *her* Nate. She had to blink twice and look away quickly and couldn't help herself but smile. That's when he turned her way, returning her grin.

They walked in and chose one of the small wooden tables in the back of the cafe before Nate got up and ordered their tea. There were hardly any people around them, the bad weather kept most of them away.

Lucy should have chosen peppermint tea too, to calm her nerves, her emotions still running on overdrive. It felt surreal. *There he was.* She still couldn't believe he was actually sitting in front of her. If she stretched out her arm, she would be able to touch him.

That's when reality hit back equally hard, reminding her it wasn't *her* Nate anymore and she wasn't allowed to touch him. Her chest tightened at the thought, past weeks pain running down her throat, tears building. She blinked quickly to blink them away and could feel her guard rising. Wishing she could take back her prayer. The idea of feeling squeamish sounded a lot easier to handle than trying to control the hurricane bubbling underneath her skin.

Nate returned to the table with their table number, and two glasses of water.

"What's new with you?" he asked, sitting down. Lucy thought for a moment, her brain drawing a blank.

Walking to the café, she asked her heart to guide her this evening and her brain to take a backseat. Looked like it had already taken her up on the offer and gone on vacation.

She had *nothing.*

What did she do the past couple of weeks? Apart from crying her eyes out, obviously.

What was worth sharing? *Nothing* felt important right now. All she wanted to hear was what was going on in his head. That's why she came. To know what he'd been thinking, why they were no longer together and if he felt as miserable without her, as she without him.

She looked up and found him waiting for her reply. So, she started category by category, her work plans first and how she was thinking about expanding her region; the meditation Annabelle had persuaded her to do, an investment idea that came to her during, the meeting she had this afternoon, the old man she randomly met connecting her to another designer from Bairu and the project she had in mind for her new designs.

She could hear herself waffle off one after the other... as well as the constraint in her voice. Words were coming out of her mouth without meaning. Disconnected somehow... She sounded like a bloody news reporter, she thought, and not a very good one. Like a kid expected to read out an article it had zero interest in.

This wasn't the way she meant to come across, but holding it together took all her energy right now. There was a moment she wanted to stop and ask him to skip the small talk. To just tell her what he came here to say, but she just couldn't get herself to do it.

Maybe this was what he needed to build up the courage to say what he needed to say. After all, in a gym, one doesn't automatically start with the work-out either.

Not that she'd been to one lately, but from what she heard, one always started with the warm-up. So maybe this was his warm-up into the real part of conversation.

So, she continued her monologue, as well as she could, rattling off one thing after another before exhaling deeply. Her part was done. She could finally turn the tables back to him.

This was the moment she was waiting for, all these weeks. The moment she would finally get her answers. Understand... or at least try to. But to her surprise, Nate started telling her about his trip back to the family and how it was both good and sad being back again for the first time in years. She got that.

He told her about the time they spent together, and she listened, trying to respond in the right way, at the right time. As well as she managed, at least.

Her brain had taken her quite literally, hung up a big **do not disturb** sign and disappeared.

She heard herself responding to Nate, struggling with her words all the way through it. When she finally finished, she wasn't not sure she understood what she said herself. Seeing him was hard enough… listening to him even harder. Pretending everything was ok, was killing her.

Maybe she should just sit and listen, she thought. And so she did. For the first part of their conversation at least. The second she spent crying.

It took all her strength to look him in the eye. Both went silent. There was nothing else to discuss but them. They had covered all areas, quite systematically one could say, the elephant in the room growing bigger and bigger every second, filling the otherwise empty room entirely.

Lucy looked down at her tea pot and started playing with the lid. She couldn't look up. Couldn't face him. Couldn't meet his gaze. He was just as she remembered him.

Warm eyes, kind, caring… thoughtful. It was killing her.

She knew he was watching her, and she knew she was breaking, right there in front of him, in the middle of the café. She could feel it build up, yet there was nothing she could do to stop it.

There was a long pause, neither of them knowing where to start. Nate finally broke the silence.

"How have you been after the break-up… after us?" He asked. Lucy glanced up for only a split second. She had thought about this question before, anticipating it would come. There was only one possible way to answer it in a somewhat acceptable form.

"I've been," she simply replied.

There was another long silence after that. Usually, she would have jumped in, tried to make it easier, shared. But she couldn't... Not this time. She had laid her heart bare to him on too many occasions, and her heart didn't allow her to do it again this time.

This time she needed answers.

"I'm sorry about what happened..." Nate started after a while. "I do feel really bad about it, I really do..." He paused for a moment. "But I also feel it was good."

"The Break-up?" Lucy asked stunned, looking up for just a moment and he momentarily pulled back.

"No," he replied quickly, but she was longer sure he meant it. "I still don't know if that was the right decision," he continued.

"I'm the wrong person to ask that question to," Lucy replied, stirring her cup.

What did this mean? Did he regret their break-up? Did he want her back?

Just some of the questions that shot through her mind. She listened anxiously, her heart filling with hope.

He told her he missed talking to her and the fun times they had. Told her he wanted to come back to the person he was six months ago, asking her how to do it.

"It usually requires working through the stuff in front of you," Lucy offered quietly, drawing from her experience working with Dr John.

"I miss our catch ups," Nate continued, and Lucy waited. Waited for him to say it. Tell her it was all one big mistake. That he did want to be with her. He didn't.

"What are you thinking?" he asked instead.

"I'm listening," she told him. "I came with the intention to listen, to understand and to try to make sense of it all."

"Do you know why we broke up?" he asked, and she shook her head.

"I never did," she replied honestly, "and still don't." She paused. "Knowing the reason would have probably helped a lot," she added after a while.

"There were many," he replied to her surprise. "Things had gotten crazy with work, he started," pausing for her reaction. She already knew that one.

"What were the others?" She managed, getting ready for the next blow.

"I felt like I was constantly letting you down," he added quieter, "which caused a lot of additional pressure." Another pause. The irony of being *let go* by someone convinced *he let her down* didn't escape her. She knew she sounded bitter and hated herself for thinking that, but that didn't stop these thoughts from pushing their way in.

It is safe to hear other viewpoints echo's in her ears. She took a deep breath, not saying anything. When she looked up, she found Nate struggling for words. There was much more he was trying to say, wrestling with his words, unable to speak them out loud.

Lucy looked down at her cup again, hoping it would make it easier for him to share.

Silence kept building between them, before Nate inhaled deeply.

"My mental state hasn't been great this year," he started slowly, "and I didn't want to end up disappointing you."

"Disappointing me?" Lucy looked up again, astonished by what she just heard, meeting his gaze.

"Women want a strong man," he continued, "and I didn't want to come across as weak." He shrugged his shoulders. "I wanted to be seen as somebody who has his shit together." Pain was written all over his face as he said these words out loud and she knew how hard it was for him to say them.

There he was... *her* Nate. Always so incredibly hard on himself. Not seeing he was exactly what she wanted. Not knowing how else to show him.

She thought telling him *she loved him* would be pretty clear, but he was never able to receive it.

"I never asked for a strong man," she told him. Did he forget it was a soul connection she craved? That meant allowing the other to see you, fully, at your best and at your worst. It means having those difficult conversations, speaking about the hard stuff... the regret, the shame, and guilt that comes with it. That wasn't weakness... that was power. An incredible strength many couldn't claim these days. A true connection.

She looked back at him, watching him more vulnerable than she had ever seen him before. Lucy considered her response for a moment.

"I wish you would have given me a chance." She told him. "Shared with me what you were going through and seen how I'd respond. I have done enough work these past few decades to try to move past *my own shit*, I would have probably understood better than most. I know how much it takes to be vulnerable, and I see it as strength, when you build up the courage to share things that feel impossible to share." She paused for a moment. "And I wished more people would talk about these things... you'd be surprised how many people I see at the market every day, hiding their pain in public, suffocating under it behind closed doors."

"I still have these conflicting thoughts about us," Nate jumped in, relieved by what he heard.

"You got yourself into a loop," she replied. "You will keep going round and round in circles for the next ten, twenty years unless you start acting on them.

We could have tried to work things out together," she added. "Understood each other's needs, insecurities and boundaries and tried to find a way to work around it. Together. There would still never be a guarantee of course, that it would have worked out, but at least we would have come to that conclusion together. Instead, it was one conversation and a shut door in my face."

Tears rolled down her cheeks as she said it, reliving the hurt his actions had caused. He took her hand. Lucy remembered her thoughts about how she would feel if he tried to touch her and thought she wouldn't be able to handle it. Wouldn't want him to touch her... but it just felt right... So stupidly right when his hand was on hers and his eyes waited to meet her eyes.

When she finally managed to look back up, blinking through her teary eyes, she answered his question. With trembling lips trembling and more tears coming.

"I've been hurting," she told him honestly. "That's how I have been. Hurting real bad." There was no holding back anymore at that point, like a dam breaking under rapid, uncontrolled release of impounded water, her tears broke free.

She turned towards the wall trying to hide them, suddenly grateful they were the only customers on that side of the café.

"I'm so sorry," Nate whispered over and over again. "I should have checked up on you." He paused for a moment. "I didn't mean for this to happen."

Lucy registered everything he said and knew he meant it. She knew it was hurting him to see her like this and wished he didn't have to. She believed him. The problem was, it didn't change anything.

"I feel really bad about this," Nate repeated, and she looked up.

"If it's forgiveness you're after," she looked him sternly in the eyes, so he knew she meant it, "You got it." Nate shook his head.

"That's not what this is about." He paused. "We can talk anytime," he offered, and Lucy broke out laughing. Nate, taken aback by her reaction, gave her a bewildered look. Possibly because of the sound she released. It sounded less like a laugh and more like Pennywise. Adding to the mess he had in front of him, Lucy could understand his dilemma.

She took a deep breath and looked at him firmly.

"Tell me everything but that, Nate." She pronounced his name strongly, to make a point. "Not after I tried talking to you for the last eight weeks and you kept pushing me aside." He looked genuinely surprised.

"Has it really been eight weeks?" he asked, nodding slowly. "It doesn't feel that long." Lucy's gut clenched at his words, as if to say, yes it did.

"I'm glad you feel that way," she managed. It came out a lot harsher than she expected, so she took another deep breath and told him it took two to tango. That she clearly didn't give him the platform to share and opened up as much as she should have.

He looked at her and smiled.

"Want to take a walk?" He offered.

"You mean, do I want to continue crying outside?" She replied. Nate shrugged his shoulders, tilting his head.

"How did you get here?" He asked instead.

"By bus" she replied. He looked outside for a moment.

"I'll drive you home."

They walked to the car, and she told him how those past weeks had been reflective for her too. That she understood how her circumstances added to the situation. And that because of it, she probably expected more of him than she would have otherwise.

She told him her reality. How lonely it had been for her and how what she earlier called her golden bubble had turned into a golden cage.

"You can't change your circumstances right now," he interjected softly.

"Yes, I can," she replied. "But for that I need to get my butt into action."

Once they were in the car, Nate brought up their first conversation from a few weeks back, telling her it had also taken him by surprise.

"I wasn't expecting to have that conversation that day," he added, reinforcing he still didn't know if it was the right decision. The air in the car got thinner and thinner.

"It was right of you to share what was going on in your mind," she told him and noticed his relief. "But wrong to run after.

I still don't get it," she added. "I thought we had something real good going on."

Her voice broke at that point. Sitting in this proximity with him only made things worse.

She looked outside following the road signs without paying much attention. The road was clear. Nate drove on.

"I've become more conscious of my thoughts and feelings lately." He shared.

"Stopped pushing them down as much as I did before."

"Sounds like great progress," Lucy told him, but he disagreed.

"Everything just came together Luce…" he told her instead. "Or so it felt. And once those conflicting thoughts were added, it all became too much." He looked at her softly.

"Something just had to give in that moment," he tried to explain.

"As long as you don't regret '*the something that had to give*, later,'" she replied, hit by a wave of sadness. She was 'the something' he didn't choose. He didn't reply.

Lucy learned a while back not to misunderstand it. As much as she wanted him to give her a clear answer right that moment, it usually meant he really didn't know.

"I've been numbing my emotions," he told her instead. Lucy wasn't surprised. Dr Jones had mentioned this to her many times after her parents died and reminded her of it again after she went silent when Jamie disappeared. It was a common response to dealing with trauma. She nodded and told him how she used to get angry in the past and then even angrier for getting angry.

"I wasn't an angry person and didn't want to be one," she explained, "and couldn't understand what was happening until Annabelle explained it to me. Anger happens to be a secondary emotion. In a masochistic kind of way, it was actually *good*. Looking out for me.

I just had to learn to understand it before I could start dissecting it. Turned out it carried a lot of messages for me," she continued. "Messages I had previously ignored. So, once I started paying attention to them and taking note every time I got angry, I realized she was right.

It *was* good."

They arrived in front of her house way too quickly.

"Maybe we can do this again sometime?" Nate asked, stopping in front of her gate. Lucy thought about it for a moment. There was nothing she wanted more, but she also knew it wasn't healthy for her. Knew she would always be waiting, hoping... for the possibility that *maybe one day*, he would change his mind. She knew there was only one answer.

"Think about it," Nate said quietly, sensing her dilemma. She shook her head, tears running down her cheeks again.

"No" She replied softly, but firmly. His face changed momentarily, he was visibly hurt.

"I can't be your friend Nate," she explained. "I wanted nothing more but to see you these past few weeks, but when today came, I started resisting it. I knew it would be hard to see you, but I didn't realize it would be this painful." She paused for a moment. "I never learned to do that half hearted love thing," she added, "and I won't be able to just sit there and make small talk with you, because it wouldn't be real. Sooner or later, you will tell me you have moved on, and I would be happy for you, but I would also be lying, if I said it didn't matter." She wiped her tears from her cheeks before continuing.

"Thank you for driving me home tonight and I'm glad you think it was the right decision."

"I don't know if it was," Nate said, his voice pleading. Lucy couldn't go there. Not until, he was sure.

"And I'm glad you're making progress," she added, before looking at him one final time. "Take good care of yourself, hey?" She got out of the car and moved towards her red gate as quickly as possible, shutting it behind her without looking back.

She knew turning around even just for one second would make her change her mind. She wouldn't have the willpower to hold back, be able to stop herself from running back, begging him to stay. She closed her front door behind her, hearing his engine start and began sobbing. Already regretting what she told him. Already missing him….

Knowing what her heart really wanted deep down inside, also knowing it would be suicide.

~

TATJANA GENYS

CHAPTER 12

The Homeless Man

"Hello…" a small voice came through in the distance. *Who is this?* he wondered.

People didn't talk to him very often, unless to tell him their piece of mind. And it usually wasn't good. He blinked through his eyes but couldn't see anyone.

His dirty fingernails grabbed hold of the whiskey bottle beside him and checked how much was left in the bottle. It didn't matter how much he drank, or what time it was, he stopped caring about that a long time ago.

He took a big swig and lowered his head. The liquid moved down his throat quickly, burning it every inch, releasing, and soothing the throbbing head. His heartbeat slowed down and he sighed. That's better, he thought.

]"Excuse me?" that little voice came again. He sat up and turned around when he heard it the third time. It took him a moment to understand what was going on. Maybe because he wasn't expecting a child, though in hindsight the little voice should have given it away. *Where were her parents?*

He looked around expecting mum or dad to come flying at him.

Last thing he needed was to be called a child molester. Another figure was standing by a tree to his left, looking petrified. *Was this a joke? What punk would let her do their dirty work?*

He really wasn't in the mood for this.

He looked back at her and found her in front of him now, hands in her pockets, smiling from one cheek to another. She reminded him of somebody, he thought, with her big fringe and dark brown ponytail hair, turning from side to side in her polka dot dress.

Don't go there, a firm voice came from inside him. He took another gulp.

I won't.

She giggled, her teeth sparkling bright at him.

"What do you want?" he barked. She looked at him curiously, unimpressed by his bad temper, her eyes wandering him up and down, before landing on the hole of his shoes.

He cringed inwardly as her eyes lingered there for a moment too long, before they landed on the bottles to his side.

That's enough, he thought furiously. He was used to people looking at him in disgust, turning away or pretending he wasn't there. But what hurt the most, were parents moving their children in another direction quickly, whispering into their little ears what not to become.

"You think I can't hear you???" he once screamed at them angrily. "Think this is the life I chose?? I too had dreams!" He sighed watching their horrified faces disappear.

That was then.

They needn't have bothered. Nothing they said to him could come even close to what he told himself. As if he didn't see what he'd become. But back then he still cared. Didn't want to sleep outside. Tried knocking on many doors trying to find a job or place to stay and had too many of them shut in front of his nose again. *He deserved it…* he thought. All of it.

This was his punishment. He took another big gulp, his nostrils flaring when he felt his eyes water. Not today. He wouldn't let anyone see this side of him anymore.

"What do you want?" He asked again, his voice sharp. He wanted her to go away.

She didn't move, even after grinding his teeth.

Why can't she leave me be…? he wondered, craving to be left in the company of his only friend, the one he was holding in his hand.

He met her eyes and was surprised when he didn't find the hostile look inside, he was expecting. She just kept looking at him with deep brown eyes.

"What are you drinking?" She asked.

"Whiskey," he replied.

"Does it taste good?"

"No."

"Can I try some?"

"Hell no!"

"Why not?" She sounded surprised.

"It's not good for you," he replied. Her eyes watched him slowly as she took in the empty bottles next to his sleeping bag.

"Is it good for you?" she tried again. He didn't reply.

"Then why do you drink it?" She asked again.

"To forget."

"Forget what?" She probed.

Who I am, what I am, what I've done… Those blue eyes…. Whoa, where was this coming from?? I need to slow down, he told himself. Not going there today.

Is that who she reminded him of?

"Doesn't matter." he replied.

"It does to me," she countered and paused for a while.

"Does it help?"

That question made him pause for a while. It was so simple, yet he never thought about it before.

"For a while," he replied honestly. She didn't seem surprised.

"Why do you keep doing it?" She asked instead.

"I don't know what else to do." He looked at her and noticed another wave coming. Brown eyes mixing with *her* blue in front of his eyes, pulling him where he didn't want to go. Couldn't allow himself to go.

He tore his eyes from her quickly, overwhelmed by the emotion.

She sees me... he thought. Sees me like *she* used to see me, with those big eyes full of love. Not understanding that I am the monster... A scumbag.... That I should have been the one... not them.

"They didn't deserve this", he finally managed and his voice broke. There was no holding back anymore. Word after words came flooding from his mouth like water from a waterfall. Were they just waiting there? He wondered. It sure felt that way now they came shooting out of him like out of a canon. He could hear himself talk but lost all control to stop them. Was that the whiskey talking? Couldn't be... and yet he found himself telling her everything. Things he hadn't told anyone before and things he didn't allow himself to even think about.

Yet little by little it was coming out one by one, as one memory pushed to the forefront before the other, his heart clenching as it did. His mum's eyes and dad's big laugh, their family dinners for Christmas, sitting around the big dining table in Christmas crowns or birthday hats, his sisters' giggles, and funny faces. He saw himself chasing her around the living room and hearing her squeal in delight. And then...

No, not that… he begged, anything but that. And yet it came, merciless and without warning. Flash back after flashback rolled off in front of his eyes as he relived the day, he tried the hardest to forget.

Instinctively he grabbed for the bottle as the fight played out in front of his eyes.

"I hate you!" he heard himself yell. Tears were running down his cheeks as he saw fire trucks and police cars in front of the house, excruciating pain washing over him repeatedly. He should have been there. Her cry rang deeply in his ears, piercing through his heart hard. He gasped in agony. *Not her…* she will know by now. Know what he had done and he couldn't bear to look her in the eyes once she understood.

It was his fault. He wasn't the victim here, he was the monster. Big sobs were leaving his mouth as he laid his dark soul bare in front of her. His mind was trying to step in, trying to put brakes on, but it was too late. The train crash already happened on the inside and all he could do was watch it derail. He looked up at her briefly, embarrassed, ashamed and guilt ridden. She caught his gaze and locked eyes with him before he broke the gaze and looked down at his feet. The look on her face was too familiar. His heart ached at the thought of it. And yet the way she looked at him… through him, felt like she looked right into his soul.

"That must have been hard," she suddenly said softly, taking his hand. "I'm glad you told me," she added after a while. "What was it like for you?"

"For me??" he repeated in disbelief. Was she for real?

"Doesn't matter," he simply replied.

"It does to me," she countered quietly. He looked at her in disbelief, his expression half pleading, half mortified.

"Don't you see, it's all my fault??" They sat in silence for a moment.

"I see," she started, nodding her head slowly. "But that's not all I see."

Tear after tear rolled down his cheeks, landing on his hands softly. He released the second big cry, surrendering to the pain in his chest and the ache in his body. Shame was washing over him as he told her how he wished he could turn back the time. Take back those words. Get back to that day and do everything different. He would give anything, to have one more moment with them.

"What would you tell them?" She asked softly.

"So many things..." he replied. "I'd tell them I'm sorry. That I love them... how I never meant for this to happen... How living like this has been the worst kind of living. That I regret everything... every day! That it's been eating me alive *ever since* that day. And that it still haunts me. No matter how hard I try to erase it from my brain. But I deserve it. Because its all my fault"

He wiped his face with his sleeve and took a long, big breath.

His eyelids got heavy, his body drained by the emotional outburst of past years catching up with him. He leaned back and closed his eyes when he felt her lean in closer to his ear.

"You matter," she whispered softly in his ear.

His body pulsed and sank into a deep sleep, an unfamiliar peace growing inside his chest.

When he woke up hours later, he remembered Annabelle squeezing his hand, telling him it was going to be okay. Feeling light in his chest, he woke up in hope... and the idea that maybe his life was worth living after all.

Luke

Luke passed by the newsagent and caught a glimpse of the headline

'Innocent man killed by burglars in his own home'. Innocent… he snorted. As if….

Served him right, he thought.

He'd been pondering the event for a long while once reality hit. At first, he was scared, horrified by his actions… He knew what he did was wrong, but the more time passed, the more he couldn't help feeling the world was a better place for it.

Especially once he saw her, but that wasn't for another day.

He went straight back to Sue's place that evening, freezing on the spot when Nate stared right at him at the fire pit. He was sure they'd both be asleep by now.

If it wasn't for Annabelle… his whole cover would have blown. He didn't plan for this to happen of course, didn't think he was capable of it either… yet it all somehow happened in a blur.

Luke went in through the backdoor once Nate went back inside and inspected himself in the mirror. A big cut on his lip, Luke had dried blood around his face and neck and a big swollen black eye. His ribs were bruised heavily but didn't seem broken.

He put an ice pack on both, wincing under the pain. I need a plan, Luke thought, his hands shaking.

He couldn't continue with Nate and Annabelle in the morning, that much was sure. It was only a question of time, before they saw his injuries, especially Nate was too suspicious.

He knew where he wanted to go, but also understood the small window he had.

Right now, police were searching the grounds. If they came here, which was unlikely, he had an alibi, as long as they didn't see his bruises and cuts. So for now, he had to stay put.

Sooner or later, they would seize the investigation for the night and re-start again in the morning. By then, he had to be as far from the crime scene as possible, if he wanted to go unnoticed.

That only left him with one option.

He lay awake for another hour, before he finalised his plan. Sunglasses on, he left the house three hours later. Breakfast at their doorstep, he left Nate and Annabelle a little note, telling them he would meet them in Central later. *Later* was non-committal, he felt, and exactly what was needed right now. It was non assumptious, since it could mean later today, or in the week.

Hesitantly, he set off in the opposite direction of the house, his heart beating fast.

It didn't settle down until hours later, when he took a swim in a lake ten miles further south, where he changed his soggy bandages and into fresh clothes. He packed everything in his bag, which he burned a few days later. That way no one could assume the mileage he already had behind him. Another thing *he* taught him, he thought. Funny how all came in handy suddenly, and probably not the way Malcolm had in mind.

His feet moved fast, even though his ribs were hurting, he knew exactly where he was headed. She had been on his mind ever since he left the house.

I must tell her, he thought, no matter what. One way or the other.

He also knew he couldn't get caught or risk never seeing her again. That thought made him sick to his stomach. *You know what to do*, he told himself as he strolled through the city, looking around. His eye wouldn't heal for another few days and the sunglasses would only get him so far.

He bought a sandwich from a vending machine and sat by the fountain, knowing it wouldn't take too long before someone would show. This was *'their'* meet-up place, easily identified by the sneakers hanging from the power line and the cigarette buds and empty beer cans on the ground.

He was intruding, purposefully. Luke looked at his watch, it was almost noon.

So far, he managed to go mostly undetected. *Perfect,* he thought. Midday meant people would be around sooner or later. He just needed one to witness this, but few were always better. It also meant chances were higher, someone would break them up eventually.

Last thing he needed was another round like last night. His rips stiffened at the thought.

From the corner of his eye, he saw three men approaching, just as he finished the rest of his sandwich. He observed them silently, waiting for them to make the first move.

"Hey punk, what time is it?" one of them shouted in his direction. He shaved half an hour off the time, just for good measure.

"He meant it's time for you to leave," the other jumped in, hailing a big laugh.

Luke looked at the three of them. They were of average weight, one short, two tall, and two too many. Even though they looked more like talk than trouble.

"Nah, I'm good," he replied. "Kinda like it here." He looked around and nodded appreciatively.

"Don't think you heard us punk," the short guy came forward. "We're saying you're not welcome here." Luke looked directly at him this time.

"Oh, I heard you, alright. Just don't feel like leavin' quite yet"

The three of them exchange a quick glance, weighing up their options. The short guy nodded at the tall guy to his right, who balled his fists in reply. *Just as I thought*, crossed Luke's mind. It was never the loudest. I could probably take him down, he thought, but that wasn't part of the plan.

"Looks like you need a hearing aid," he heard, as the tall guy stepped forward, his friends howling behind him like dogs.

Luke got up slowly, brushed his crumbs off his pants.

"Maybe you do," he replied, matching his tone. It didn't take long for the first fist to fly. Nor the second. Both men tumbled to the ground. This guy was strong but inexperienced, Luke thought. He mostly used his weight to pin him down. Which wouldn't have been a problem if Luke's ribs weren't hurt. Luke kicked him between the legs and caught two fists in his face before he heard a male voice.

"Stop!" The guy was torn off his body. "I warned you last time," he heard the stern voice. "I'm calling the cops."

The man took out his phone and started dialling, at which point the three of them jumped to their feet and disappeared. A hand reached out for Luke, which he took only too gladly, tapping his lip to feel for the cut, wiping the blood off his chin.

It didn't take much for the cut to re-open.

"I'm Ted," the man introduced himself, pointing towards the promenade. "I live just there. Come, we'll get you cleaned up." He paused for a moment.

"How bad do you hurt?"

"Not too bad," Luke replied as Ted continued.

"Didn't look too good when you fell backwards. You're not from around here, are ya?" Luke shook his head slowly, feeling for a bump.

"Nah, just visiting."

"Well, some nice welcome you got here, ey?" Ted replied jokingly. "We're not all that bad here. Lemme make it up to it."

TATJANA GENYS

They went inside the building and up the grey staircase. Inside the apartment, Ted brought him some tea and an ice pack. His home was practical, a little like gramps, Luke thought.

"How ya feelin'?" He asked, putting the cups down.

"Better," Luke replied, looking around. "Thank you," he added.

"You don't fight much, do ya?" Ted continued, and Luke shook his head.

"Never seen much point in it," he lied. "Who's that?" Luke asked, pointing at a picture behind Ted to change the topic.

"My daughter," Ted replied proudly, looking at the picture fondly. That gave Luke time to take off his glasses and place the ice block over his eye. "Cammy," Ted continued, still looking at the frame. "And those rascals are Baxter and Joshi, her little boys. Just hope they don't turn into kids like those guys." He grinned.

"It's not that bad," Luke assured him, when Ted spotted his eye.

"Jeez... that's quite the shiner you got there. That guy got you good!"

"I should've left when they asked me to," Luke replied, applying more ice.

"No, you didn't," Ted countered. He really was like gramps, Luke thought. "They act like they own that place. I swear to God, one of those days I'm gonna be true to my word and call the cops." He sighed.

"Been at it long before I came?" Luke shook his head.

"Lemme take a look at ya," Ted continued. Luke removed the ice pack.

"Is it bad?" He asked.

"Keep it on a bit longer," Ted replied, "I'll grab the cream to take down the swelling.

Luke looked at him appreciatively and took a sip of his tea. The heat stung his lip and he winced, pulling backwards.

"Where's Cammy now?" He asked when Ted returned.

"Lives out in the country," he told him. "Moved there 'bout a year ago but visits every so often." He started applying the cream to Luke's eye. "Stings like a bitch, that one, but it'll be gone in no time," he added. Luke gave him a wry smile.

"Good, there's someone I gotta go see." Ted looked at him warmly.

"She better be worth it," he told him with a wink. Luke nodded.

"That she is." He emptied his cup and got up to leave. "Can I use your bathroom before I go?" he asked, and Ted showed him the way.

In the bathroom, he checked himself in the mirror. The cut on his lip felt worse than it looked, his eye freshly swollen from the fight. Perfect, he whispered. He took his sunnies from the table and got ready to leave.

"Won't need those twenty minutes from now," Ted told him. "Cream's on your backpack, just in case."

Luke paused for a moment, before pulling Ted in for a hug.

"Thanks Ted," he told him. "I hope Baxter and Joshi have someone like you to look out for them if they ever need to," he added. "Don't know what I would've done without you." Ted waved it off quickly.

"It was nothing," he said. "Anyone would've done the same."

"Maybe," Luke told him. "But you did. Boys are lucky to have ya."

And with that, he was out of the door.

He looked at his watch, which showed two pm. No time to waste now, he thought, and ran towards the rehab centre. He passed Bill, the security guard by the gate, gave him a quick nod and greeted the lady at the front desk, before making his way up the stairs. First floor, second floor, third floor, taking two stairs at a time.

"Looking fine today Maggie," he told the lady at reception. She didn't, but that didn't matter. He knew it would cheer her up and mean she'd take extra care of her.

"Did you do somethin'with your hair?" Maggie blushed, shaking her head.

"Well, whatever it is, it's working," he added.

"Welcome back Lucky Luke," Maggie replied. "Haven't seen you here for a while."

He took off his sunglasses exposing his shiner and gave her an apologetic smile.

"Got a little held up," he told her.

"Dear lord," she replied. "What happened?" But he just waved it off.

"Just a run-in with some locals... it'll pass."

"Why don't you go straight through," she told him, "I'll fetch you a compress."

She got up from her desk and turned to leave.

"She awake?" he asked.

"As awake as ever," Maggie replied.

That meant she was hanging onto the machine with her dear life, like she had done for years now. Too weak to fight her injuries and yet too stubborn to let it go.

Luke sometimes wondered if he should release her... flip that switch on his way out, kill that machine. And her... He knew she was holding on for him and wished he could help her find peace. He worried for her very often, blamed himself for not looking out for her better, but there was also that small nagging thought inside him, that she didn't just hang on like this for no reason. She always had a plan. Knew what she was doing.

Well, up until she met that prick, that was, he thought grimly.

He thought how she always believed in the best in people, even the ones who gave up on her. Always told him off when he reminded her, that many of them turned their back on her. "Look where it got you," he sighed.

Something must be telling her to keep fighting, he thought. That her time had not yet come.

With that on his mind, he sat with her often, telling her everything he could possibly think of, hoping one of those things would bring her back to life. That's when he remembered the ring inside his pocket. The one he was beaten up for, but finally managed to retrieve it from the house. Her family ring. The only thing of value to her and the first thing Malcolm took off her when he had a chance.

Luke took a deep breath and stepped inside the room. He always did before he entered, to centre himself and collect the energy he needed inside.

There she was... the white hospital gown hanging off her frail, skinny body sadly, a big bandage covering her forehead and scar. He looked back at Maggie and gave her a big smile.

"Thank you," he mouthed. He didn't miss that her receding hair was freshly combed. He touched it carefully, remembering how she looked when they brought her here.

Her head was split open at that time, half her brain hanging to the side. He couldn't look at her then and it still pained him to look at her now. Doctors worked on her for hours trying to stitch her back together. Like a stuffed teddy bear, he thought, sick to the stomach.

And yet, she still looked beautiful to him. Even now, all these months later, wires and cables still sticking out of her. She was still pale, but the bruises were mostly invisible now. He pulled a chair up behind him and sat down to the left of her, taking her hand.

"Hey Ma," he said softly, pausing for a moment. He always did, hoping for a response. It never came. He knew it was silly, as if she would just wake up and greet him cheerfully, like she always did.

"I missed you," he told her after a while. "Did you miss me?"

He paused and smiled wryly.

"You look good today. Should wear your hair down like this more often." Silence. Taking a deep breath, he moved closer to her ear.

"I did it Ma…" he whispered, placing the ring inside her palm. "Took care of it, like I said I would. There's no need to worry no more, he can't harm us any longer."

Her finger flinched as if hit by lightning, setting off the machine next to him. It started beeping vigorously.

"Out of the room!" Maggie screamed storming in. Doctors and nurses came rushing through the door. Before Luke could comprehend what was happening, she pulled him by his arm.

"Wait in the hall," she repeated firmly, shutting the door in front of him.

Never knew how strong she was, he thought, staring at the closed door behind him, his heart in his throat.

Nate

She disappeared behind her red gate, leaving me stranded in front of it. *Again.*

This is the second time I'm sitting here, aghast. *Don't go!* I want to scream after her, but she doesn't look back. *Don't give up on me... please...*

I arrived extra early for our catch-up today, knowing she doesn't like it when I am late. Man, was I nervous. What would she tell me? Where would this go? She had a lot of time to think about things... Where was her head at?

But when I turned around and saw her, all of it disappeared. *There she was.*

She didn't see me at first and by the time she spotted me, I was grinning like a little schoolboy. Man was it good to see her.

I walked back and forth between the counter and the water station, just to collect my nerves. But when I asked her a couple of questions once I got back to the table, she didn't look at me. *Look at me!* I wanted to tell her, not knowing how much pain I caused her and how broken she was.

She gave me some high-level answers, like she couldn't care less. Wasn't she happy to see me? She looked so beautiful today. I wanted to tell her, but I think what left my mouth was '*You look healthy*'. That's when she finally looked up. *Healthy...* great compliment.

Nate shook his head.

She asked me about my holiday, but she was just being polite I could tell and when I asked her for her opinion, she just trailed off. Wasn't she listening?

She said she wanted to see me. *About time,* she even told me when we last spoke... and yet she declined every offer I made. Even times I had already committed elsewhere.

I shifted uncomfortably in my seat, not knowing where to take it from there. Wanting to tell her how much I missed her and how I lay awake at night just thinking of her.

Yet when I did, she didn't hear me nor when I said, I made a mistake.

And now she's gone inside of her building and I'm at a loss on where to go from here. Because all I know now is that I want her near.

~

Luke

Luke was sitting in the hallway downstairs, Bill, the security guard, watching him closely from his booth. He was given instructions not to let Luke out of his sight after he kept pacing back and forth in the waiting room, bumping into the nurse twice on her way out, trying to get a glimpse of his mother.

How could he not? He thought. He couldn't just sit there and listen to all those beeping noises from inside the room. There was urgency in the doctor's voice, he could hear it clearly. *What did it mean? Would he get to see her again?*

The carpet in front of him, dark and grey, smelled of hospital. Stale. The doors opened and closed every few seconds, the young receptionist greeting everyone in an overly jolly way. Most people ignored her, which she didn't seem to notice, or mind.

The most human person on this level, Luke thought, and likely the most underappreciated.

The soles of his feet were still buzzing from the walk and so were his thoughts, making him more receptive to the sounds around him: The tapping of the keyboard of the person signing one in. The whispers of two young doctors in the corner down the corridor, the shallow breathing from the man sitting next to him. He was observing it all, as if it wasn't happening to him, but in front of him.

What if she didn't wake up? He thought. Or needed caring for the rest of her life? Or worse… What if she didn't remember him? He wouldn't let her stay in that house after what happened. It had way too many memories and was far too remote.

He'd take her to the city, he thought. Somewhere with a garden. She would love that very much.

Please wake up, he kept whispering underneath his breath,

promising to take care of her if she did. The man next to him shifted uncomfortable, unsure what to make of it.

Luke didn't care. The only thing he could think of right now, was to pray. He tried to negotiate and beg and offered anything he could think of, in exchange for her life. Promised to be good and to stay out of trouble. Promised going to church… every Sunday, if he had to. Or volunteer. Whatever the price was, he was willing to pay it. As long as she wasn't taken away from him.

The phone rang and the receptionist listened intently. She nodded gently at Luke, her expression blank. "They're ready to see you now," she told him.

His stomach in knots, Luke sprinted back up those stairs.

~

"Am I too late?" Came shaken through the phone. There was a brief pause on the other end of the line.

"Never" came back the reply. Stay where you are, I'm coming to get you.

Claire hung up the phone and grabbed her bag. This was bad. Whatever happened between them, had to be big. She thought of the way they had parted and the conviction in Lucy's voice when they did. Jumping in her car, she raced out of Bairu. Because if one thing was certain, heartache, she knew.

~

New beginnings

No more. Lucy made that decision this morning. She wasn't going to just sit around and wait any longer. Wait for life to happen, for Jamie to return, or for Nate to finally choose her. That's all she ever did and for what?

Her brother didn't come back, and Nate didn't want her either. She had to put an end on the past and focus on her present. She didn't have much, but she had enough.

These past few weeks, as miserable as they were, also showed her she was much stronger than she thought. Capable of handling more than she ever imagined. If she could survive *this*, the rest would be a piece of cake.

What she realised in all of this, was that she had given up more and more of herself each day that had passed. Handed over her power like a piece of string. Anger built inside her at that thought. Maybe it wouldn't be easy, but anything would be better than *this*.

No longer would she allow her life to be determined by others.

She grabbed her bag and started packing. No longer would she accept being poor Lucy.

"I AM NOT WEAK!" She called out, packing her clothes and toiletries.

"I AM STRONG" she continued and moved to a jar hidden behind her spices. She took out her savings and placed them in her pocket.

"I AM POWERFUL!" She told herself thinking about how long she had saved that money for another day. She shook her head. Today was the day that new life would begin.

"I AM CAPABLE!" She stepped out of the house and closed the

door firmly behind her. She now understood why Jamie left without looking back.

"I AM BRAVE," she said a little more quietly and stepped towards the car.

New life… here I come.

~

Carpe diem

Nate was walking for days now, haunted by the expression in Lucy's eyes. He remembered her hand falling heavily to her side when he questioned their compatibility.

She was gone before he had a chance to explain. *Call me any time!* He had called after her, wanting to talk this over with her, but she just shook her head and left.

She had this all wrong, he thought, frustrated with himself for not making it clearer. He had to do something. Had to make it up to her. Show her that *he did* care. But how?

That's when fate stepped in.

They were walking past the garden café when Annabelle spotted Dan and Ellie, his crush, inside. Leaning over the bar counter, they were laughing over a set of photos laid out in front of them, her hand touching his forearm.

Ellie saw them and waved them inside.

"Nate!" she gushed. "I heard so much about you." She gave him a big hug.

"And you must be Annabelle." She squeezed her tight. "Thank you!" she added, whispering in her ear.

"We're just going through some old photos," Dan told them, clearing his throat when Ellie came from behind and hugged him. This was still very new for him.

"Let me see! Let me see!" Annabelle jumped in, clapping her hands. "Is this you?!" She squeaked looking at the faded picture in front of her. Dan nodded.

"Ellie found them in the attic," he told them proudly, squeezing her hand.

"Is that Lucy?" Nate asked, looking at the little girl in the picture in front of him. He recognised her instantly. Ellie nodded.

"And that beside her," Nate looked up at Dan briefly, "is that…"

"That's Jamie," Dan confirmed. Nate took a closer look at the picture. Funny that, he thought, he looks just like…" he turned to Annabelle.

"Ellie, could I borrow this?" He asked, stuffing the photo inside his pocket.

Ellie nodded.

"Sure, but what would you want with this old thing?" She asked. "I'm sure Dan has more recent photos." She thought it cute of Nate to want Lucy's picture.

"That one will do just fine," Nate confirmed. Looking at Annabelle, he added, "we better get going. Annabelle." He nodded at Dan and Ellie and grabbed Annabelle by her arm before she had a chance to protest. Dragging her outside, he stopped by the water fountain, leaned down to her and held her firmly by her forearms. Annabelle giggled until she saw his expression.

"Annabelle… your friend Bobby," Nate started, "is that his real name?"

Annabelle looked at him with big brown eyes.

"I don't know," she replied hesitantly, "he never told me his name. I just thought Bobby suits him well." Nate released her hands and pulled the picture from his back pocket, his heart beating fast.

"Is this him??" He pointed at the young boy next to Lucy. Annabelle looked at the picture in front of her when Nate ripped it from her hands and started sprinting.

He didn't wait for her reply. If he was right, and that was barely a possibility, this would change *everything*.

This was his chance. His moment... and he wouldn't let anything stand in the way.

He thought about how happy Lucy would be and what this would mean. Then of his stillborn child and wife and how it felt losing both. He never wanted anyone to go through what he had, especially when they still had the chance he didn't. But first, he had to find out if he was right. There was so much at stake here and so little time.

He thought of Lucy's big blue beautiful eyes beaming at him if he reunited them. And with that thought, he ran and ran, as fast as his legs would carry him, even when his lungs hurt so bad, he thought he was going to pass out.

Back to where they started and where it all began. What if I don't find him? crossed his mind. He pushed that thought aside, pushing his legs even harder. Not an option.

Not today. Not when I finally understood what I have lost.

Nate

I went back to the lake and the nearby city, describing Jamie to anyone and everyone I met along the way. Nobody had seen or heard of him.

The reactions I got were mostly the same: confusion, disgust, or apathy. It was hard to miss it mirrored back where I was just a few months ago. Back then I, too, would have turned a blind eye. If it wasn't for Annabelle, I would have pretended not to see him and walked right past him, absorbed in my own day. I've come a long way since.

But where was he? And where could he have gone? I marched through the heat of the sun and the fall of the rain. My stomach rumbling for a long while before it finally gave up. I wouldn't, I promised myself, wondering how often Jamie would have gone hungry. Turns out we do only realize how fortunate we are when things get taken away.

I asked a young boy for directions at the station, and he looked at me so appalled, I questioned my own doing for a moment. But then I guess it didn't happen very often, that someone came looking for a homeless man. Especially as desperately as me.

I rubbed my temples to release the headache that had been brewing since morning and sat down on a rock. A piece of fabric fell to the floor. I picked it up and smiled, brushing off the dirt. Lucy gave that to me. I had cut my finger cutting the baguette, watching her instead of where the knife was going. It wasn't a deep cut and only bled very little, but Lucy had run upstairs so quickly, I worried she would fall. She was back moments later, a basket of plasters in hand, cleaning my wound and patching me up, giving it a little kiss when she finished. *Just in case*, she had whispered, and wrapped the fabric around my finger.

I took it with me ever since.

I will find him, I whispered, squeezing it tight. Looked up at the sky, wondering where I might go. That's when Luke crossed my mind, like he did many times. Problem was no one knew where Luke these days resides. He knew this place best, all its path and terrain. Who else could now guide me? His friend entered my brain. I thought from a moment, trying to remember the way, trying to piece back together, where last we did stay. As I walked further on, I looked up at the sky. Seeing Lucy in front of me, as if she was nearby.

I'll come back for you," I said, as if to her face. Many miles from there meanwhile, Lucy heart began to race. She sat up in bed and for reasons unknown, started calling for Nate, on her face a big frown. "Come back to me," she called out in the dark, but all that Nate heard was another dog's bark. "Please wait for me," he then whispered more quietly… as Lucy got up and excused herself politely.

I see you. All of you…
Body and light, spirit, and soul

Past the imperfections you now call your being &
past the mistakes you regret for so long

I will always see you.
Past the past & post the future

For what you cannot - or do not dare
With the glimpse of a hope
that one day you might 🧩

Lucy

Lucy thought she knew what love is. What it felt to have it, and what it meant to lose it. Yet her relationship with Nate challenged all that... and all of who she was.

She always felt her life guided by love... she was lonely in its absence, joyful in its existence, experiencing excruciating pain in its loss. But things had changed. Her ideology of love had shifted, as did she.

Lucy didn't need saving anymore, she realized, she needed to save herself. And for the first time, she knew how. She understood she didn't need to wait for a lifeboat but had to grab a life jacket instead. How unhealthy it was, to solely rely on the other person and that she needed a life outside of the one she would share with another.

That she needed to prioritize her own passions and spread her wings wide. And that she couldn't continue avoiding people and needed to call them in instead.

She understood how she had caged their relationship, asking to be chosen above all else.

Yet learned that as much as it was great to be selfless, she also needed to be selfish at times.

But most of all, she learned the importance of loving herself. From her big wonky toe to her overthinking crown. Especially on days she messed up, like she did that day.

To surrender to what is and break wide open, wider than she had ever imagined possible, and still be able to forgive. She learned the true meaning of unconditional love, at its purest essence. And the importance of setting boundaries, if you were lucky enough to find it in front of you.

TATJANA GENYS

Finally, she also learned that even when nothing made sense, it could feel okay sometimes.

And that this too became a form of closure. Unless it was truly the end-end.

Sometimes my words fall out too fast,
My mind tells me, this will not last

When I know well inside my heart
This will not keep us either apart.

Sooner or later, we will both see
That you and I belong to be

Right now, is the time for us to heal
to reconnect with what we feel

For each other, ourselves, and our path
And individually do then do the math

That life together is best it can be
It just took us that long to finally see

Lucy met Annabelle at Claire's a few months later. It was the first time she saw her in a long while, and she couldn't wait. They agreed to a movie night and were browsing the selection when Lucy's eyes lit up.

"That one," she said matter-of-factly.

"That one?" Annabelle and Claire queried in unison, frowning.

"**How to be single,**" Lucy read cheerfully, "Exactly what I need right now."

She knew she couldn't stomach a chick flick. They stopped for cakes and deserts, and settled on the couch, getting each other up to speed on what they missed.

Lucy felt monotonous. She was plotting along helping Claire on her project and yet something was missing. Claire could see it too but gave her friend time.

"My heart still aches, you know?" Lucy told Annabelle, "and I find myself *bitter* lately."

"Bitter?" Annabelle questioned, putting a fruit basket in her mouth. "What are you bitter about?" She asked, chewing.

"This situation," Lucy replied truthfully. "The hurt in my heart is big and there are days I keep asking myself if I could ever move past this. If I could ever forgive him..."

"What's to forgive?" Annabelle asked, surprised. The innocence in her voice was evident, she truly meant it. "You know he always thought of you first, right? And I'm pretty sure he thinks he did right by you." Lucy shrugged her shoulders.

"He could've asked," she replied.

"I'm also pretty sure he wants to talk to you," Annabelle continued, "but is conscious of how you left it." Lucy snorted silently.

"You know the funny part, Annabelle?" She said instead. "Some part of me still doesn't feel like it's the end." Her voice deepened as she continued. "The other part gives that part a *very* hard time." She smiled at Annabelle, knowing how crazy it sounded. "After all, I have no indication he even remembers me. I haven't heard from him since we last spoke. So, I can't help but judge myself for still buying into the fantasy. That's what I'm resenting." Annabelle gave her a long look.

"You shouldn't be so harsh on yourself Lucy. For what it's worth, I also don't think it is over." She said it softly, gauging Lucy's reaction. "It doesn't feel like it's over because it isn't." When Lucy returned her look, unsure where Annabelle was going with it, she continued, smirking.

"I have a feeling he will be in touch with you very soon."

"What makes you say so?" Lucy asked, her heart beating faster. "Did he say anything?" Annabelle shook her head.

"No… but I know he is missing you. And I have a feeling he is fighting with his decision. You made your choice Lucy, I don't think he has yet."

Lucy dropped her shoulders. She couldn't understand why unlike before, she couldn't just let this go. Close this chapter and move onto another.

"I spend days reviewing the past, you know?" She told Annabelle. "Trying to understand if I'd always been like this… but I haven't. So why now? Why am I giving this relationship the power to determine my life?" She paused for a moment. "It shouldn't, and I shouldn't be allowing it. But since I did… I need to find a way to change that."

Annabelle looked at her expectedly. "I need a bigger purpose and my heart needs a break, " Lucy concluded. This would be the beginning of her and not the end.

The making of her, not her undoing.

She thought about Claire and how she came to the city, her dream so big. Right now, Lucy was making her dream come true, and as great that was, she needed to find her own. The little voice inside her was getting more and more vocal.

"I didn't listen at first," she told Annabelle, "though I knew it was there. So, it found a way to make me listen."

"Go on," Annabelle encouraged, "I want to hear it all." She helped herself to an éclair.

"This week was long," Lucy started. "I was trying to juggle Claire's project on top of my own and by the end of the week, I reached my limit. Claire invited me out to dinner with her friends, and as much as I wanted to, I knew I had to decline." Annabelle nodded in sympathy, placing her fork on the plate. "When I finally finished on Friday," Lucy continued, "I promised myself a duvet day. I spend Saturday in bed, in my pajama bottoms, eating chocolate cookies and cheese and ham toasties, watching one show after the other mindlessly. I dozed off a couple of times and didn't care, giving my body a chance to restore.

This show comes on about life choices: a life of freedom, fun and much heartbreak, against a life of safety and security. The main character chose the latter. Few years in, she felt a gap in her life. I could understand her decisions and somehow relate to her, especially when she kept convincing herself this was what she wanted."

Annabelle listened intently.

"It wasn't enough," Lucy continued, her voice strong. "I got out of bed the moment it hit me. And it never would be. I started pacing around the house, cleaning the kitchen. This was what I had been doing, all this time. It hit me. The *right* thing... Yet if it was the right thing, why did it make me feel so miserable? *Because it wasn't enough.* It came as both a relief and a wake-up call. One of those defining moments, even if mine came whilst I was scrubbing the kitchen counter in my pajama bottoms.

I need to create a life that *is* enough. More than just enough. And for that, I need to start fresh. Get out of here. After all, what I have to leave behind, I can count on my fingers. So, what am I so afraid of?"

"Choosing you…" Annabelle replied. She looked at Lucy, meeting her gaze.

"Nate became your distraction," she continued. "A welcome one, but a distraction, nevertheless." She pointed to her camera. "He enhanced the picture and minimized the glare, but the picture underneath it didn't change. You just took away the filter."

"I don't want a filter anymore," Lucy replied. "Or anyone to come in and enhance my picture. I want a different picture. One that doesn't need enhancing and one I want to stare at, every single day. One with so much life in it, I won't tire of it. One that will wake up my soul," she added whispering. "I am ready to be brave, Annabelle, and give it my all."

"What would it take?" Annabelle asked.

"A few things," Lucy replied, "but I just need to start somewhere." She thought about it for a moment. "I could move to Bairu," she said, more to herself, and heard her inner voice reply. *Yes, you could do that.*

"I could quit my job," she continued. *Yes, you could do that too,* the inner voice agreed. She looked at Annabelle with tears in her eyes.

"I am saying yes to me, Annabelle, and it is the most liberating feeling."

Annabelle got up and gave her a big hug.

"Time to carve out a plan," she told her. Lucy nodded, grabbing her phone from the counter when it beeped. A message from Nate was staring back at her.

"You have got to be kidding me."

~

Jamie

There he is! Nate took a double look and then another, just to make sure he wasn't imagining it. It was *him*. Gone were the rugged clothes and dirty hands, his face was shaved too, and yet the closer Nate came, the surer he was. No wonder no-one had seen or recognised him.

Nate was on his way back from the post office, looking for a register to see if Jamie's name was listed. When the whistle blew, signalling a departing train, he noticed a man running towards the station. *You'll never make it*, he thought, watching from afar. That's when another person stepped into the light, put his foot in the door and held it open, ignoring the beeping and angry whistles of the operator. The running man jumped on, breathing hard and nodded gratefully as the doors closed behind him.

That's when Nate started sprinting too, startling the operator once more.

"Too late!" he told Nate in passing. "You'll have to catch the next one."

Nate ignored him. He didn't need that train. He had one goal and one goal alone.

"Jamie??" He asked breathlessly and eagerly when he finally reached him, catching a bewildered look.

"Are you Jamie?" he half screamed at him when he didn't get a reply. Joy, exhaustion, and hope hitting him all at once.

"Who are you??" The man demanded. Nate took a deep breath. He didn't have the time or energy to explain.

"Is Lucy your sister?" He asked instead. He couldn't make a mistake, not after coming this far, his hope fading each day that passed. The only thought that kept him going was her. Exhausted and exhilarated, he just kept staring at Jamie, waiting to hear those words. So much so, he didn't notice the change in his expression, until it was too late.

Jamie grabbed him by his throat, anger written all over his face.

"Who sent you??" he screamed, shaking him hard. "WHO SEND YOU??"

His voice was sharp. Jamie didn't care if somebody came after him, but he wouldn't let anything happen to his baby sister. Not after he spent all these years away from her, trying to protect her.

Nate, at a loss on how to respond, simply shook his head.

"I am going to ask you *one more time*." Jamie repeated, emphasizing the last three words. "Who. Send. You??? Was it Sergej?" he asked, his eyes sparkling furiously.

Who was Sergej and what did he want from Lucy? Nate wondered, shaking his head again. The grip to his throat was so tight, he couldn't speak, all that came out was a croak.

"No... one... send... me," he squeaked, blood rising to his head.

"I swear to God," Jamie continued, "if you laid as much as one finger on my sister..." he tightened his grip, "so help you God."

Nate gulped, thinking of all the ways his fingers *had* touched Lucy. Many times.

He understood arguing was pointless at this time and that he had to convince him otherwise.

"It's... not... what... you... think," he tried again as Jamie pulled him onto his feet and locked eyes with him. Nate tried taking his hands off him, but Jamie didn't bulge. Driven by his love and protection for his sister, he was even stronger than usual.

A woman passing by, turned around midway, disappeared hastily in the opposite direction. Whatever this was, she didn't want to get involved.

"Then what do you want??" he barked at Nate again. One hand dangling next to his body, Nate fumbled in his pocket with the other. With a sigh of relief, he grabbed hold of its content and raised the picture to the level of their eyes.

Jamie looked at it for a moment, unsure what to make of this. He would recognise it, wouldn't he? Nate wondered, now also eyeing Jamie suspiciously. Jamie finally released his grip.

"Lucy is... *my friend*," he told Jamie, rubbing his throat. He would come to the 'girlfriend' part later he decided once Jamie calmed down.

"I wouldn't dream of hurting her," he told him instead, drawing a cross across his chest. Jamie's face relaxed.

"How is she?" he asked, his voice croaky.

"She misses you..." Nate replied, watching him closely. "Talks about you all the time. So does Dan." Jamie's eyes light up for a moment, a flicker crossing his face. *He found him...* Nate couldn't help but grin at the thought. He couldn't wait to tell Lucy.

"What's with the face?" Jamie asked, confused.

"You don't know how long I've been looking for you," Nate replied. "Although, that wasn't quite the way I imagined we'd meet," he chuckled, and Jamie broke out in a laugh.

"Yeah... sorry 'bout that. Got a bit carried away there. Why'd you look for me anyway?"

"I want you to come back with me," Nate told him honestly. Jamie shook his head.

"No chance. I'm not going back there." he told him. "What's it to you, anyway?"

"I care for Lucy," Nate replied, "and know she's still waiting for you. She's been looking for you everywhere."

"How did *you* find me?" Jamie asked. "That picture is hardly very telling."

"You don't remember..." Nate replied hesitating "This isn't the first time we are meeting." Jamie raised an eyebrow.

"Last time we met, you were a bit... scrubbier, if we can call it that. Plus, Annabelle called you Bobby for the longest period of time, which didn't help."

"The little girl..." Jamie replied, his eyes softening. "How could I forget? You were the punk behind that tree..." Nate looked down at his feet. This wasn't the way he wanted to be remembered by her brother.

"A lot has changed since," he told him. "I'm not who I was back then." Changing the subject, he continued. "Lucy and you share the same expression. I thought it looked familiar when we started dating and that I'd seen it somewhere before but couldn't remember where for the life of me. Until it hit me when I saw that photo. So here I am," he told Jamie proudly.

"Dating?" Jamie repeated, raising an eyebrow. Nate's cheeks flushed. In all his excitement, it simply slipped off his tongue. He shrugged his shoulders apologetically.

This time it was Jamie, who looked *him* up and down.

"My intentions are honourable," Nate told him quickly, regretting it instantly. Jamie laughed out loud.

"Honourable, hm?" he repeated sarcastically.

"I care for her." Nate replied softly, shrugging his shoulders. "And I think she cares for me too." Jamie watched him for a moment. Nate didn't seem the bravest of guys, but brave men didn't always make the best boyfriends.

He wanted his little sister protected, but more than that, he wanted her taken care of. Whoever this guy was, must care a lot, coming all this way, he thought.

"What did Dan say?" He asked, knowing Dan was a great judge of character.

"He approves," Nate replied, wondering briefly if that was still the case, hoping Ellie would distract him long enough or until he returned home with Jamie. Jamie nodded slowly.

"Guess it's time I meet the boyfriend," he told Nate. "Follow me."

Goodbye

Annabelle squealed in excitement when she saw Nate's message. Could have also been for Lucy's mortified face.

"I knew it!" she exclaimed, utterly pleased. Lucy, meanwhile, lay wide awake that night, watching the glow in the dark stars Claire had stuck up the ceiling for Annabelle.

She smiled when she saw what Claire had done to the room for her arrival.

The bed was pushed to the corner by the window, so a big Egg chair could now take its place. Fairy lights, pillows, stuffed animals and throw-on blankets were spread across the room, her keyboard resting in the back of a corner. Annabelle pulled it out and played some uncoordinated notes.

"I'm pretty good at this, right?" she asked, beaming, hitting another wrong note. Lucy smiled, watching the picture above her bed.

Claire and her family, smiling into the camera happily. It must have been quite the shock for them when she left. Especially since Claire didn't have her own children.

A little like the Baker family, Lucy thought, remembering how happily they took Annabelle in as their own and their warm smiles at her, eyes filled with love.

"They are so good to me," Annabelle said, reading her mind. "It will be hard to say goodbye." Lucy looked up, surprised.

"You're leaving?" She asked. Annabelle had never mentioned such thing.

"At some point." she answered. My work here is nearly done," Wisdom and sadness were playing in her voice. "Soon I will wake up and know it is time."

"Where will you go?" Lucy asked, wondering briefly if the same would apply to Nate.

"Wherever I'm needed," Annabelle replied.

"You could come with me?" Lucy offered, not wanting to lose her friend. Annabelle gave her a long hug.

"Let's not think of this today," she said. "Plenty more for us to do here first."

And with that, she jumped off the bed, grabbed a pillow, and threw it at her face.

"Oh, you're on!!" Lucy laughed, reaching for another and chased Annabelle down the hall.

They were up early the next morning. Or Annabelle was. Lucy woke up from her jumping on her bed, pulling up her eyelids.

"Yoouuu awake?" She asked as soon as Lucy made a sound.

"I am now," Lucy replied, rubbing her eyes.

"Come on then!" Annabelle exclaimed excitedly. "Lets go, lets go, lets go!"

The sun was shining bright, when Claire dropped them off at the giant staircase, vigorously declining any offer to join them, blaming it on her heels. She handed Annabelle and Lucy a pretzel and donut for later and wished them farewell.

Climbing these stairs felt harder this morning, Lucy's legs felt heavy.

Annabelle counting each one of them didn't make it any easier. "145... 146... 148..." she happily exclaimed, jumping from one to the next.

They made a big loop through the reserve and sat by the water, Nate's message swirling around Lucy's head. He said he thought of her.... *Often.*

That he wanted to reach out many times but wasn't sure if it was okay to message. Lucy wasn't sure what to make of it. At first, she was happy when it came through, but then she wasn't sure.

"Will you reply?" Annabelle asked.

"I don't know," Lucy answered honestly. She had just turned a corner.

Finally made a bit of progress, at last. Her heart still ached for him, but it wasn't as unbearable as it was before. Did she really want to go there again? She meant what she said to Annabelle last night, she didn't want somebody else to play the main role in her life anymore. Something was waiting for her, something big, even if she didn't know what it was yet. Did she really want to risk it all? After she had come that far? She stuffed her phone in her back pocket. This would have to wait.

This was her time with Annabelle and she wasn't going to let it pass her by. Especially not when Annabelle had thoughts of leaving.

$\sim$

Nate

I have been contacting her on and off ever since I got back. Minus Jamie... couldn't convince him to come with me for the life of me, no matter how hard I tried.

Even when I thought I broke through to him, he came up with another reason why he couldn't. I recognized myself in him too. Or in his fear rather. Fear I had known for decades and fear that made me lose the best thing that crossed my path lately.

"Consider it," I pleaded again before I left.

You can imagine my surprise when I returned and learned Lucy was gone... by no other than Dan, too. To say he a bone to pick with me, would be an understatement. Man, was he mad... thought his head was going to explode for a moment. It wasn't until I told him about Jamie, he finally softened. I send her a text an hour later:

Hi, how are you?

Regretted it as soon as I hit send. So, I followed it up with another.

Hope you don't mind me checking in.

Regretted that one even more. What was wrong with me?? So, I finally sent her what I wanted to send her all along.

Guess I've been thinking about you often. Been wanting to make contact, but not sure if it was appropriate or not...

Couldn't have known it came on a day she had her turning point. Annabelle finally came out with it a few days later. Thought she was acting all weird.

Lucy wasn't sure if me thinking of her was enough. *Women…*

So, I told her about this dream I had. She was there too. We were swimming in the water when a big butterfly landed on her arm. It was surreal and very beautiful, but it died under a big wave. Right before all the water disappeared and before I understood a tsunami was coming. I woke up scared, breathing hard.

I never share shit like that with anyone. Still don't know why I told her… guess the thought of us going the next part alone was freaking me out.

"That makes a lot of sense," she told me calmly. "What does?" I asked. None of this made any sense.

"Natural disasters are signs of inner turmoil," she replied. "You're restless and out of alignment. And you're resisting what's in front of you, which is why it's hard. And will stay hard until you surrender. Have you been overwhelmed lately?"

I nodded.

"I thought so," she simply replied. Lucy thought I was overwhelmed? I panicked. Last thing I wanted her to think about were my insecurities.

The butterfly meant change was around the horizon, apparently. For her, since it landed on her arm. A sign of change and transformation and given its size, a pretty big one. Since it died, a cycle was coming to an end.

"Yaaaay!" Annabelle said, raising her arms in celebration when I told her. I looked at her blankly and she lowered her arms.

"Thanks?? What cycle was coming to an end?" The thought of losing her was petrifying. She told me to lean in and allow it. For my sake, first and foremost.

And that she missed me too... that last past I must have read a million times.

~

Lucy

I told him I missed him, and he went radio silent. Again. Aaarrrghh!!! Why do I keep falling for this??? Do I never learn??

Nate

'As long as you don't regret that something that had to give...'

That sentence has been circling my head ever since she said it. Lean in, she now told me. How the f#ck does one lean in? I wouldn't be in the mess I am if I knew how to do it.

I went to the physio the next day and blurted everything out. Should have seen her face. Fifty minutes of word vomit.

"We have a lot of work to do," she told me when my time was up.

"No kidding professor" I thought. I couldn't believe it. I closed the door and went back to my car, gobsmacked. It just slipped off my tongue. *All of it.*

I had never talked about my childhood to anyone, not even Lucy. I wanted to, but the words got stuck in my throat. Decades ago.

I didn't want Lucy thinking any different of me or worse... *pity me.* I wanted to be the person she saw in me. The guy she believed I was... or *could be.* So that one day, I could believe it too. I almost called her after the session but didn't know if it was okay.

She reached out a few days later, telling me it was okay wherever I was and to see the progress I have been making. It felt encouraging, yet also like she was saying goodbye.

Had the change that was about to happen, already begun? I wasn't ready to say goodbye to her. Not ready to let her go.

I told her about the therapy, and she said she was proud of me. Proud?

Why would she be proud? And yet... *She was proud of me...*

Don't recall the last time anyone said that.

Lucy to Nate (via Text Message)

I don't know what triggered this message, but guess if I learned anything from the past, it is that these are the things important to be said. When you told me, you didn't know if you made the right decision, I heard you. Every time you said so. Foolishly, I waited for you to say, 'I didn't'. When you told me you missed me the other day, I waited for you to say 'I want you back'. You didn't... Last night was my final attempt to see if anything was missing. There isn't. You're happy. And I want you to be, always! And now I know that you are, it's time for me to find my own. Please take good care of yourself and do follow your heart, at least once in a while. Life's too short to be lived in the mind ♡

Nate

What?? Where did that come from? I checked in with her over the weekend, asked how her project was going. We chatted, everything was fine. Why is she sending me this?? And why does she keep saying goodbye?? I told her before that I miss her. And obviously care for her, I wouldn't be reaching out if I didn't. And clearly *not* everything I wished for came true.

I take out my phone and start typing

> **Hey, thanks, I am happy... but I didn't say that there was nothing missing... I'd like to see you again if you'd be up for it?**

My phone beeped hours later.

> **What would seeing me look like, this time?**

That question kept me up all day. It took all my courage to send her my next message.

> **I was thinking/ hoping something along the lines of a date...**

There. I said it. Can we finally get this over with? Just let me see you already...

But of course, she doesn't.

> **Does the idea of spending a few days with me still scare you?**

I'm a simple girl Nate, with an honest heart and a complicated brain. I want the real thing. A partnership that's true and honest... not just on paper. I want to build a life with someone. One where you grow and heal and move through the ups and downs life throws at you... together. Is that what you want? If you're serious about this, let's talk.

Otherwise let's save each other the heartache

~

Ping Pong

Lucy felt good. She had finally said what she wanted to say. Got it all off her chest. After reading the message a hundred before, that is, and about a million times after, but still. It felt right, honest and to the point. A yes or no question, with no room for fluff.

What if he says No? she panicked at the thought, but only for a split second. Then it would have never worked anyway, she thought and took a deep breath. Now it's out and up the universe.

> 36 hours later, no response.
> She took her phone out and started typing.

> ~~Fool me once, shame on you.~~
> ~~Fool me twice, shame on me.~~

She put her phone back to the side. Counting to ten, she took three deep breaths. She got back to her designs. Her phone beeped. She walked over and saw his number flare up and the beginning of his text. *Oh god...* Her heart was pounding fast as she restrained herself from opening it straight away. Focus on your work, she told herself.

You're being ridiculous, her mind told her.

I know, she whispered back.

It won't change what he said, it continued.

I know... she repeated. But it will what's inside of me, she added quietly, finalizing the garment she was working on. She took a deep breath and opened his message.

> **The last thing I would want is to cause any more heartache, lead you on or anything like that.**

Ultimately, I want everything you just described. And btw, nothing has changed. That was always what I wanted. But I understand why you are cautious. Guess I thought it would be good to meet and see how our chemistry was between us, if you were up for it.

He doesn't know... staring at her screen Lucy kept re-reading the message.

He still doesn't know. Tears started rolling down her cheeks. He hadn't answered her questions either. She started typing.

~~Maybe it was what you always wanted, but you didn't want it with me and if nothing changed, we already know how this will end.~~

~~Chemistry was never our problem~~

She wiped her tears from her cheeks but more kept coming. Nothing changed... her heart started aching again, pulling once... twice... harder the third time.

Why did it still hurt so much?

~~You really don't get it... do you?~~
~~I'm still in love with you.~~

She didn't want to be in love with him anymore... how could she still be in love with him? She wondered. After everything...?

Because it wasn't over... and it still isn't over. Her brain mocked her, quoting a scene from the notebook. She ignored it. She didn't want to hurt anymore, and she didn't want to be broken anymore. She wiped her nose.

Glad you're feeling better ♡

The moment she hit send, her mind started scolding her.

NO! You are not leaving it there. No more being polite. No more hiding. You will speak your mind. Figure out what you need to say and say it.

Lucy hated her brain sometimes, but she knew it was right. Most of the time at least.

Maybe I should meet him? she tried.

What?? The disapproval of her brain was evident. You are insane… Where did that come from?? She could literally hear it snort. I knew this would happen, it continued. We both know how this will go. You will meet him, and it will be great, blablabla blablablabla. Then you will start hoping again that it will become more, like you always do, and it won't. *Like it always doesn't.* And we'll be right here again, hearing "I told you so." We both know it.

Lucy nodded, her brain was right.

What if it won't? her heart whispered. She re-read the message.

He did say he doesn't want to hurt you, it continued.

Oh geez, that's what he said last time too, her brain countered. And look where *that* got us.

～

Annabelle came over again that same weekend, a bag of croissants in her arms.

"Goood moooorninng," she sang happily, holding the bag up in the air. "With compliments from the Bakers family."

She handed Lucy the bag and stopped when she saw her face.

"Oh dear, Luce… what happened? You look awful!" She gave her the longest hug.

"Gosh, I needed that." Lucy replied. "The hug, not the compliment." She winked at Annabelle and filled her in quickly whilst pouring some tea. Annabelle listened and watched her closely, sipping from her cup.

"What are you going to do about it?" she asked as Lucy plated the croissants. Lucy shook her head helplessly. Every option she considered didn't feel right.

"I am going round in circles, Annabelle." She had promised herself to figure this out herself but found herself at a loss. "He doesn't get it," she told her, for the fifth time that morning, shrugging her shoulders.

"I think he does," Annabelle replied calmly. "Want to know what I think?" she asked hesitantly as if reading her mind. Lucy nodded.

"I have no doubt he loves you, I told you that before. He does love you," she reinforced, waiting for the message to sink in. "He wanted to give you what you wanted Luce… and initially he did. Remember how happy you were."

I don't want to remember, crossed Lucy's mind.

"But he wasn't ready," Annabelle continued, taking another sip. "You know why he keeps contacting you?" Lucy shook her head. "Because he wants you in his life, simple as. Think about it Luce, before you throw it all away. He never said he didn't want you. He got cold feet." She shrugged her shoulders.

Lucy wanted to protest but she stopped her softly.

"I know what you're going to say, but there were a lot of things he hadn't figured out. You're stronger than him, Luce. Even after everything… and he knows that. He couldn't see the path. Couldn't see how he could possibly be what you want. Let alone offer you what you need…" She grabbed a croissant and took a big bite. "Let him catch-up with you."

~~"Maybe… but you didn't want it with me, remember? and unless that has changed, we don't need to meet, we already know how this plays out. Chemistry was never our issue."~~

~~I am battling with this… my brain tells me one thing, my heart another.~~

~~So tell me Nate… if our cards were reversed, what would you do?~~

Lucy took a deep breath. Let's try this again.

I don't want to make this more complicated than it needs to be, but I need you to know what's going on in my mind before we do this. My brain tells me, even if you did want all of these things before, you didn't want them with me, and unless that's changed, we already know how this will play out. My heart tells me "What if?" but I am petrified of going there again if you're just going to disappear again once I do. That's why I asked you if it scares you. Chemistry was never our problem. Yes, it might be awkward at first, but we'll move past it… like everything else. IF we're both committed to it. And for that I need to know – are you going to let me in this time?

If the answer is yes, I can meet you this weekend. If that still scares the frickin` daylight out of you, I rather wouldn't.

She hit send and stuffed her phone in her bag. Time to go for a walk.

Nate

Her words echo loudly in my ears. *If you're just going to disappear again… PANG.* That one hit hard. Is that what she thought of me? *You didn't want it with me.* She said it so matter-of-factly. Does she truly believe that? I chew my lip. Why would she feel that way?

Will you let me in this time? I want to… but how can I promise her that?! I start pacing around the room. It's not something I simply decide on, it just sweeps over me.

And if I break the promise, then what? Will she leave me? It's not a switch I can flip to make it go away. Can't she see that?? This weekend. This weekend. She gave me twenty-four hours to decide. It's been thirty-one. *FUCK!* Why couldn't she have just said yes??

I run my fingers through my hair, pulling it hard. I don't want to mess this up… What do I tell her?? My anxiety kicks in again, creeping up my back and neck.

The last time I committed to someone it nearly killed me… I don't want to go there again, but I don't want to lose her either. FUCK… Judging by the tone of her message, I am about to. She is giving up on me… *FUCK!* Don't give up on me.

Not when I'm so close. I even started talking to that guy last week, like I said I would.

Dr Dee says I'm getting better… making progress, isn't that enough?!

I open my phone.

Hey… thanks for being open. Like you said, the issue was that I didn't let you in. But I can honestly say that it wasn't because I didn't want all those things with you. I've been feeling very positive

about everything lately, I assume from being less stressed and also from the work I've been doing on my mental health. And it's great. And the reason I had the courage to reach out to you. That said, I do have more work to do and unfortunately for both of us, we won't know how it will go unless we try...

I hit send. Then re-read the message from her perspective. Too fluffy, she will say.

I start again.

Guess what I am trying to say is that yes, if we were to try again, then I would commit completely. I would want our relationship to reach a much deeper level than it was before. And though I feel confident that it would, I can't deny this tiny feeling of anxiousness I get sometimes. I really don't know what it is and where it comes from, but I know it's not part of me and I will overcome it. I don't want to pressure you, nor do I expect you to take any risks. But if you do feel like catching up, I'll be around

Lucy - Two weeks later

I'll meet you by the fountain, she told him, just past the square. And there she sat, her heart beating fast. Anticipation, anguish, and a ball of mixed emotions competing inside her. Minutes passed, which felt like hours. Passengers walking past watched her curiously.

She was wearing her black mini dress, one too dressed up for the occasion, but she didn't care. She wanted to look good. For him. For them. For that new moment.

A memory she hoped they would cherish many years from now. She looked at her watch. Was it really just one minute since she last checked it? She tapped the watch lightly, making sure the arrow didn't get stuck inside and held it to her ear to check for the ticking. It wasn't broken.

A group of men passed her, shouting something in her direction. She ignored it. Her eyes were glued to the fountain, screening the crowd for that one familiar face. And then she saw him. Running. Screening the crowd like she just did.

She spotted him not just because he was wearing the woolen jumper, he once wore on their third date. 'Just an average Joe', he would later tell her. 'Everything but average and anything but Joe,' she would reply.

He looked left to right trying to find her, looking anxious... Was he nervous too? Was his heart beating as fast as mine? She wondered. Her heart made a somersault at the thought. That's when she got up and waved him over.

The next 12 months were an uphill battle, kind of like the runs Lucy completed that year. She often compared them to what they

TATJANA GENYS

were facing, each staircase and hill a reflection on them. So, she pushed even harder, to climb all these mountains and find strength within her, to continue their path. Because as much as they wanted, they couldn't just move past that, what one fought for so long.

It was during those runs the idea came to her, her own fashion show like Milan in Bairu. She crafted and drafted her designs and creations and convinced Winton High to catwalk her show. Claire helped with the contacts and sourced the right venue, Tim calculate a clean balance sheet. Within a few months, her show was then ready and months after that, it was in full flow.

Nate in the meantime, saw Dr Dee every Tuesday, more often in weeks, when things got too real. They re-worked his schedule and what he gave focus, narrowed down what he needed/ what was important in life. It was in one of these sessions, he finally moved past it, removing the cause, which he carried so long. He sat and he grieved, like a boy not a grown up, releasing the pain he had suffered so strong. His words had cut out and his throat started burning, excruciating pain running wild through his frame. His muscles were flexing and tensed in reaction when something kept building, trying to escape from within.

The rumbling grew strong, immobilizing for a moment, grew bigger and bigger as he gasped up for air. He was trying to fight it but that made it stronger and whilst he felt helpless, the strike came from nowhere.

It pushed from within him, then slowly took over, his body jolting backwards, his chest breaking open. An unspeakable scream escaped from inside him, whilst grief and bereavement kept urging for more. His body was pulsing, his heart pumping faster, the attack came much fiercer than the ones he had known.

He screamed again louder, more violent, and longer and much

more aggressive than moments before. It kept pouring and pouring like the spread of wildfire, unable to stop and get under control. He screamed over and over, a dark cloud emerging, growing bigger and bigger, with each scream he let go.

Adrenaline kicking, he threw himself in it, understood only then what it meant to lean in. So, he screamed even louder, euphoria rising, his head meanwhile blurry, getting fuzzy, and light.

After twenty more minutes, he sunk to his forearms, now covered in goosebumps and shook to the core. Emerging from the frenzy, he looked around frantically, expecting a reaction to the damage he'd done.

But with no one around him and the dark cloud no longer, he stood by a mirror, confused and unsure. Because his reflection, unlike he expected, showed Annabelle standing, the dark cloud in her hand.

"I don't understand," he said walking towards her. "What does this all mean and how did you come?"

"It's actually quite simple," she replied very slowly, "it means that my job here is finally done."

"How can it be done?" he asked, taken aback as she took his hand softly and held onto his arm. Inside the mirror, he could now see all others, yet they all just walked past her, as if she didn't exist.

"I don't understand," Nate continued to whisper, watching Mrs Baker now join them, which just felt so wrong. He looked back at Annabelle, her eyes sad and teary as all others continued, a smile on their face.

"Wait!" he kept screaming, seeing her disappearing, as she stumbled and crumbled and fell to the ground. We didn't change the world, it suddenly hit him and nobody learned, but he understood. It finally made sense, all that which she taught him, he could finally see what she wanted him so. That's when Annabelle smiled and mirrored his action, her hand tapping lightly, where he'd placed his own.

"Tears aren't all bad," Annabelle then started softly, "or else there wouldn't be tears of joy. It is my way to cleanse and prepare my next adventure," she continued, looking at his puzzled face.

"We did more than you know and if you cannot see it, you missed the most important part.

"Look around you," she told him, and he found himself standing in the bookstore they first met, the leather band firmly in hand.

"I don't understand," he continued to whisper, not seeing the difference until he opened the page.

Then you don't see what I see, came back in bold letters, and was quickly replaced by the following part. **_You_ changed, and as a result, so did people around you. This journey started with you and was about you all along. Touching one heart can impact an entire village and as one cruel person can change the course of history, so can a good one. It might just take that little while longer.**

"But what about you?" he asked, and she repeated his question. "What will happen to you?" he then tried again.

"I'll go where you'll go," she added more firmly, **"didn't you say you understood? I'm in every soul that is aching, in every person who feels at a loss. I am in their pain and their resolution and there when they need me once their moment has come.**

It will come as a whisper, a wish, or a plea and one that's so honest, I will dare not ignore. That is how I first heard you, long before our adventure, when you weren't yet ready, yet your path already began. Until that one morning, when in-between darkness, a small spark of hope came straight from within."

Nate thought back to that morning and how he'd arrived here, like something had pulled him, that he'd usually ignore.

"Didn't you wonder, why I reminded you of someone, why you followed me places, without a return? How you could feel, all these emotions… see what I saw and feel what I felt? I am inside you and all around you and have been forever since our day one. Now that you see and know what you need to, your time has come, to carry the baton. Help heal yet another, there are plenty around you and give what I gave you so they'll do the same."

"Was none of it real?" He asked the ink fading, but as he had asked it, she was already gone.

~

CHAPTER 13

Puzzled, I stare at the bound book inside my palms. Opening it slowly I find the story of a man going on a journey with a little girl. I read on. This is my story I'm reading.

It doesn't mention any names, but right there in front of me, I find it printed in black and white. How is this possible? Does this also mean… scanning the pages, my eyes start searching for something, not allowing me to reminisce in my thoughts.

And there she is… Sitting on the bench beside me, waiting for me to lean in for our first kiss. I read on. To the first time she told me she loved me, my heart clenching at the thought when I couldn't say it back. I move along quickly. *Will you let me in this time?*

An elderly man in glasses moves my way.

"Can I help you find anything?" he asks from a distance, lifting them higher up his nose. I shake my head.

"I've got everything I need right here," I reply, lifting the book in the air, my finger holding the passage I last read very firmly. I need to know.

The man leaves, and I open it up again quickly. Only this time, all I find are empty pages in its place. I turn the book upside down, shake it, flip it, turn it sideways… Nothing. What does this mean?? Is this the way things will end? I pay for the book and leave the store, finding myself back on the pavement I stood, what now feels forever ago.

I look around. Everything looks familiar yet I'm completely out of place. How long was I gone? And where do I go on from here? Is life meant to just go on the way it was? Impossible... Annabelle was right, I changed... and I didn't want to go backwards.

I finally understood what was holding me back, how to get my life back on track and say yes to living. I felt ready. Ready for a life without fear and a life with Lucy.

And yet now that I was, I found myself back to square one. Literally...

Contemplating Annabelle's last words, I started walking down the street. I was gutted... I didn't get to say goodbye to anyone and never got to tell Lucy what she meant. How she was, by far, the most genuine, kind, caring and all-round amazing person I ever met. And that I owed all my progress to her if I was truly honest.

Instead, she would forever think I was some confused guy with issues...

I marched on, cursing myself underneath my breath. I thought I had time...

Hands in my pockets, I kicked the stone in front of me, ignoring the doorbell to my right.

"I'll need it by Monday," came a voice from inside. A man carrying two crates in his hands made me stop. I recognised that face. And come think of it, I recognised that voice.

"There you are!" Dan appeared next to me beaming.

"Dan?" I asked and felt a clap on my shoulder. "What are you doing here?"

"What am *I* doing here?" he asked, confused. "Where else should

I be? Ellie will bring your order out in a minute," he continued. "You coming?"

"Ellie...?" I repeated. "Yeeesss..." he stated equally slowly. "My girlfriend!? How hard did you hit your head?"

"Annabelle told you I hit my head?" I asked, trying to connect all dots.

"Who?" He queried, walking inside. "Might want to get it checked out mate."

I couldn't believe it. There he was in front of me, talking about Ellie. I pinched myself just to make sure it was true. Overwhelmed, I gave him a big hug, relief building inside me.

"You alright there bud?" he asked and I nodded. There were no words. I didn't lose them all... Could this also mean...?

"What about Lucy?" I asked hopefully. He looked at me puzzled and my hope disintegrated. *Please let her be here too...*

"What about her?" He asked, his voice unreadable. "Did she ask for me?" I tried again, heart in my throat.

"Ask for you?" he repeated. "She's waiting for you, you numpty."

"Waiting for me?" I repeated, a wave of relief washing over me. *She was waiting for me!*

"Thought you did a runner again," he continued, eying me suspiciously. "You better not screw this one up again Nate or I swear to God..." I grinned, remembering our first encounter.

"I know, I know..." I lift my hands up in the air as if to surrender, "or you'll kick my ass." *She is waiting for me...* He waved me off.

"Nah, won't have to"

"Where do I find her?" I ask, my heart beating fast, watching Dan cramp in one of his cupboards.

"She asked me to give you this." He hands me a folded little note and I literally tear it from his hands.

N1 café, Victoria square, 12pm.

That's all it said. I look at the clock, 12:05pm.

"Gotta go," I shout and run out the door.

"Don't you want your…" I hear Dan behind me but I'm already gone.

⌒

I'm sprinting down the street as fast as my legs carry me. Past the train station, I take the staircase up to Regent Hotel to scrape off a few seconds.

Wait for me… I run across the bride towards the city park and back down the stairs leading me to the water bay, inhaling and exhaling deeply as I continue down the promenade. My heart is pounding fast, my lungs hyperventilating.

Thought you did a runner… Ironic. This will be the longest run I will ever run.

Towards her, towards us and wherever she will go.

I'm coming for you, I whisper. Choosing you, like you always wanted me to.

I sprint towards the square.

"Where is N1?" I ask a guy in passing, but he just shakes his head. I try the lady beside me.

"2nd floor," she tells me, pointing to the building to my right. I speed up, running past pigeons and surprised tourists as the tower clock showed 12:25.

Common… common, common, common…. I run up the first flight of stairs and up the escalator. One more and I'm there.

CLOSED FOR REPAIR

the sign reads in front of me, blocking my entry. *NO!* I look around frantically.

"How do I get up there?" I ask a guy with a name tag.

"You won't be able to get up there," he tells me. *No kidding professor.*

"Where *can* I go up?" I ask instead, trying to stay calm.

"There's an elevator round the corner, past the.." I start running before he finishes his sentence.

"Thanks mate," I shout after him, turning around the corner and push the elevator button frantically. *Common, common...* The elevator doors open and I jump inside, pressing the 'close door' button several times.

Please be there, please be there... heart pounding in my chest the doors open in front of me.

Heart pounding, hands sweating…
Knowing that the reunion is near
The sweet sensation, of anticipation
Knowing the path is finally clear
What will it look like and how will it feel?
once integrated, there's much more at spiel
What once a concept too hard to understand,
Now one can feel the body expand
Ready to unite two hearts & one soul
Ready to make that union whole

Their eyes lock when they see each other, past months melting away in front of them. No words are needed as they move towards each other, unable to break the other one's gaze.

I see you.. Nate thought as he slowly moved closer.

All of you.. Lucy whispered, embracing him tight.

Something moved in the corner of her eye.

When the shape stepped forward, she could see one arm nervously pulling at the other. Nate felt Lucy freeze in his arms, inhaling sharply.

"Jamie!" She whispered, her eyes filling her with tears.

CHAPTER 14

You

Finally!! What took you so long?? Days I have been lying here or could have been years… I must have lost count… Dusting away on this godforsaken shelf, waiting for the right time to come.

Stop doing the same thing over and over, without real purpose or impact. Stop wishing you would have done more, seen more, visited more, laughed more, slept more… or actually been happy. When was the last time you were happy?

It can't just be anyone, you know? It's not as simple as that. Congratulations, you are 'it'!

You look different than I imagined… not that I knew what to expect of course, but different somehow.

Haven't you figured it out yet my friend? You and I are going to change the world together.

Contract

I hereby consent to fully immerse myself in this experience. To push myself beyond imagination and challenge everything I believe in. To enter with an open heart, and mind, and commit to bravery, especially when faced with my biggest demons

_____

Signed: Your Name Here

PGIL2024USA